Ersatz Nation

Tim Kenyon

Lidia,
I'd prefer your homeland's
beautiful sterling to our ugly American
money, but what the heck. I'll take it.
Enjoy the book and thanks for
your support!
Love, Tim

Big Engine
PO Box 185
Abingdon
Oxon OX14 1GR
United Kingdom
www.bigengine.co.uk

Big Engine cover design concept by Deirdre Counihan

Cover typeset by Paul Brazier, www.brazier.mistral.co.uk

Produced by publish2day Oxford, www.publish2day.com

ISBN 1 903468 07 8

For my mother and father

I'd like to express heartfelt thanks to those who made the completion of this book possible. First off, my family. Thank you all for enduring my absence during this journey. I love you all; Sarah, no one person has ever inspired me so much; Susan, I will never forget the sacrifices you endured for me; Mad Dog, for talking shop when we should have been working, but without it this story would not exist; Jesse, Randy, Cynn, Leanne and Mook, for making it all worthwhile and a little more bearable; Jane, for telling me I could; Mariana, for your fresh perspective; Claude, you always seemed to know where I was coming from, and where I'd be going; Mark Smith, for toughening me up from the beginning; Mike Gillis, for all your insights on my writing; Jim Kelly, for your critique and wisdom; Paula Wellde, for helping when I had to get technical; Philip Kogan, for reaching out; and finally to Jean and Spencer, for believing in me and my words.

One

His stomach grumbled loud enough to hear it. Dinner was all Dolan could think about as he waited in an endless line of cars, still blocked by a paver slowly pressing a fresh layer of tar onto the road. He looked out over the dashboard, then turned off the engine. There was no point wasting gas; the traffic wasn't going anywhere. The pudgy man to Dolan's left leaned on his SLOW/STOP sign and yawned, the pole buckling under the man's weight. Dolan smiled, but the man seemed uninterested, distracted by whatever turmoil filled his private little world. It was tough, but Dolan tried not to make the man's problems any of his own concern. The people on Earth dealt with their internal lives personally. Mother was not here to direct them. The troubles eating at this guy was nobody's business but his own. What a lucky bastard.

The cars still weren't moving, so Dolan removed the envelope from the pouch of his briefcase and looked it over again before finally tearing it open. This time he'd held out for three days before opening it, but that seemed long enough. He couldn't go on waiting. The doorway back was closed to anyone else, including Mother. And while on this side of it, the occasional letter was the closest tie he had to the Unation – the only real home he'd ever known.

The letter was from Theman, Mother's liaison, and it began with the typical, overblown salutation: *Attention Mr Patrick Dolan, Defender of Mother Necessity and Her Unation.* He kept reading. Theman was reminding him of the importance of his job on Earth, and how much Mother appreciated what he was doing, and that no matter what happened to Dolan, She was still willing to destroy it all if he ever–

There was no point reading more. Letters like this were just Mother's way of reminding him that She was still in charge, no matter where he was. Since he was the first and only person to come here from the Unation, She was taking every precaution to protect both worlds and the secret passage between them. Of all that She had ever created for the citizens of the Unation, She claimed that doorway as Her most important and influential discovery. She created the rift, She created Earth, and everyone in the Unation believed that as fact.

But nothing could convince him that this place wasn't real, at least to him. Rich sunsets and lush, green fields, places where he could see no one, all that was no fantasy. It was no dream, so naturally it was okay to dream about staying if he wanted to, even if Mother ruled that thinking about it was completely unacceptable. For the most part he was a reasonable man. He couldn't stay, he knew that. Mother hadn't yet pulled him from this assignment for that simple reason.

He was still well aware of his job description: Find suitable candidates for Mother, collect them and return them to Her. 'Kidnap' was too strong a word, he hated using it, as much as he disliked referring to his victims by name. Kidnap, collect – it all meant the same to Her; that would never change. Neither would Her policy on the world She had sent him to: *It must be undeniably recognized that Mother created the rift, therefore She created Earth – No questions asked.* And he had no plans to do so, but if this world around him had been created by Her, he wondered why She was allowing these people to have the liberty to love and earn and think solely for their own personal benefit. What could She possibly want to learn by studying them? That too was a topic he didn't want to question. Especially that one.

Dolan picked up a pad and pencil and started sketching. Out the passenger's side window he saw a busy recreation area. Groups of people lounged in the grass, children played curious games as adults watched. Others flew kites, making them turn and dip as they pulled on their strings. A chain-link fence separated the park from the busy arena of machines. The construction site crawled with orange vehicles, littered with rows of concrete barricades and enormous piles of dirt and stone. He sketched the two different worlds on one sheet. Removing a soft green pencil from his brief-case and rubbing it across the white paper, he began adding color to the outlines. Off in the distance the unfelled trees swayed in the breeze. Along the edge of the road several earth-moving vehicles sped by dodging piles of stone, broken limbs, and men wearing soiled clothes and bright yellow hats. He stopped drawing and turned his nose toward the gap in the window. The tar was like nothing he had ever smelled in the Unation, and he found the curious odor very appealing.

Returning to the page, he added in the fence between the park and construction site. It was important to make the drawings as life-like as possible. Accuracy was the key to remembering what he was seeing here. Mother could take the memories from his mind if She wanted to, but he was intent on making this portion of his life permanent. No matter what happened, no matter what She would consider unauthorized memories, he'd always have the sketches to help him remember. There was no way he was going to spend the rest of his life with a twelve ¿year gap in his head. Of course, that wouldn't be an issue if he could only find some way to remain. If he could he'd be in control of his own life, keeping his thoughts to himself rather than needing to go back and contribute them to Mother. He touched the back of his neck, making sure his hair was still hiding his well kept secret. No matter how comfort-able he felt here, he knew damn well that no one could ever see, no one could know the truth. But that wouldn't have to be, if only he could find a way ... if only he could stay ...

The ground suddenly shook and both he and the car jumped. The vibration resonated like the footfall of some invisible pres-ence coming to take him back to the Unation. He spun around, looking beyond the stopped cars and empty fields. Children con-tinued to play, men continued to work. They were oblivious, but

Mother was out there somewhere, he was sure of it. Even though he'd always felt safe on Earth, he still needed to return to Her every twelve hours. Had Mother become fed up with his desire to remain? Had She been playing a waiting game all along? He hoped not; he prayed on his life that wasn't the fact.

A grinding noise to his left caught his attention. An enormous yellow crane opened its rusty jaws, dropping a cut tree to the ground. Another tremor shook the car. In his mind, the presence had taken one step closer. *Let that step be the last*, he said to himself, and he forced away the thought of staying on Earth. It went reluctantly, but he knew Mother could still find it if She wanted to.

He popped the cap off of the aspirin bottle he kept in the ashtray, tossed three pills into his mouth and chewed. His stomach churned on the pasty pills and growled sourly, reminding him again how little he'd eaten. Retrieving Mother's recent candidate from across the state in Walpole – he'd nicknamed this one the Fighter – had taken two hours longer than expected. He wasn't scheduled to return to the Unation until early the next morning, but his patience quickly wore thin when he realized the time – it was already 4:45. Because of delays the three hour trip had taken six. How stupid to have brought only one sleeper. A single injection surely wasn't enough to keep her out for the whole trip. She was bound to wake soon with sharp memories of the damage he'd done to her during the abduction.

Traffic finally began to move, so he started the car and made a right turn onto Route 101, heading east toward Epping, and beyond that, the quiet little town of Garrison which for the meantime he was calling home. Mother had sent him to other places over the *i*-years: Sheridan, Wyoming. Mopeka, Ohio. Bridgton, Maine. Interesting, but all too average. These had been some of Mother's preferred sites – the most successful ones, by Her standards – but Garrison, New Hampshire was by far his favorite. And for no particular reason. Small town, a lot of the old, a lot of the new. The mix was just right for him. The people were friendly and there were enough of them that he could move around unnoticed. Garrison just felt like a comfortable place to hide, and that was good enough for him. And for Her.

The traffic stopped again and he gripped the steering wheel until his knuckles swelled, knowing that his cozy living situation wouldn't mean a damn thing if he didn't get this girl back to his apartment soon. Sitting idle in the hot weather was going to kill her very fast. Even though the sleeper could sustain her with very little air, she certainly wasn't safe from dehydration. The car was low on fuel, but he decided to chance it and activated the air circulator. The engine chugged as it worked to pump cool air into the trunk. If he had to explain to Mother how he'd lost another candidate, She would no doubt consider that one mistake too many. He couldn't fail Her – not after what happened last time.

Several of the cars in front had been directed around the construction vehicles in the road. He edged forward, a pace that was too incredibly slow. He couldn't help but stare at the gas gauge as it hovered just above 'E' and using the air circulator was only using more fuel. When he looked up the traffic had stopped again. He stomped on the brake, nearly hitting another car. The driver, unaware how close Dolan had come, stepped out and peered down the road. He yelled something, honked the horn and climbed inside again. The pudgy man directing traffic turned to him with half-closed eyes. Whatever the man in the car had yelled did no good – they still weren't moving. Several cars behind him tried to use the sandy shoulder to pass, but were stopped by a police officer. Dolan wondered if he might be able to pass on the opposite side while the officer was occupied with the others. He backed slightly, then edged out and peered down the side of the road, but the shoulder was blocked by felled trees piled along the edge.

Once he had pulled out he realized being in the middle of the road was attracting too much attention. The last thing he wanted was to irritate one of the police officers. They just might make him pull to the side and wait out the traffic as some kind of punishment. What if they asked to search his car? What if the woman woke up? There'd be no way he could sneak away to shoot her full of sleeper agent. If only he had thought about buying gas before the pick up that morning, but instead he had become preoccupied with his Earth fantasies, arguing with himself about staying focused on his job. Mother or the police, either way his delusions were sure to be the end of him.

Dolan reversed again, pushing back into the lane of stopped cars. The piercing scream of a car horn flared from behind. He jumped, worry becoming reality at that moment. The law men had snuck up behind him while he wasn't paying attention. Maybe if he ignored them they'd go away, but he felt compelled to not be taken without a fight, he owed himself that much. He turned. The front end of a monstrous pickup truck loomed no more than a foot away. Inside the white truck a young man was shaking his fist and mouthing words. The boy leapt from the truck, his wide lips still shouting some unknown, mute message. Dolan watched him, amazed at how much the young man looked like his brother's son, Jacob. Dolan peered through the glass at him, a tower of a man seeming to grow in size while he waited outside the window. The boy finally knocked hard on the glass. Dolan fumbled for the handle and the boy bent down, sticking his nose in the window crack. The face was certainly Jake's – yet deep within the young man's eyes it wasn't him at all.

"Mister, what the hell's your problem?" the young man barked.

"Noth ... noth ... " Dolan couldn't get the words past his lips as the strange replica of his nephew stood over him.

"You almost drove right into me!"

Even the voice was his. His brother Rodney had that same cracked, nasal tone.

"I'm nearly out of gas," Dolan managed to say.

"We all have our excuses for being in a hurry, don't we?"

The confrontation was becoming less a matter of paranoia as Dolan stared at the small red scar on the young man's forearm, identical to Jake's. But this man was not him, could not have been him. Jake had been dead for more than six *i*-years, after disobeying Mother one too many times. Though his REMOVAL from the Unation had never been clear. Jake simply disappeared one day, and Dolan had to read about it in the *Incorporated*. Mother obviously had Her reasons for keeping the truth from him, and now he knew why. Mother had sent Jake to Earth. But something had gone wrong, terribly wrong, because he wasn't even recognizing his own uncle.

"Jake, don't you know me?"

The young man furrowed his brow. "What goddamned planet you from?" he yelled, then walked away. "Pay attention next time!"

Dolan watched in the side mirror as the young man who was Jake kicked the rear panel of the car. A dull thud echoed from the trunk. The car rocked as he kicked it a second time. Dolan turned and watched him get back in the truck. Over the whirl of the air circulator he listened for movement in the trunk. He prayed the sleeper would keep the woman under. If she woke up, Dolan would have nowhere to go. She'd easily be discovered. Maybe that had been Jake's plan all along. Or Her plan.

But he heard nothing. She was still asleep.

The young man who was Jake pulled out from the line of cars and passed Dolan on the right side, driving along the shoulder. Sand and rocks pelted the exterior of Dolan's car and a cloud of dust circled into the air. A police officer yelled for him to stop but Jake kept going. Dolan gave up brushing off all these strange sightings as coincidence. Only six months before he'd sworn his brother Rodney was alive and riding in a car, right alongside him, on that very highway. Mother was using Jake for something. Something that was becoming disastrous. He needed to find out why.

Dolan swerved around the police officer and followed the pickup down the right shoulder. His tires sank into the soft sand slowing him down. The truck pulled away, disappearing momentarily over a crest in the road. Dolan fought his way through the soft shoulder, speeding alongside the endless line of halted traffic. The steering wheel pulled, wanting to control itself. He fought it, trying to keep the car from sliding into the line of concrete barricades and the occasional police car stopped along the side. He ignored those officers too as they yelled for him to stop. At that point, the discovery of the woman in his trunk seemed trivial. He wanted only to confront the young man who was Jake once more, find out why he was on Earth, how he had gotten there. Dolan had the only way mechanism. There were supposed to be no others.

In the distance, he could see several orange construction vehicles, but no white pickup. As he reached the crest in the road, Dolan suddenly felt a thousand eyes upon him. He slowed and looked inside each car as he drove passed. All faces were turned to him. The drivers, the passengers were glaring in rage and utter amazement as if by some mass epiphany they had become aware of why he'd come to their world. Jake must have somehow alerted them. And Dolan knew that if this moment ever came Mother was going to abandon him, close the door forever. But he couldn't stay here alone, no matter how much he wanted to. He needed Her, his life depended on it.

As he continued to pass the stopped cars, he realized the drivers were not as much looking at him as they were looking *past* him. Their interest was focused on something else, and that relieved him. He turned, looking in the same direction, and was horrified at what he saw. A large billow of black smoke rose into the air from something engulfed by fire inside a busy construction site. As the black stuff swirled and lifted, the shape of the white truck became visible in the center of the flames. It had rolled onto its roof. Although everybody was noticing the demolished truck, absolutely no one was making an effort to help Jake.

Dolan parked in the soft shoulder and sprinted down the sandy embankment. He approached the wreck, shielding his eyes. Intense heat pushed at him, as if giving a warning to keep his distance. A rare silence hung over the yellow flames; there was a strange absence of crackling glass and roar of rushing air. He circled the vehicle looking for some sign that the young man who was Jake had escaped before the truck burst into flames, but there were no signs, no footprints in the dirt. Mother had likely forced Jake to wreck the truck after Dolan recognized him. He wished he never had; Jake would still be alive. Losing him a second time twisted Dolan's stomach. This time Jake's blood was on *his* hands.

As he moved to the driver's side he noticed a charred black

limb pressed against the glass. He tried to step in but the flames shot out, forcing him back again. The heat became unbearable and he fell back into the sand. Saving Jake was hopeless, and a hatred for the people of Earth flared in him for the first time. They all just stood and watched him die. Dolan wanted to bring everyone of them to Mother. *Let Her do what She will with all of them,* he thought.

Slowly, a dark, distorted form took shape within the flames. A body of sorts, but not Jake's. With Jake gone She would need to send another to take his place, someone to spy, someone to tell the world who Dolan was and what he was doing. Who better to send this time than Theman himself? The spot where he was sitting was going to become his grave. The freedom he had been working for, all his dreams of staying on Earth, lost. He was a man of two worlds, though neither would have him.

Theman moved closer to his reality, the dark figure taking a more human form. Twisted licorice fingers reached out for him through distorted ripples of heat. In a single flicker of the flames the emerging figure resembled everyone he had ever taken from Earth: The young child from Barrington he had removed from the arms of a sleeping mother; the elderly man, Reginald Wells, whose unexpected death was Dolan's first grave error. Two faces, and a thousand others, all at once.

The silent flames spat the black form onto the ground in front of him. The image stopped, loomed over him. Dolan covered his face, forced in scorching air and tried to scream. He sensed the smell of burning hair, the rise of blisters on his skin, his tongue melting and running down his throat.

"Hey, buddy, you okay?" a voice asked. There was a surprisingly cool touch on his arm, and Dolan jumped, scrambled back a bit and looked up. A burly man loomed over him, skin covered with soot. Dolan looked down at his own unburned arms. The man didn't move in on Dolan, instead he held his hand out. It wasn't Theman, but it was someone from the Unation. She had sacrificed Jake to replace him with another, someone Dolan didn't know. He looked up into the man's face, studied it. He didn't want to forget it because he knew this man would be watching now. Mother was never going to take Her eyes off Dolan, he knew that for sure.

After a moment, Dolan glanced to the right at a group of men standing extremely close to the raging fire. One of them was almost in it, unharmed by the heat. They stared back, puzzled and grimacing. The one in the fire absently patted dust from his jeans. To Dolan's left, people in cars were no longer staring at him or the burning wreck. They merely crept forward as a short distance back the pudgy man turned the sign from STOP to SLOW.

"I asked if you're okay." The sooty man reached down to touch Dolan's arm again. Dolan recoiled, then scurried away and climbed up the soft shoulder on all fours to his car. If only Jake had recognized him, if only he hadn't run. He could have saved Jake from Mother. But now Jake had been replaced. For all Dolan knew Mother could have been watching him through any of the people around him. He turned the ignition and kept his eyes on the sooty man as he turned and retraced his steps, walking back through the truck's hollow shell still engulfed in flames.

He forced his car back onto the road and eased along with the rest of the traffic. He occasionally turned toward Jake's burning truck. The smoke swirled and hovered until the hungry air devoured it. Each time he looked the sight became more faint until in one brief moment the flames and the smoke dissipated, leaving nothing. The truck had vanished.

"Move along!" a policeman yelled, thumping his fist against the trunk of Dolan's car.

Dolan accelerated, following the others past the obstruction and onward toward the open highway. His anger toward the people around him had faded, there was nothing they could have done for him, or Jake. But the image of silent blue flames still burned in him. He felt Mother in him too, stronger than ever, and he knew She wasn't going to set him free. What he had just seen was only a taste of the insanity that awaited him if he stayed. Returning to the Unation for good one day was an absolute. He'd been born with a lifelong obligation to thought-contribute to Mother Necessity, and if he violated *that*, his mind would shut down completely – he'd be as good as dead.

The parking lot of Mick and Herb's gas station was anything but deserted. Too many people came and went, all attentive to what others were doing. Dolan turned away from whomever he thought might look at him. Cars lined either side of the lot, drivers waiting to fuel them. From the north side of the traffic circle a small van carrying a group of teenagers entered the lot, tailpipe scraping the ground. Yelling and laughing, the teenagers crawled over each other to get out, one of them kicking the trash around that had fallen out. A taller boy grabbed one of the girls around the waist, spun her in a circle, nearly dropping her. She screamed, flailed her arms, kicking her feet in the air, begging to be let down. Next to them, an inattentive mother and her two children hopped across the stained asphalt with bare feet. Thankfully none of them were curious why Dolan had backed his car into a shaded corner beside the building. Regardless of their aloof behavior, he knew that any one of them, maybe all, were spying on him for Mother. He slouched further into his seat and glanced at the gas gauge as it hovered below empty. He turned off the engine. People came and went, none of them passing through without Dolan's getting a good look. He had attracted enough attention for one day and didn't want any more of it; just fuel.

The woman and her two children came out of the store, and the resemblance she had taken on made Dolan's heart sink. She had become his wife, and the pain that had run through him as he watched Maggie die came back like the crash of a wave against his chest. But that was long before he'd ever heard of Earth, more than twelve *i*-years before. They were both living well and both had worked hard to gain Mother's permission to have a child. He didn't know a couple that was happier. Life from then on was supposed to change forever. They were going to bring another life to Mother, another person who would someday give their thoughts and ideas to Her. That was every couple's goal. But their fantasy did not end as many others had. Maggie had a condition that, as Mother put it, was quite unprecedented. Uterine atony, genetic bleeding disorder – the doctors made up plenty of descriptive names, but they had never seen it before and Mother had created no technology to cope with the condition. The people that were supposed to be Her professionals could only stand there and watch Maggie bleed to death.

When they wheeled her out she looked so synthetic, having lost so much blood. The confusion had overtaken everyone in the room – the doctors hadn't even taken the time to cover her over. He tried to pull her blood-soaked gown back down over her waist. Parts that had been inside her were lying between her legs. Except the baby.

The doctors inundated him with profuse apologies, but he ignored them. He just wanted to touch Maggie's cheek, and when he did he finally understood what had happened. Maggie had given her life bringing Mother a child. At least that was what he believed until one doctor told him that his daughter had died too.

Dolan ran his hand against the stubble on his cheek and watched the woman shuffle her children across the lot and into the car. Losing Maggie had left a hole in him which he'd filled with his preoccupation with Earth. This place had kept him going for so long, but now the space in him was empty again. At that moment he just wanted to walk away from everything, leave his job behind him, his life, his status level in the Unation. But he knew better, he couldn't give up now. He had too much to lose here, and there was nothing to return to in the Unation. He had agreed on a transfer to Earth right after Maggie's death, hoping his new assignment would give him a chance to grieve peacefully and at the same time keep his career on track. No matter what had happened, losing focus on professional life would have guaranteed him a personal life much worse than he was living after he lost Maggie. And to think, an entire world all to himself. What incredible opportunities to pick up the pieces of his torn life.

But as it turned out Earth wasn't what he expected. Mother had a set of strict rules to follow: NO unnecessary contact with the inhabitants, NO fraternization. Soon he found himself more alone than he could have ever imagined. The only people he mingled with were those he was collecting for Her and they always had to be knocked out. His job became his only outlet for grief, and it had done little good except give him an excuse to bury the hurt.

Sounds of stirring came from the car's trunk – a soft, broken moan, a rattle of the toolbox which he knew was snug behind the spare tire. With only fumes left for fuel and no more sleepers, he had to make a decision and fast. He sat up straight and peered across the lot at two men filling their cars. At that moment, neither seemed to pose a threat greater than the woman in his trunk. It was time to buy gas.

Dolan started the car, eased it across the lot. Both men looked up slowly, faces pale with curiosity, though neither resembled anyone he knew. Regardless, he was compelled to keep his distance, reminding himself of the lengths Mother would go to protect Herself. Anyone could be watching.

"Clear off your windshield, mister?" a boyish voice came from behind as Dolan replaced the nozzle.

He spun around, half expecting to see a miniature version of Jake staring up at him. However, this boy too resembled no one he knew.

"Your windows," the boy said. "You know, clean them?" He moved the squeegee around in circles.

"Please, don't," Dolan pleaded, cringing at the desperation in his own voice.

The boy stopped moving the squeegee, stared at Dolan for a moment, then walked off, holding a conversation with himself. Dolan turned to watch the two men drive away. He was relieved that neither looked back to catch him staring. When they were out of sight, he moved his car as close as he could to the front of the store where he'd be able to keep an eye on it.

"Evening, buddy," the man behind the counter said as Dolan went in.

This guy didn't look familiar either, which probably would have convinced him that Mother wasn't playing games, except for the fact that Dolan *should* have recognized him. "Where's Mick?" Dolan asked finally, half expecting the old man to tear off a clever mask revealing the younger face of the store's owner, the same person who'd been selling him gas and cigarettes for *i*-years. He clutched his wallet tightly, stared at the elderly man behind the counter. Everything in the store had been reversed. The cigarette rack was now to the left of the soda cooler, the cash register had been moved to the other side of the counter. The place was its own mirror opposite.

"Vacation." the old man said, refusing to look at him.

Dolan waited for a more convincing explanation, but none came. "When's he coming back?" he asked nervously.

The old man looked Dolan straight in the eyes. "You're asking the wrong guy. Theman has all the answers."

Dolan could feel that his feet had frozen into place. With each passing moment, everything he'd experienced seemed less like a dream. His throat began to tighten, as if Mother had gained total control over him, even more than She already had. The pain in the tips of his fingers, his nagging headache, the dull cramps haunting his stomach – none of that compared to what She could do if She really wanted to. He was at Her mercy. Was Theman somehow spying on him right now? Did he know the brand of cigarettes Dolan smoked, or the number of coffee cakes he ate on a daily basis? Dolan felt that strange, bulging eyes were fixed on him through the knot holes in the wood slats on the wall as the old man's words rattled through his head again.

"*What* did you just say?" Dolan asked, eyes fixed on the holes in the panel. The old man continued punching keys on the register as though he hadn't said a word.

"I said, the man's son has all the answers. You know, Mick's boy." He paused, staring blankly. "The little guy cleaning windows out there."

Dolan reworked the man's words in his head trying to make sense of it. At the same time it all seemed too unreal to believe, but too real to deny. One thing was for certain: The boy outside was not Mick's. "I've never seen him before," Dolan said finally, removing the last four coffee cakes from the metal rack that had been moved to the right of the register.

"He's here whenever Mick's here." The old man pointed thoughtlessly toward the window. "Can't help you with your memory none."

"No, guess not." Dolan laid the money for the gas and cakes on the counter and turned to leave.

"Hey," the old man squawked. "Want your cigarettes?"

Dolan spun around just in time to catch the pack of Pall Malls flying at him. His brand. He didn't dare say another thing, just laid a handful of pocket change on the counter without counting it and headed for the door.

"Have a good one, buddy," the old man said. Dolan sped to the door. "I'll tell Mick hello for you!"

In the lot he passed the young boy, squeegee and rag in his tiny hands. He flashed Dolan a crooked smile. Dolan dug through his memory, but it did no good – the boy's face was not that of Mick's son. Though at this point, any recognition at all seemed unreliable. In a matter of an afternoon, he had lost any sense of distinguishing those he knew from those he didn't. And that would be Theman's best cover if he chose to follow him. At that moment, he felt there was nowhere he could go without being watched. The image of eyes staring through knot holes remained lodged in his mind. Once he got back to the car, he looked in the mirror and noticed his own eyes had begun to resemble those same holes in the wall. They'd become unrecognizable. All he could see were two black empty pits.

His preoccupation with Maggie made him oblivious to the road signs and his assigned routes, so he drove the rest of the way along roads he'd never taken before. Fiery headlights rushed by making him squint and look away, as if his oversensitive eyes were warning of danger inside the passing cars. Once the vehicles were out of sight, he returned to staring at the lines in the road, thinking of his wife, the old man, the Pall Malls, the burning truck. During his *i*-years of crossovers from the Unation, he must have been carrying pieces of mental baggage that now were unraveling the reality he'd built out of Mother's creation, Her dreamworld. If asked, he'd certainly call this place home, but admitting that to Her would get him REMOVED. And that wasn't an option at that point.

He continued to follow the signs directing him to the Route 16 intersection. Once there, he turned north toward Garrison. The last two miles seemed to take an eternity. He sensed that each car he passed was creeping by, the driver glaring at him. One of them was bound to be someone sent by Mother, perhaps Theman himself, searching him out. But if Theman found him, he certainly wouldn't be as obvious as Jake had. No, Theman was smarter than that. He'd just watch, wait for Dolan to screw up again before moving in. Then there'd be a confrontation, face to face. That's how Dolan would want it.

He drove by his apartment three times before finally turning in. He backed his car in the dark corner of the driveway. Two more vehicles passed by the house at a curiously fast pace. By now it was completely dark and Dolan couldn't see if the drivers were looking at him like the others were, with their burning curiosity and disdain.

He lifted the heavy briefcase off the seat and, before opening the door, removed a small pocket knife from a zipper pouch on the side of the case. He pulled the interior light out of the vinyl roof and cut the wires. After tossing the knife and the light onto the passenger's side floor, he softly opened the door. Because of the extreme weight of his case, he had to use both hands to carry it. Mother had certainly designed an exquisite piece of machinery, the mechanism that opened the doorway to Earth, though he wished She had considered the fact that he was going to have to carry it around. But he was not about to let the case out of his sight since the mechanism inside was his only means of return. He had decided long before that where he went, the case went with him.

The scuffling of his feet against the pavement quieted the symphony of crickets in the grassy hedge along the edge to the house. He found the lack of noise disturbing, as if it had been something else other than his footsteps that caused them to stop. It had been that quiet after the doctors left him alone with Maggie. That was the only other time he could ever remember being aware of the absolute silence. Even now, late at night, he would still find himself restlessly searching for a light to leave on, one that would buzz and shatter the noiselessness. Listening to it sustained him like air.

He lugged the case up the stairs to the porch outside his the apartment. He carefully set it down and the boards squeaked under its weight. He made his way back to the car wishing the crickets would start singing again, but his attention was quickly drawn to another noise. From inside the trunk he heard a faint, metallic scrape followed by a muffled whimper. Time had completely escaped him. Counting the number of hours that the girl had been under the sleeper was impossible. Days could have passed by in a single minute and he would have never noticed the bright orange streak across the sky that was the sun. With clumsy fingers he searched for his keys. After frantically feeling his pockets he cursed quietly and retrieved them from the ignition. He slid the key gently into the lock, turned it, and listened for the soft click.

The trunk lid sprung up, tearing the key ring from his hand. He pulled his face back just as the edge grazed his chin, swinging set of keys flashing by his eyes. The throaty wail of terror inside the black compartment echoed across the field. He took one step back and watched as the Fighter rolled out of the darkness, to her feet, and leapt with a limberness that could only have been energized by pure fear. The wrench she was clutching came down hard on his left shoulder, her other hand found his right forearm. Her fingernails took several layers of skin near his elbow, sure to leave scars. Both of them fell to the ground, her on top, air rushing out of his lungs as he hit the pavement. She brought the wrench down again, slower this time which allowed him to grab it before it cracked his skull wide open. He squeezed her hand, felt the cartilage in her knuckles give. She howled and the wrench slipped free, just missing his head. Through fear alone, her strength had doubled since their earlier encounter. He started to feel overwhelmed as she remained perched on his chest, continuing to scratch and hit him. The panic in her had blurred the logical ease of her escape – she only needed to run. Managing a small, pitiful breath, he lifted his legs, wrapped them around her neck and pulled down, whacking her head against the tar. Her bellowing cries ended abruptly. The deafening silence he loathed so much had returned.

With a twist of his hips, he slid out from under her limp body, positive he'd killed her. As he searched for a pulse, a trickle of blood ran out onto the ground. In the dim moonlight it looked like engine oil seeping through her thick hair. After finding a faint thump in her neck, he hoisted her over his shoulder. The scratches on his arm were bleeding profusely, leaving dark streaks on her pants. He'd have to wash those out before bringing her to Mother. But washing the blood from her clothes would not cover the marks he'd left on her body – add a head gash to the list of injuries. It had not mattered at this point if Theman, or even Mother Herself, were watching because his preoccupation with this world, his incompetence, were clearly evident by the cuts and bruises on her body.

With the woman securely over his shoulder, he stood by the back of his car and sighed. The trunk key was bent. To avoid breaking the lock he removed the rest of the keys. He carried the girl up to his bedroom and gently set her down on the bed, disregarding the streaks of blood he was leaving on the bedding. He retrieved a small bag inside the closet and carefully removed a sleeper. Adjusting the dose to full, he rolled the girl onto her stomach and, after removing the sheath from the needle, pressed it into the base of her skull and activated it. The transparent blue liquid inside the glass vial slowly moved from the tube into the woman's brain. A dose like that would keep her out well into tomorrow, which was fine. He needed no more confrontations for the rest of the night.

In the bathroom, he ran water over the scratches on his arm and the dark blood turned into a pale, red liquid as it ran down the drain. Luckily, the wounds hurt far worse than they looked. The blood had already begun to clot. He looked at himself in the mirror, shaking his head at the mess he saw. But right then the girl was more important.

He sat on the edge of the bed and softly wiped the drying blood from her matted hair and scarred neck. He used another clean cloth against the spot where the driveway had cut her head. The sleeper had slowed her breathing down so drastically that she could have passed for dead in this world, though Mother would know the difference. She always knew.

The girl looked oddly peaceful, much like Maggie had looked when he saw her for the last time, as they wheeled her away to the REMOVAL bays. Mother took Maggie as part of Herself; even the love she had had for Dolan was now part of Her. But he couldn't remember ever feeling Maggie's presence when he gave his thoughts to Mother. He was all alone then, too. He had given up on the chance to talk to someone about what had happened. To have someone listen, and understand. Mother never looked back, never considered Her past; Her wisdom came from what other people contributed to Her.

Any of the people here would sympathize. Surely this woman would know how he hurt. What would be the harm in waking her and confessing who he really was, all that he'd lost, and everything Mother had forced him to do? He could show her the back of his neck, and even though she'd be first frightened, then prejudiced, she'd still find it in herself to help him.

But he knew better. There was no helping those you couldn't understand.

After filling the bathtub with water, he turned her over and removed her stained pants. He dropped them into the hot, soapy bath water and the fabric sank slowly, blood seeping out in a rolling cloud of red.

Then came a hard knock at the door. He moved quickly into the kitchen. Through the window he saw two dark blue uniforms, badges gleaming dull yellow in the porch light. Any thought of revealing himself was suddenly washed away as he stared out at the men that could end his life as quickly as Mother, if they happened to discover his true intentions. With all he had done since he first arrived, all the scenes he'd caused collecting Mother's candidates, the police had never become involved. He assumed for a moment that they had been sent by Theman, but passed off the possibility when he recalled the ruckus he'd had with the woman in the driveway. It had been loud, really loud. They were no doubt just doing their duty, but that worried him even more. A second knock came as he reached out to open the door.

"Evening," the first officer said in a husky voice. "Garrison Police. Is there a problem here?" He poked his head in and carefully scanned the room.

"Nothing, nothing at all," Dolan said in the calmest voice he could manage. "My ... my wife got a bit noisy. I realize now that I see you here."

"Now why do you think we're here for *that* reason?" the second officer piped up. He was much younger and stood a full head shorter than his partner. The first officer turned, furrowed his brow, clearly chagrined by the young one's sarcasm.

Regardless, it was a keen observation. Dolan had only assumed he knew why they were visiting him. One more false move could land him in a situation he'd always anticipated but never expected. Though he should have, at any time. Theman was sure to have words with him about this. Mother would see to that. "She fell again," Dolan said, praying he wasn't backing himself into a corner with his explanation. "Happens every so often. It's some kind of balancing problem." He pulled on his ear.

"Are you sure that's what all the yelling was about?" the first officer asked. His partner stepped back and peered in the kitchen window, looking around curiously.

"Yes, sir," Dolan said, keeping his eyes on the shorter one who was moving his nose as if sniffing for some sign that Dolan was lying. The young man returned, one side of his mouth turned up.

"We're not going to find out that you've had a fight, are we?" the younger one asked.

"No." Dolan winced, thinking of a hundred things he could have said besides a curt *no*. The two men stared at him and said nothing for a moment. He knew they were studying him, memorizing his face, because he had just given them the invitation to watch him. Whatever he did, wherever he went, these two would know. Now Mother had people here working for Her, and She didn't even know it.

Both men took a step forward. "Would you mind if we came in and checked on her," the first one asked, more as a statement than a question. Dolan stayed on the threshold but felt repelled by their advances. If he let them into his house there was a chance they'd realize the truth just by looking around. No time to prepare. He'd slip somehow, make reference to something this world had no right to know. Allowing his two realities to merge was out of the question, but there was no way his mind could keep the two separate. Not while these two men stood over him and drilled him with questions. He rubbed the back of his hair flat and stepped out of the doorway. The officers sauntered into the kitchen.

"Where is she?" the young officer asked.

"Asleep in the bedroom." Dolan moved quickly down the hall, staying in front of the men. Hoping he had put away the sleeper apparatus, he slid into the bedroom a few steps ahead and glanced at the table. It wasn't there. As furtively as possible he glanced around, hoping what was in the room belonged there and not back in the Unation. Everything looked normal to him, but that didn't mean a thing. His two outwardly different worlds had mixed into an opaque mess inside him. The two men stepped in and looked around. The taller officer stood over the girl, hands on hips. "I'm sorry," Dolan said, "I missed your name earlier, Officer ... ?"

"*Sergeant* Delvechio." He shook Dolan's hand. "My partner, Officer Theberge." Delvechio's partner moved behind Dolan, boxing him in. He tried to wedge himself between the two officers and the bed, hoping to stay close to the woman. The last thing he wanted was for either man to take a good look at her and think she was dead.

"And your name, sir?" Delvechio asked, producing a note pad.

"Patrick Dolan." He pointed to the half-naked stranger on his bed. "My wife ... Maggie." *That hurt.* He pulled the comforter from under her feet and laid it over her.

"Your date of birth, Patrick?" Officer Delvechio's pen hovered over the pad of paper.

Date? He'd calculated the Earth date so long ago, but – "Thirty-eight," Dolan said.

"You were born in 1938?" Theberge said. "You're awfully spry for your sixties."

"Years," he said. "That's my age."

"So, 1960 then?" Delvechio asked after pausing to calculate.

"Yes, sorry ... second month, fifteenth day." Dolan said over the lump in his throat. Why hadn't he spent more time memorizing that stuff? "Of 1960," he finished.

"Her date of birth?"

"Same year, twelfth month, twenty-third day." Dolan glanced at her. "Do you mind if we finish talking in the kitchen? I hate to wake her up after what she's been through. She's very irritable afterward." He stepped between the men and moved toward the door. Delvechio leaned over the woman and examined the bandage on her head. There was nothing to do but hope they wouldn't notice the absence of breathing. Dolan held his own breath and waited for the two men to join him. At the last second, he felt his eyes bulge slightly as his body fought with him for air. Finally, Delvechio tapped his partner and motioned for him to follow. Dolan followed them out, closing the door behind him.

"You sure she's okay?" Theberge asked Delvechio. "Maybe we should roll the med team. Have them look her over."

"Really, she's fine," Dolan interrupted. "She doesn't hurt herself that often when she falls. Looks worse than it is."

"Convenient that she can't speak for herself," Theberge said, turning away from Dolan mid-sentence.

"In the kitchen," Delvechio snapped, motioning to his partner.

Dolan lead the men straight to the back door. "I'm sorry you had to come out here for this."

"We need to follow up on every call, Mr Dolan," Delvechio said. "No matter what it is." He closed his notebook and returned it to his breast pocket.

"I appreciate your concern," Dolan said, opening the door. "She just wanted to sleep it off before going to the doctor's. I'll leave it up to her come morning."

"Good night," Delvechio said. The man nodded to his partner, then slipped out the door.

Officer Theberge moved across the room with one eye on Dolan. "We're going to be keeping an eye on you from now on," he whispered, then slipped out and followed Delvechio.

Dolan watched intently out the kitchen window as the officers walked down the stairs, quickly past the spot where the Fighter had bled onto the driveway, and to their car. The unthinkable had just occurred. He had just become a permanent part of Earth, though he couldn't figure out if it was a curse or a blessing. His name was on record in an official capacity. It seemed absurdly exhilarating, as if before he had never existed. Someone here knew who his was. Mother wasn't going to be pleased when She extracted the thought from his head.

He slid his hand under his hair and fingered the cold metal protrusion he'd kept hidden from the officers, and the rest of them. His knowledge implant was Mother's only way into him, and his need to thought-contribute was the only thing that kept him going back to Her. He had to go back, there were no two ways about it. Sharing his mind through his KI was the only way he knew how to live, the only way he knew how to survive.

Two

Dream, reality. Dream, reality. Dolan couldn't tell the two apart anymore. The defining line that he'd been crossing for i-years was gone. Both worlds start to bleed together to make one, and the tangible things around him no longer seemed as reliable as before. He was even afraid to lean against a wall, worried that it might not really be there. He stood very still in the center of his kitchen, craving food, but that too might do nothing more than vanish before he could eat it. All he could do to calm himself was to walk slowly through each room tapping his fingers against the walls and furniture. He saw his case and he touched it. A white flicker of static electricity crackled under his fingertip and he yanked his hand away. The mingling fluids that were his two worlds separated again as he quickly remembered that there was only one way mechanism. And he had it. There was no one else from the Unation on Earth, there never could be so long as he was there. That was a fact, and facts only existed in reality. Dreams, on the other hand, had their own set of rules.

Only after his stomach settled did Dolan feel like eating. He made himself a turkey sandwich, ate it hastily, and chased it with a coffee cake. He'd have to make that his last meal before crossing back to the Unation with the Fighter the next morning. Making the dizzying trip on a full stomach had proved to be a bad idea.

His next assignment was already sitting in front of him on the table. *No rest for Mother's dedicated workers*, he thought. Once the Fighter was safely delivered, he'd have to come right back and collect another candidate. Mother only allowed him time to contribute, then he had to leave. Fine with him. Staying away from Earth for more than an hour had become too long a time.

He broke the seal on the envelope and removed the small plastic tube. Inside were three memory caps, one distinguishing each of Her potential candidates. Mother had tapped into their minds, in what way he did not know, did not *want* to know. Regardless, what made each of them a person was locked away inside the small cap that was designed to fit snugly onto a KI ... *his* KI. He wondered what kind of thoughts he'd find. Their identities were always a mystery; they were always faceless, nameless, until he snapped on the cap and became them. Children this time though. That much he knew. Mother had become interested in young minds. Deviant young minds. And one of these three was going to go back with him, because She was intent on discovering how these people have survived without someone like Herself to counsel, protect and provide for them. That was the one concept that eluded Her, though Dolan had no trouble seeing how they managed. The people here cherished their internal lives; it was what kept them human.

Before putting the first cap in place he went to the counter and poured a tall glass of warm root beer, opened the fresh pack of Pall Malls and lit one. When he had first arrived on Earth he found smoking kept him occupied; no longer did his mind carry him back to Maggie's bedside, watching the memory repeat itself, her dying over and over again. There was a consciousness in the smoke that wasn't Mother. She had nothing to do with its creation and that made taking in the smoke all that more pleasurable. He pulled on the cigarette. With each drag the tobacco tasted sweeter and he grinned as he held his breath, a little more of Earth inside him.

He removed the first pellet-sized cap from the tube and held it gently between his fingers. After crushing the half-smoked cigarette and taking a hearty swallow of root beer, he reached for the back of his neck, peeled off the fleshy tab covering his knowledge implant. He snapped the memory cap onto his KI port and waited for a flood of stranger's memories to come rushing into him.

The numbing sensation in his hands and feet always happened when he connected a memory cap, but the dull, persistent pain across his whole body was an entirely new feeling. As he slipped deeper into the familiar euphoria, the space between the edge of the table and his chest shrunk with each breath, closer and closer, as if he were about to move right through it. The surface of his upper body had become so sensitive that even the light touch of his clothing burned his skin. Unable to bear it any longer, he slowly guided his numb fingers to each buttonhole, then slid the shirt off just in time to see a barrage of dark purple bruises appear suddenly across his chest and arms. One was shaped like a hand, cupped around the biceps near his left elbow. The marks were too big to have been caused by the woman in his bedroom. He watched them grow, become darker. The pain intensified, but the pain was not his. The bruises belonged to the person coming into his head.

His vision began to weaken. The kitchen became a negative of itself, light and dark trading places. Then the room changed. Shallow images of walls began to appear where none had been before. He saw shapes forming in the new room – a circle, a narrow rectangle, a perfect square. From inside the square a face surfaced, one Dolan didn't recognize at first, then he realized it belonged to the child in his head. A boy of maybe fourteen, with a rough, disquieting face and a full head of blonde hair. The young man's eyes became Dolan's too, and the two looked at each other in the mirror. Dolan could only make out hatred. It blinded everything else until the young stranger's memories began to flow ... and a passing memory left its mark behind: *my name has become Jeremy Baines ...*

... You purposely wake up early after deciding last night that the only answer to your problem is to kill your father. For the first time in quite a while, you smile and watch curiously how your face moves in the mirror. You no longer see a thirteen year old grinning back at

you in the cracked mirror. Right now, you look ageless. As you keep looking at yourself, you realize how old that bastard has made you feel. You always wished you were in a different place, a home far away, experiencing a different love besides the painful one your father gives to you.

You turn your head sideways, stretching to see your profile in the mirror. You feel so old because of your father, who has taken away everything you wished you'd discovered on your own. You feel so weak because you're unable to defend yourself from him. Retreating inside yourself only allows the memory of his hurt to torment you, but remaining outside means contending with the real thing, because that's where he is. So you have to remove the cause of your misery. You smile at yourself in the mirror, carefully studying the curves of your lips and cheeks. You decide you're not so old. It's not too late to fix things.

Your father's straight razor rests in a glass on the shelf in front of the medicine cabinet. You continue to stare at yourself in the broken mirror, contorting your face and counting the wrinkles that appear when you squint and grimace. You grab the razor, the metal cool on your fingertips. The thought of it mixing with hot blood intrigues and repulses you at the same time. Sharp acid creeps up the back of your throat and you spit into the sink.

A slam echoes down the hallway – your father's bedroom door. He is up earlier than usual. Shit. Your plans to do it in the kitchen are shot. There's no time to hide.

"Get out of that bathroom. I have to take a leak." There is a stomp of footsteps and then he begins pounding on the door. "What the hell are you doing?"

Your eyes glance on your own neck in the mirror. The color suddenly runs out of your face and you wonder if that's what death is going to look like. Your stomach heaves at the thought of flesh splitting apart under the cool metal, though this time you swallow the small amount of bile that makes it to your mouth. You turn and reach for the bathroom door while twisting open the straight razor behind your back ...

When Dolan opened his eyes he found himself in the bathroom watching youth and hatred wane as the lines in his face returned. The bruises on his arms and chest faded along with the young man's memories, though Dolan swore he could still feel the warm drops of blood that had landed across the boy's face. The expired memory cap popped off his KI and fell into the tub with a *plunk*. He headed back to the kitchen. Imitating movements and actions of those in his head were not uncommon. A wave of relief passed through him to know he didn't own a straight razor.

He splashed two handfuls of water on his face and returned to the kitchen table. He snapped on the second cap, not giving himself time to think about what he'd almost seen. The boy's memories of his father were his own business, but if Dolan needed to join with him for Mother's sake, then so be it. Now time had passed, and this boy was just fine for Her. He had found Her a child capable of killing. Was there really a need to go on? What he'd find in the next one might even be worse, but the pain he felt from the first could only be squashed by letting in the next. He was at the epicenter of a vicious circle of victims that had been spinning inside him for too long.

The second cap started to slip off his KI and he pushed it on tightly. Daylight from another place began to pour into the room. He squinted at the brightness as he watched waves of greenery rise up out of the floor. His bare chest began to cave in, the muscles atrophied in a matter of moments. It was not unlike how he felt when Mother came into him and took from his mind what She wanted. He was becoming a child again. *I am now Justin Marcotte ...*

... No little bitch sister is gonna get away with telling everyone at school that you still wet the bed. But what will your parents do to a girl who can't do a damn thing wrong in their eyes. Nothing, that's what. Not a goddamned thing. So it's your job to straighten Amy out before she ruins your life. A good scare ought to do the trick, and you know the perfect place.

Amy follows annoyingly close behind as she usually does every day after school, singing her stupid songs she's been learning for chorus. You both wander home along the path through the woods. At the lip of the clearing, Amy grabs your hand until you reach the bank of the brook that empties into the quarry on the other side. The quarry ... You smile.

At the edge of the brook you shake your hand loose and disgustedly wipe your palm across the seat of your pants. You turn and follow the water through a group of trees to the rocky cliff on the other side. There it is.

You grab Amy's hand and try to pull her to you. The rain has filled the quarry higher than you've ever seen. Maybe you'll send her for a swim.

"I don't want to stand so close to the edge," Amy says.

"Don't be such a little shit," you say.

"I'm telling mom you said that."

"Go right ahead, little shit." You lay down on your stomach, inching forward through the tiny chips of granite and dirt to peek over. You throw a rock over the edge and wait for it to hit the water. It takes forever. Amy finally takes a step forward and stops. "It's all right," you say. "Look over here." She takes another small step, then crawls on her hands and knees beside you.

"I don't like this," she says, starting to cry.

"Good. Be scared," you say. "And don't tell lies about me," and you punch her hard on the arm, then bound away. You turn back, ready to run just in case she decides to chase you.

Pushing herself up, Amy tries to stand quickly. The grainy stones under her hands stir, causing her to slide forward. Just like a rubber ball, she bounces off her stomach making a dull grunting sound. She slides and vanishes over the edge. The tips of her fingers grappling the granite are all you can see.

"Justin, help me!" she screams.

You don't move. "Just climb back up." She continues to scream, petrified. You can hear her feet scraping the wall. "Calm down," you say, walking toward her. You stop at the edge and look down at her. She's scared now, more than you've ever seen in your life. Maybe *that will teach her. Or maybe it won't. People don't change that easily. Maybe you should just take care of it for good. After all, she did slip. You wouldn't be lying ...*

You find your foot hovering over her bloody fingertips. You step down hard. Her screams become silent the third time she smacks into the granite wall, then you see her disappear into the water ...

The boy flashed away the moment Dolan opened his eyes, and he found himself staring down at the floor. This time his body's mimicry had left him lying across the table on his stomach, head hanging over the edge. He'd knocked over the root beer and bits of glass was scattered under the table soaking in the brown liquid. He didn't care about the mess, he was just happy to be alone in his mind again.

Shards of dread and remorse for the little girl twisted around inside him. The feelings weren't from the boy, but from himself. He had never felt so cold inside. To Dolan, at that moment, murder seemed so easy, so legitimate. How had that boy's mind become so cold and adulterated? Even though the boy was gone, Dolan still sensed no distinction between right and wrong in him. Dolan wondered if his own daughter might have grown up thinking the same way, or if Mother would have prevented it by conditioning her, or REMOVING her. Without Mother, would he have ever been able to kill as the boy had?

Put it behind you. No more thinking. Just act.

And so he did, pressing on the last cap. The memory of Maggie tried to make her way back into him, thankful that he was taking the time to think about his daughter, the one he'd never seen. As his vision glazed over he became less aware of the hole inside him that Maggie had occupied and more conscious of the wall clock tapping in his ears: *tick tock tick tock tick tock.* Then a young woman slid into his head and his pelvis began to ache. That was fine; he'd become used to the push and pull of letting a female inside. He slowly slid behind her eyes as his mind tried to cope with the physiological impossibilities of being both sexes. But the battle wasn't about gender this time. This girl was different. Every part that made her a woman had been blinded by rage. Such intense emotion before the visions came was a first. He'd never sensed anything stronger than the hatred buried deep inside this girl. Her world in his head came into focus, and suddenly he began to loath the fact that friends and family called her Missy when they knew damn well, *my name is Michelle, Michelle Brenahan.*

"You don't believe me?" you say. "Come here, I'll show you how easy it is to put someone in danger." Julie follows you to the middle of the bridge.

"Stop talking trash, will you?" Julie says.

"Pick up that rock," you tell her, pointing at a stone by the bridge railing. Knowing better than to disobey you, she grabs the rock and holds it out over the edge the same way you are.

"There, now look at it," you say in a strained voice, using almost all your strength just to keep the rock from falling. "Can't you feel the rush when you stare at the rock? Doesn't it make you curious what would happen if you dropped it?" Your arms begin to burn, making your eyes water uncontrollably, but you're not about to stop. This is what you've been waiting for – a chance to prove that you're not full of shit. That you can do it too. The killing is easy.

"Everyone that goes by in their car is still alive because we're letting them live. That's what I've been talking about, Julie." You continue to stare at the rock. "I always wonder if those assholes were thinking the same thing," you say. "When they drove their car into me and my sister."

Out of the corner of your eye you see Julie's hands twitch and she steps back quickly dropping the rock to the ground by her feet. "You're too fucking crazy," she screams.

You turn and smile. "Let me show you fucking crazy." Silently, your rock slips from your hands and plunges to the road. It smashes through the windshield of a brown station wagon. The car skids into the other lane and starts to spin, leaving black marks on the road that swirl around like a spyrograph. Eventually it slides down the embankment, tumbles twice and comes to rest along side a large green highway sign. Beside it lie the ejected, deformed bodies of a woman and a child. Wait ... wait. There it is. You can see blood now, so much blood ...

When Dolan opened his eyes he found himself outside, moon hovering round and weighty above the dark tree line. He tried to shake the images of twisted bodies from his mind but couldn't chase the girl out of his head in time. The shadow of grass waving in the field, the trees, the clouds – they all took the shape of the people he'd seen die on the road. The face on the moon screamed like a dying infant, becoming the daughter he'd never seen. Through the young woman's eyes he had watched the dead body in the road become Maggie, and next to her was his own child. He had witnessed their deaths a second time, and he realized right at that moment that he never had the chance to give their little girl a name. But finally he had seen her face. She was no longer a dream.

I'll name her now, he thought, caring very little that Mother may not have agreed. *My daughter's name is Whitney.* And that was final. He knew Maggie would have loved it.

The young woman faded away into nothing. Dolan was alone again, though his arms still ached. She must have pulled a muscle lifting the boulder, but the pain should have disappeared with her. Then he suddenly became aware of a weight pulling on his clenched hands. He was holding something – and it was very heavy. He looked out over the edge of the porch railing and cautiously stepped back, scraping his bare feet across the wood. He slowly placed his briefcase down in front of him. He tried to inhale, but could only collect a few short, quick breaths, picturing the case smashing on the pavement below. He turned and vomited over the rail.

He carried the briefcase inside, returned it to the space between the arm of the couch and the wall. Without bothering to undress any further he fell onto the couch, wishing for his own bed. The room spun and his mind flooded with a thousand distorted images. Had he dropped the way mechanism, he would have followed it down. He'd want to die by his own hand if it ever came to it. Without another thought, he quickly fell asleep and dreamt only of people he didn't know.

A succession of loud thumps awoke Dolan from a light, uncomfortable sleep. He sat up on the couch, back stiff and screaming with pain, to peer around the corner of the hall, half expecting to see the Fighter stumbling out of his bedroom, a look of death in her eyes. He could see his bedroom door – it was still closed. Maybe she was just waiting, armed with a coat hanger, pretending to still be unconscious. After what had happened the previous night, he was not about to underestimate her again. Fear was on her side and it made her strong. He stood and walked down the hall, then he heard it again – three loud thumps. But this time the noise came from the kitchen. Someone was at the door. The policeman hadn't had enough, at least the younger one, and they were coming back. At first he didn't dare move, hoping they would leave. Had something else happened during the night that he wasn't aware of? The younger officer might be returning alone this time. After all, he seemed convinced that something had happened to the woman besides a simple fall. The young officer knew more than that, something he shouldn't know. There was nowhere for Dolan to go now without being watched, the apartment was no longer safe. It was time to move on. Time to hide again.

Dolan moved quickly to the door, but stopped short of opening it. Through the wispy curtain he saw a woman. Not in a policeman's uniform, but in a dress. Her shoulder-length brown hair was pulled off her face and tied in a pony tail. Much the same way Maggie used to wear hers. He leaned closer to the window until his nose touched the fabric. The woman didn't notice him. She rocked on her heels, holding a piece of paper steady in the breeze, her eyes bouncing back and forth across the page. A lock of hair around her finger – she even twisted it just like Maggie used to. There was nothing unnatural about her. Mother had no influence over this woman, the first unfamiliar face he'd seen in days, and that was refreshing. Although, the more he stared at her through the curtain, the more he recognized and even predicted the subtlest movements. The line in her forehead, the way she moved her lips as she read. The two worlds were blending inside him again and talking to this woman was only going to turn that mixture to concrete. Nevertheless, he felt compelled to open the door. At this point, he didn't care what Mother thought. He had to talk to her.

She was turning to leave as he opened the door. She spun around, startled. "Oh, you scared me. I didn't think anyone was home," her voice cracked and trailed off, just as he expected it would. Her likeness to Maggie became even more real.

"I'm home," he said.

She took a step toward him, extending her hand. "Susan Reil."

He forced himself to take her hand and shake it demurely. "Patrick," he said, voice cracking slightly. "My name's Patrick ... Dolan."

"I represent the Coalition Against Urban Sprawl. Can I take a moment of your time?"

"Absolutely," Dolan said quickly.

"This neighborhood, and many others in Garrison, are in danger of rezoning by the city council." She handed Dolan the paper she'd been reading. "If the new zoning ordinances are passed this whole area will be overrun by businesses. Noise, pollution. It'll be awful. And that will mean more traffic, construction, and even worse, we'll lose our parks. The Coalition could really use your support by signing this petition," she held out a pad, "which will help us voice our opposition to the members of the council."

He looked down at the pad, then back up at her. He wondered if he closed his eyes that maybe her voice would become Maggie's, and he could invite her in, ending this twelve *i*years of loneliness that he had forced upon himself. Was this Mother's ultimate test of his loyalty, by sending this woman to him?

No. Mother has no part in this. His own grief had been one step behind him the whole time and is now only catching up. Coping didn't suit him, but turning every woman he saw into a representation of Maggie was eventually going to break his sanity.

He took the pad and pen and scribbled his name. Now he only wanted to close the door and end the conversation, but she stood there smiling as if she were waiting for him to explain the obvious hurt in his eyes. Could she really see right into him? Maggie used to.

"Thanks so much for your help, Mr Dolan," she said. "If you can help out in any other way, that flyer there has information about the next city council meeting. That's where we'll be presenting the petition." She paused and smiled. "If you want to come."

"I'll look at it." He edged back into the kitchen.

She nodded a goodbye. "It was a pleasure to meet you, Patrick. Consider the meeting, okay?"

"Yes," he said, holding up the flyer. "Thank you ... Susan Reil." He closed the door and peered through the curtain as she made her way down the stairs. It pained him to look at the familiar way she moved, but he still refused to look away.

The Fighter was still out cold as Dolan carried her from the bedroom into the dining room. He placed her on the floor alongside the table. He grabbed the suitcase, made space on the table and began drawing the shades. One of the windows overlooked the front yard. He looked across the street and saw Susan Reil approaching the old man who lived in the blue apartment house across the street. In the past, Dolan had kept his distance from those who tried to talk to him. Mother insisted on it. But this woman was different. Until he'd seen her, he had forgotten how to feel around another person that he knew so well.

He watched her follow the old man inside the apartment, then drew the shade the rest of the way. He sat down in front of the briefcase and opened it. The way mechanism whirled to life as the small display screen in the case's cover activated, displaying the Unation's logo. He removed a pair of goggles from the pouch and fitted them snugly over the eyes of the Fighter, then connected the attached cord to the machine. He heard the goggles activate, retracting her eyelids and searching for a link into her through her optic nerves. Once the way mechanism's warm-up was complete, four small, glass orbs atop thin metallic posts lifted slowly from the four corners of the case. The viscous fluid inside the orbs began to glow and spin. Within the fluid were the tiny luminescent particles of Mother's dust. The dust turned and collected in the center of the orbs. The fluid spun faster, turning green. Next, he meticulously positioned the briefcase until the rays of light coming from the orbs illuminated each of the four walls. He removed another cord from the side pocket of the case, connecting one end to his KI and the other to the way mechanism. He touched the start icon on the display screen, leaned back and waited. Without blinking, he studied the glowing wall in front of him. Watching the transformation was the only way he remained convinced that he was actually traveling between the worlds.

A soft, swaying motion caressed the wall like ripples of water. He felt his head move up and down as he followed the faint, vertical waves. The sharp, distinct corners of the pictures on the wall became blurry, colors washing and blending with green light from the orbs. As the ripples stretched and extended across the ceiling, the machine's light became substance, collecting in globs along the edge of the ceiling, moving slowly down the walls, erasing the paper's floral pattern and leaving behind the drab gray of the crossover room. As the thick jelly slid down, it absorbed the furniture; the small table by the window wavered and vanished, the carpet faded. All the color in the room had disappeared. He was unmistakably back in the Unation.

The heavy door swung open and struck the wall. A young man in a scout uniform entered the room, his rifle raised. Dolan slid the chair back, pulling the way mechanism with him, eyes focused intently on the barrel of the rifle, ready to dash under the table with the Fighter, moaning now. By the grimace on the guard's face, Dolan was sure that Mother was putting an end to his long line of mistakes. He'd brought back damaged merchandise, once again.

"Sir," the scout said sternly. "Please proceed with the check-in procedure immediately."

Dolan stared up the sights of the rifle into the wide eyes of the young man. "I can explain –" he started to say.

"Please proceed, sir," the young man interrupted, his voice wavering. "I will not ask a third time."

Dolan removed the cord from his KI and dropped it to the floor. "Dolan, Patrick M. SL12," he said, as his vocal cords tried to form a knot.

The guard was silent, unmoving, rifle still raised. "You're not finished yet, sir," he said, firming his grip.

Dolan moved to the check-in station against the wall. He activated the unit and waited for identity verification, never removing his eyes from the barrel of the rifle. The emitter activated and waves of green light encircled his head as Mother scanned and calculated Dolan's cephalic index. For a moment he worried that the three-day-old bump above his temple was going to throw off the extremely sensitive measurements. "Clearance approved. Mother welcomes you back, Dolan, Patrick M.," the androgynous voice said. *Nothing to worry about,* he thought. He had been accepted back to the Unation and She didn't seem to be holding him responsible for anything. At least for now – but he had yet to thought-contribute. His mind was full of violations. Mother wasn't going to stand for it any longer. The hammer was going to fall, he was sure of it.

The guard lowered his weapon, slung it over his shoulder. "Thank you for your cooperation, sir," he said, turning toward the door.

"A bit over-zealous, wouldn't you say?" he asked, breathing more easily.

The scout stopped and turned. "Any job Mother gives me, I take seriously, sir."

"What's your name?" Dolan asked.

The scout snapped to attention. "Douglas, Henry A. SL8, sir."

"You're already at status level eight? How *old* are you?"

"Twenty-five, sir."

Unbelievable that Mother would promote young people so quickly. Her greatest concern had always been loyalty, and that only came from *i*-years of dedicated service. Had things really changed so much since he'd gone to Earth that no one needed to prove themselves to Her anymore? What was the rest of the world like by now? During his brief returns to the Unation he hadn't once stepped outside. He wondered if he'd even recognize the place.

Dolan removed the cord from the way mechanism and laid it on the table. "Well," he said gesturing toward the door, "If you don't mind, Henry Douglas, I'd like to contribute now – in private, if I may?"

"Of course, sir. Would you like me to call someone to collect your shipment?" Douglas pointed to the Fighter, who was quiet again.

"She has a name." The one he'd given her anyway.

Douglas stared at him blankly. "Is that important?"

"Just bring her into the hallway and wait there."

The guard hoisted the Fighter onto his shoulder, bouncing her back and forth.

"Take it easy, will you?" Dolan snapped.

"Her pants are soaking wet," the guard said, holding out one hand and shaking off the moisture.

"She had an accident," Dolan said almost in a whisper, wondering if Theman would accept that same excuse for all her bruises and the gash on her head.

Dolan watched Douglas leave, trailing drops of water. He was alone again and he looked around the room for something familiar. It still resembled the general shape of his kitchen, but that wasn't good enough. He felt a strong urge to reach out, activate the way mechanism and go back. But there was no returning yet. His KI was nearly full and he needed to thought-contribute. This *was* still his world, even though there was nothing in it for him. No family, no home, no possessions. He was as alone here as on the other side, but over there he *could* survive without Mother, even if it was only for a very, very short time.

He reluctantly moved to the far wall and connected his KI to the core node. Mother came to him, as did the faint silence of the rest of the Unation. Maggie was in there somewhere, but this time he couldn't sense her, the one time he really longed for it. His KI emptied into Mother but the connection was less than refreshing. Dolan pressed his eyes shut to watch bits of the past day rush out of him and into Her. Jake, the flaming truck, the pack of cigarettes, the Fighter's pool of blood, Susan Reil. Everything that had happened, everything he had thought and contemplated the previous day was now part of Mother. While She was in him he fought hard to convince Her that he didn't really want to stay on Earth. He repeated over and over: *It's all just a pipe dream, Mother.*

As he detached himself from Her, the vidcon on the edge of the table activated. He had a good idea who was calling him. Theman was never known for his patience. The projector lit up and cast a blurry cloud on an image on the floor next to him. "You're late," the image of Theman barked.

"Good afternoon, sir," Dolan said.

The dark, faceless image shifted in the chair, missing from the vidcon's projection. His image hovered above the floor. "You've been smoking again," Theman said angrily.

"Just to blend in, sir," he said, chagrined by his quippy, but very lame excuse.

"No more. I won't tell you again," Theman said, pointing at him. "Now, progress report."

"Well, sir, I've brought you the candidate–" He didn't want to say her name; he wanted to call her the Fighter – "Julianne Morrow, and now I'm crossing back to –"

"You're lucky she's not dead," Theman grumbled, shifting his weight. "If I learn you've pulled another stunt like that, I'll cut you down to SL1. Do you hear me?"

"I do, sir." He hadn't even considered demotion as a punishment. Losing his status level was even worse than REMOVAL from the Unation. It had become an unwritten code. Death before humiliation.

"I understand twelve *i*-years is a long time to be away," Theman said. "Mother and I have been talking over your ability to continue. The incident with this candidate tells us both there's something wrong. You've built quite a career just to throw it away because of something foolish."

"Bad judgment, sir," he said. "That's all I can blame it on."

"You've done excellent work to this point, despite other ... complications. This Earth scenario is working quite well, certainly to our advantage. I don't want to see a change in our progress now. Mother has learned a great deal to this point, and the Unation must continue to benefit from your work."

"I live and work for Her prosperity," Dolan said, knowing it was what She liked to hear.

"It is possible that you need a short hiatus? To become ... re-enlightened to the real world?"

"I still feel capable."

Theman grunted and paused. Dolan could only hear the buzz of the vidcon. "Well, then. Let's discuss your next assignment," Theman said.

"I'm sure you'll be happy to hear that I finished reviewing the candidates' profiles. I think the best one of the three –"

"Mother wants them all," Theman interrupted.

Dolan said nothing, waiting for Theman to repeat himself, sure that he'd misunderstood the man. But Theman just sat there. "All *three*, sir?"

"I know collecting even one is difficult, but Mother and I have decided that we need to take this step. It's important. Very important that She have all three." He seemed adamant. Dolan didn't dare rebut. "After these three, you'll find and collect data on ten more."

That was sure to be the job that would end him; Mother didn't need them, She only wanted to find his breaking point. And She certainly wasn't far from discovering it.

"None of them will be domestic cases," Theman continued.

"They'll be destitute, runaways, but with equally violent tendencies as the others. Don't worry. In the time you kidnap them and return them to Earth, no one will ever know they were gone."

Dolan took a deep breath and held it. Watching three memory caps in a row had pushed him to almost destroying the way mechanism. The thought of letting in ten was painful. Why did Mother want him to suffer like that? Theman should just REMOVE him right there instead of prolonging the inevitable. He fought the urge to be so agreeable, but he couldn't help it. "No problem, sir," he lied. He had a very big problem with it.

"Good. I want you back here before zero hour tomorrow." Theman looked down at a report folder. "Dolan, I'm interested in something your KI review brought out. Tell me more about this woman, Susan Reil."

He could only picture Maggie's face. "I realize I shouldn't have spoken to her, but –"

"That's fine," Theman reassured. "The last thing Mother and I want is for you to become an introvert." His reassuring words sounded so hollow.

"Our meeting was brief," he said. "What would you like to know about her?"

"What was her interest in you?"

"She had me sign a petition, and asked me to join her at some kind of meeting."

"Hmm ... " Theman's fuzzy image pondered, flipping pages, still staring at the report.

This bizarre moment of contemplation was out of place for Theman's direct and to-the-point attitude. Right then his face looked pained, almost troubled. His black image leaned back in the non-existent chair, then flickered out and reappeared almost instantaneously.

"Mother and I have thoroughly discussed this issue. We've decided we want you to go to her," he said.

"Go to her, sir?" The haunting images of Maggie moved in on him as he thought about Susan. The two women were meshing together, much like the two worlds he'd been straddling.

"We want you to join in the meeting and use the position to scan new, potential candidates. Mother is anxious to learn more about them."

"Sir, becoming involved is so risky." Not that he had any right to be dictating rules, especially to Theman.

"You seem to be handling it all right so far. Just remember, Mother can do away with that world as quickly as She created it. That should help you keep it all straight."

"I'll contact her as soon as I return," he said, but that was the last thing he wanted to do.

"You're doing a wonderful job, Patrick. You'll become an SL19 before you know it. Just don't forget, Mother has been adamant about not becoming involved with these people. For now, She's making an exception. But we won't tolerate anymore foolish thoughts of staying." Theman fingered the report then slammed the cover shut. "Understood?"

"Understoo –" The call terminated before Dolan could finish. The room darkened as the vidcon image faded. Convincing Mother that his thoughts of staying on Earth were harmless now seemed like a terrible idea. Theman hadn't made a case of it, but he hadn't needed to. Mother was planning to punish Dolan, simply by resuscitating his memories of Maggie in Susan, and for that he'd rather just be REMOVED. It'd be a lot less painful in the long run.

Three

After waiting nearly ten *i*-years for a promotion that never came, Selmar Rayburne finally convinced himself that Mother Necessity had deserted him. All of his friends and colleagues had moved on to become uppers, climbing the social scale to SL7 quite some time back, leaving him behind to continue struggling as a lower. As an upper, they had gone on to work less difficult, more important jobs. Each couple was given a stylish single-family home with all the trimmings but, to him, none of that really mattered. The material items Mother offered each person for their hard work had come to mean little. He wasn't jealous of their fancy homes, the show-off clothes, any of those things. His own dreams were shattered only when he found out that Mother had issued each of the couples a progeny pass. They had all been given Mother's permission to start a family of their own. All except him. He was more than willing to forgo every item on Her elaborate list just to have a child of his own. That really wasn't too much to ask for. But Mother wouldn't allow any couple to conceive without a progeny pass, and that wasn't going to come without a promotion. It seemed as if Mother was going to make him wait until the end of time. And Sheila had already made it clear she wasn't going to wait that long. Selmar had no choice but to believe that she'd leave him if the opportunity came. He wasn't planning to let that happen. But, with nowhere else to turn, he could only continue calling Mother's bluff – if indeed She was bluffing – and keep working hard, with his mouth shut.

Though keeping quiet didn't mean staying submissive forever. So he stood again in front of the door to the job bank office, wondering if he'd given it enough time between promotion requests. Mother had turned him down for SL7 twice already. Testing Her patience was one thing, but upsetting Her was not high on his own list. He had come here time and time again to get his promotion to SL6, and that was where he had stayed, until right then. He could sense a change in his attitude that morning, a confidence he had lacked. *This could be the day.* He sounded so encouraging. How unlike him.

He had always wanted to blame his lack of progression on his own actions, maybe some shortcoming he'd suffered at a young age, but he knew damn well his father's legacy was the only thing weighing heavily on him. The name Alexander Rayburne still made everyone scowl when they heard it. How could a son disassociate himself from a father who had organized a rebellion against Mother? No chance – it was impossible, especially some forty-five *i*-years after the fact. His father had led the primes, a small group of revolutionaries, in the uprising, protesting Mother and the Incorporation of the world. Most people had welcomed the inception of the KI and its obvious benefits of thought-contributions. But his father and the others didn't want Mother tapping into their minds. Instead of negotiating a solution, She had them rounded up and banished from the Unation, left to fend for themselves while She cared for and nurtured the incorps. Now the primes were fending for themselves, in places where no incorp would want to go. His father had paid the price for his actions, but for some reason Mother felt Selmar needed to suffer as well.

No longer, though. He refused to let his father's bad judgment keep him from progressing through the status levels. One day Mother would see that he was worthy, then he too would be rewarded with a progeny pass. It was just a matter of time.

He tried to relax by taking a slow, deep breath, then straightening his tie. Even he knew a third promotion request in a week was excessive, but so was the amount of time he'd been living as a six.

Without knocking, he opened the door, stopping short of entering once he noticed no one else was waiting. The same tall, pale-skinned woman was sitting behind the small desk in the center of the otherwise empty room. This time her bright red hair was pulled tightly off her face and tied in a huge knot. Dammit, he didn't want the attendant's undivided attention again. That only raised the stakes. She might remember him, call him selfish for coming in a third time and send him on his way. Thankfully, she paid no attention, only continued to shuffle papers back and forth in a frenzy. Still clutching the doorknob, he waited for her to glance up before moving, just in case he had to run the other way. Her hands moved back and forth, papers slipping between her fingers, eyes following the sheets from one pile to another. She finally paused and looked up. Her pained expression melted away and she smiled widely, as if all her troubles had suddenly vanished. "Good evening," she said. "It's a pleasure. How are you today?"

"Fine," Selmar said, still grasping the doorknob.

"Gosh, is that the time?" she said, looking at her chron. "I apologize, but it appears we're closed for the day."

He gently closed the door and approached the woman, confident that she hadn't recognized him. The shiny gold ID plate on the desk gracefully reminded him that her name was Margie. "I need access to the job bank," he said, the words barely making it out.

Her eyebrows sunk in recognition. "Weren't you in here–?"

"I don't think so," he said, doing a terrible job at feigning confusion. "It's been some time."

"No ... I remember you now. Mr Rayburne, right?" She spoke as if he should be reeling in embarrassment just for coming in. There was no way he was about to give this woman, or anyone else for that matter, the satisfaction of seeing any shame on his face. Those days were long gone. Starting right then.

"I don't remember exactly when it was," he admitted, "but I think Mother might have processed my credentials incorrectly last time. Could you check? I mean, something *must* have been wrong for Her to reject me twice, don't you think?" He let out a nervous laugh, hoping to lighten the thickening tension. Margie remained staunch, smiling and expressing nothing more. *He* thought he sounded very convincing but she obviously wasn't going to budge. He hoped not to resort to begging. If that was the case he wished Margie would send him on his way.

"It's after closing time," she said, tapping her chron. "You should want to be home now." She began absently thumbing a stack of paper. Her grin had vanished.

He opened his mouth, decided to hold back the explanation that desperately wanted to come out. *When did making excuses for my life become so second nature?* he wondered. Nevertheless, he felt the urge to explain how his father had betrayed Mother, of his wife's impatience with his lack of promotions, the fragility of his home-life. Often the shame he held for his father infected him, as it was doing right then. Talking about it with a complete stranger would have been too difficult, too painful for him. He had a hard enough time confiding in his own wife. "There's so little to go home to," he said finally.

"Now that's really unfair." She paused to check the knot in hair. "Your family should find a better way to welcome you back each night." She returned to fingering the paperwork. "Don't your children know how much that will affect Mother's perception of them?" she said, still looking down.

"My wife and I don't have children," he whispered, as if someone else might overhear. The words came easily this time and that surprised him. But the admission was still to a stranger. The ridicule was sure to come.

She looked up with sympathetic eyes. "As generous as Mother's been lately? She'd gladly give a progeny pass to anyone who asks for one. Keep trying. It's only a matter of time." She punched the air with her fist as to say *buck up little soldier*. The response was no less pathetic than the last, or the one before that, or–

"I can't go home today without the promotion. Otherwise my life's going to change forever."

"Yes, well Mr Rayburne, I really can't authorize a third request. If your promotion didn't come with the first two tries then ... "

Margie paused, tilting her head as if he should've known better. "Maybe you should hold off till next *i*-quarter," she finished.

She was making it all sound so easy to accept, as if waiting was his best and only solution. But he'd learned that Mother never put Her neck out for those who didn't help themselves. Life in the Unation was not a free ride. Progressing through the status levels was designed to be a team effort. You work, Mother provides – and for *i*-years he'd been doing his job, very well in fact. It wasn't until recently that he started growing tired of his lack of promotions. Mother's unexplained rejections were losing their credibility, almost as quickly as Selmar was losing his patience. Margie didn't seem to grasp that. Maybe she should try living a week with the Rayburne name and see how far she got. Selmar gauged the chances of her success: one-hundred percent guarantee she'd lose her mind inside of an *i*-year.

"Do you have any children?" Selmar asked matter-of-factly.

The smile returned to her face. "I have two beautiful daughters."

"Please tell me how it feels to go home to them at night?"

"They're away right now." Her eyes sank low. "On a two *i*-quarter rotation with their prepmasters."

"Don't you wish they could be with you all the time, rather than –"

"It's tough, them leaving, but you know as well as I do that it's necessary," she explained, obviously trying to convince herself too. "There's no other way for our children to prepare themselves for Incorporation. Don't you remember how you felt when you became an incorp? For me, it changed my life."

He prepared himself for another lecture, one more person who hoped to reeducate him on the importance of prepmasters. But only a family with children needed to recruit one and that excluded him. Mother was making sure the line of Rayburnes ended with the son of the traitor. "I know the children need to be prepared," he said. "It's very important. Bringing a child into this world and raising it to appreciate Mother is all I've ever wanted. Don't you see? That's why I'm here again. I need to become a seven."

"You're only a *six*?" She made no attempt to hide her surprise, acting as if she hadn't known his status level during his first two visits. "I must have been *very* busy last time you were here not to notice that. Go on, tell me why you're only a six."

"Are you going to let me into the job bank?" he asked, losing patience.

She sat upright in her chair. "I'm sorry, sir," she said with a hint of condescension. Her formal tone had returned. "You should be well aware that closing time is the same across the entire sector. And now you've made me late."

"I don't mean to be selfish. I only have Mother in mind when I ask. As soon I become a seven, my wife and I can have a child. Don't you realize how important it is to Mother that we all do what we can to help Her prosper? Think of the service you'd be doing."

She pointed a finger at him. "Please don't lecture me about my duty to Her. You're beginning to sound like my husband."

"You do what you can, I understand that," he said sympathetically. "We all try our hardest to please Her. In our own way."

She lowered her head again. "We do what She wants us to."

"Imagine how happy it'd make Her knowing that you went out of your way for me."

"I'm really tired of hearing how little I do to make Her happy." She seemed to be talking to herself now. "My husband has no idea what it takes to run an office like this. And why should he care anyway. What I do should only matter to Her."

"Don't kid yourself. You're a good woman, Margie. She'll appreciate you helping me."

She looked up, her smile was gone again. "Whatever I do will never be enough for my husband," she whispered. Without another word, she stood and led him into the back room. Her face had become drawn, depressed. She didn't even resemble the same person he'd met coming in. He didn't mean to upset her, but his impatience had driven him to do what it took to get in. Though in the process, he must have inadvertently touched off a worry that she hadn't considered before. "You know," she said, "I'm really looking forward to my daughters coming home." Then she retreated to the front room. Triumph surged in a macabre sort of way. He'd finally relayed his misery onto someone who understood Mother's ability to manipulate. He no longer felt alone.

He approached the row of job bank podiums against the back. The stool in front of the machine he'd used last time was still broken, dangling by a couple of bent bolts. He tried desperately to prepare himself for something other than frustration this time as he moved to the podium furthest from the one he'd been rejected by. After taking his access ribbon from his pocket and rubbing it flat on his thigh, he used two hands to feed it into the scanner, sat down and waited for the Mother to give him access. Since his second rejection two weeks before, he'd struggled to work harder than usual, hoping he could make one last ditch effort to please Her with longer hours, more accounts. His clever, new method of processing and filing rejected progeny passes had certainly helped to speed up his work. He'd never seen so many disappointed couples come through his office in a single week. Hopefully She would realize all he had given up just to please Her – countless hours of sleep, many important social events, those things that would have meant more quality time with Sheila. Of course, the time he gave up with his wife was only to going to better their lives in the long run. He wished Sheila would only see it that way. If anything, it had raised the wall between them even higher. But that would change. He'd show her.

The podium churned as he waited for Mother to respond. Finally, the monitor sparked to life and She invited him to make a selection by touching the screen. Topping Her list of options was: JOB REASSIGNMENT. That was the last thing he ever wanted to consider. Once Mother granted a promotion, an incorp had to take on that assignment until the next promotion. There were no preferences or second choices. One could ask for a new job, but requesting a change in the middle of a status level was nothing short of admitting to a complete loss of faith in Mother. She guided every incorp through their lives, keeping very meticulous records of personal achievements, likes and dislikes, physical abilities. Mother always knew what was best. Nevertheless, the option of reassignment was there for those who wished it, as long as they were willing to pay the price. Humiliation was for sale, very cheap, as he was well aware. But as Sheila had pointed out, there was a lot more at stake than simply his dignity. Of course, that was just her roundabout way of threatening to leave if he didn't see a promotion soon.

The next selection was: PROMOTION REVIEW. He touched the icon and waited while Mother churned over all the details She had in his file since his last promotion. No doubt his portfolio was the longest and most elaborate of any She kept. Packed with ten *i*-years' worth of *i*-quarterly work reviews, an occasional promotion rejection stuck in for good measure. Each time he came here it took Her longer and longer to turn him down, and this visit would certainly be no different. But what did he have to lose? After thinking about that carefully he realized he had quite a bit to lose. Mother was about to break up his marriage into tiny little pieces and distribute them all over the sector – that is, if She continued to keep him under Her thumb. But maybe there really was a chance for him. A lot had happened since he'd last been in a few days earlier. She'd no doubt consider the usefulness of his recent thought-contributions, and of course he had passed along to Her all the relevant thoughts concerning his new filing method. That would allow Her and so many other incorps extra time to tend to other things. That should count for something.

But Mother obviously didn't think so. The screen flashed: *Promotion Denied.*

The podium printed the transaction receipt and ejected it onto the floor by his feet. But he wasn't about to submissively walk away this time. Margie could go home to her family but he was going to stay all night if he had to. There was going to be a radical change in the course of his life before the day was over. He swore to it.

He stood, reset the machine and pushed down hard on the screen. Rolling back and forth on his feet, he waited, hovering over the podium. He kept this up for nearly five minutes, but nothing came back. She was not about to continue ignoring him.

Not anymore. He took a step back, glanced into the front room where Margie continued to shuffle papers with one hand while holding her head up with the other. He stepped forward again, and with still no response, hit the side of the podium with an open palm. The thing was like an unmoving iceberg buried deep below the dingy gray carpeting. As he rubbed out the sore spot on the ball of his hand, the machine rang back: *Approved.*

It was hard to believe what he was seeing on the screen, though the response was quite plain. Could it have been some mistake? Maybe by hitting the machine he had confused it, inadvertently giving someone else the promotion he needed. The ticket printed and ejected. He caught it in midair and read. Yes, his name was right there next to the words: *Promotion Granted.*

The world he'd been forced to keep so tightly contained in his head split open. Status level seven – an upper. He'd finally joined the club. Sheila was going to be so relieved, all that worry in vain. Mother had put their lives back on course. He knew Mother would find him worthy of being a seven, and having his own children. He would not let Her down like his father had. Standing right there, he raised his right hand and swore on Mother's good name.

Before returning to the front room he searched the bottom of the sheet, anxious to find out where he should report to work the next morning. Ten *i*-years of the same job day in and day out made a man long for any kind of change. He would have shoveled dirt with the SL1 crowd for an *i*-quarter just for a change. His eyes scanned the bottom of the paper: *KI processing center – Criminal division.*

His heart and shoulders sank. Just when he thought there wasn't anything worse than moving piles of sand. True, the promotion was finally going to earn him the respect of his peers – well maybe not that far, though at least the ridicule would end – but there was certainly no honor in KI processing. Seeing to the REMOVAL of any incorp was not his idea of a worthy day's work, even those that had committed crimes against Mother. The thought of telling his children what he had to do to become an upper made him sick to his stomach. Once again, he'd come so far only to be stopped by humiliation. Was there any place it couldn't come from? Certainly not if Mother was taking an active part in his lifetime of hazing. Mother would never see him as anything less than the man his father had been. He stared at the job bank screen and its bold letters: JOB REASSIGNMENT. His finger hovered above the screen momentarily, but he couldn't bring himself to touch the words. He removed his access ribbon from the podium, picked up the old rejection slip off the floor and walked out, feeling no further ahead, no closer to redemption, than he did while suffering as a lower. This certainly was not the radical change he was hoping for.

The vidcon on the edge of his desk was ringing when he returned to his office. He triggered the call and waited impatiently for the person's three-dimensional projection to take shape in the center of the room. The fuzzy image sharpened to reveal the likeness of Sheila, and she didn't look happy. A separate streak of light from the vidcon tracked Selmar as he circled his desk, sending his own image back to his living room – where he realized he should have been right at that moment.

"Dinner is on the table," Sheila said, folding her arms in disgust.

He carefully covered the half-eaten sandwich on his desk with a folder, worried of the slightest possibility that she could see it. "I lost track of time. Some things here got me a little crazy."

"Every chron in this house tells me you were suppose to be here an hour ago."

"Mother gave me the promotion today." The words didn't come out quite like he'd expected. Becoming an upper should have been a time for celebrating. After all, they could finally request a progeny pass, their first step to finally having children. He wanted to feel overjoyed by announcing it, but the words went flat. He could have easily been telling her it was raining.

"The job bank let you in a third time in less than a week?"

"More like ten days," he said, unable to decide if she had actually heard what he'd told her.

"You can tell me all about your new assignment when you get here. Just tell me when you're leaving."

"I'm almost through."

"Selmar, you're finished now. That position isn't yours any-more. Just leave the unfinished work for your replacement. I need you home with me. Mr Dodd is here, and we're waiting for you."

"He's there *now* ... ? That was tonight?" he asked, knowing full well. The dinner meeting had been planned for weeks and she hadn't stopped talking about it since, but he didn't want to involve himself in anything Montgomery Dodd had to offer. Selmar didn't see anything wrong with Sheila's current job.

"We're about to sit down to dinner, less one husband. Now get back here." Of course food wasn't on her mind as much as the chance of a new assignment. Her progression through the status levels had become so important that she'd given up on just about everything else. Including Selmar's chances at a successful career. She had moved quickly to SL7, only to be suspended there because she couldn't exceed Selmar by more than one status level – the cardinal rule of any marriage. But Mother was anxious to promote her, and Dodd was there to give Sheila "an opportunity of a lifetime". Whatever the hell that meant. Selmar figured that Mother treated those who *acquire* the Rayburne name quite differently from those born with it. "Mr Dodd's offer is better than I could've ever imagined," she whispered.

"Yes, but Sheila, we've talked about that. Even you said the whole thing sounded ridiculous. Even you called the man a –"

"Shh!" She raised a finger to her mouth and took several, quick steps, though her image didn't move from its spot in the center of his office. "I don't want him hearing you say that."

"But think about what we've discussed. About all our plans when I finally became a seven."

"Selmar, let's talk about what's happening right now. Opportunities are being presented to me that we cannot pass up. Things just aren't the same as they were a couple of *i*-years ago."

"How are they any different now?" He felt like he was still fight-ing to become an upper. So far, holding the honors wasn't all it was cracked up to be. "If anything, after what happened today, our situation is better. It's all been fixed."

"I really don't want to get into this again, especially over the vidcon." Her tone turned accusatory.

"You're the one who brought it up," he snapped, pointing at her image. "We've been waiting for my promotion for a long time."

"Lately, *you've* been waiting for it, Selmar. I've been focusing on what matters now."

He paused for a moment, wishing for once she'd give in to him and really listen. "What do you think I'm trying to do here?"

"The same thing you've always been doing. To convince yourself that the world is exactly the way it used to be."

He couldn't understand it. Two *i*-years ago they couldn't stop talking about children. The person standing in front of him wouldn't even admit they'd ever considered the topic. "The world is still the same," he said. "We're the ones who've change."

She remained silent, breathing heavily enough for him to hear through the vidcon's audiophone. "I'm done arguing, darling husband," she said through stiff lips. "When are you coming home?"

He shrugged and looked down. "I won't make it for dinner."

"You're being so unfair. Can't you understand that?"

"I only have a few more cases to file." He thought he saw genuine hurt in her eyes ... or maybe it was just a glitch in the transmission.

"So you're refusing to be here to hear out Mr Dodd?"

"You obviously didn't intend to refuse his offer in the first place," he said. "Why do I need to be there?"

"I can't understand you," she said sternly, trying to move closer to him, though her image remained still. "How can you be so indifferent?"

"Sheila, I know my promotion took a long time, but I made it. Won't you acknowledge that?"

"It's too late."

"For *what* ... ? Why?" He cringed slightly at the desperation in his voice.

"I've already accepted Mr Dodd's offer. I'm leaving in the morning."

He circled his desk faster than the vidcon's viewing beam could track him. The machine beeped ferociously.

"Selmar, I'm losing you," Sheila exclaimed.

He stopped, letting the vidcon catch up, then moved closer to her image. "*Leaving?* You can't be serious about this?"

"I've never been more serious or determined about anything in my life. Do you know what this means for my career?"

"No, I don't," he said flatly.

"Stop being so damn uncaring!"

"Don't do anything yet," he said, searching the top of his desk for the promotion slip. "I'm coming home, right now. We'll talk about it."

"There's nothing more to talk about. Goodbye, Selmar." And the vidcon went silent.

She had promised for the longest time that she would remain strong while Mother toyed with him, refusing him promotions, making him the laughing stock of his friends and colleagues. At one time Sheila did care; he was her life, and she would have done anything to ensure they'd always be together. But at some point starting a family had become the last thing on her mind. Certainly Dodd's job offer wasn't the right thing for either of them. All he'd need to do was convince her of that.

He grabbed his coat off the peg by the door and left without locking the office.

As he stepped out of the lobby into the damp outdoors he noticed the pedways were abandoned. Why wouldn't they be? It was an hour and a half past closing time; everyone else was already home with their families. He turned right, walking between the buildings of the Eastern Central sector's main office complex, their tops disappearing into the high cloud cover. Bushes and shrubs grew up along the edges of the pedways where cars no longer ran.

Underground subshuttles had become the only way to travel long distances, though even the shuttles had stopped making runs by that time. His house was all the way on the other side of the sector, in the outermost housing zone. Quite a hike, but walking was his only choice. After figuring the distance, he swore at himself for staying past closing time.

Ten blocks south, then he turned right onto Fifty-first Pedway, dodging a groomed collection of hydrangea shrubs in the middle of the path. They had been arranged in a circular pattern to resemble the emblem of the Unation. At one time Sheila tried to recreate a smaller version of it in her garden. She had to have a dinner party just to use the arrangement as a conversation piece. Needless to say, she made new friends that night. *Flowers*, he thought. *She'll love them till the end.* And bringing some home with him certainly couldn't hurt.

He searched the block for a podium shop, hoping there was still one open that time of evening, but found himself surrounded only by a group of low-rise office suites, a handful of podium construction warehouses and an abandoned maintenance depot. One of the smaller, empty buildings still had a pre-Incorporation sign hanging on the outside, a artifact that had gone unnoticed. Too bad he didn't know any relic buyers interested in collectibles from butcher shops, whatever they were.

Two blocks in the opposite direction, he finally found a podium shop. Through the crack of the door he could see a pair of feet behind a closed curtain and decided to wait for the other lonesome straggler to finish. He thought he was being somewhat paranoid, but couldn't find it in him to trust anyone who wasn't home at that time of night. Finally, a man exited the podium shop, empty-handed no less. They nodded silently to each other and the stranger moved on. Selmar stepped inside, closed the door, and watched through the window until the man disappeared around the corner. He glanced around to ensure no one else was coming, then got down to business. Eight bulky, commercial-size podiums lined the walls. They were nearly a head taller than him and every corner was reinforced with industrial plastic. Even the display screen was encased behind protective coverings. There was no way anyone was going to damage or steal one of these, and he was grateful for that because he'd now be the one sending that criminal for REMOVAL. *How degrading for the both of us*, he thought.

A thick, blue curtain hung between each podium, giving the smallest amount of privacy. He approached a podium to his left. After closing the curtain, he removed his access ribbon from his pocket and slipped it into the scanner. The podium activated and emitted a concentrated ray of light that enveloped his head. Mother took her measurements, and once She agreed that Selmar really was himself, the screen displayed Her typical welcome message:

YOU'VE WORKED HARD TO EARN THESE REWARDS. DON'T LOSE YOUR PRIVILEGES BY GIVING, OR EVEN WORSE, SELLING THEM TO OTHERS. EVERYONE IN THE UNATION IS ENTITLED TO WHAT THEY DESERVE. HELPING OTHERS MAY SERVE THEIR IMMEDIATE NEEDS, BUT ONLY MOTHER NECESSITY KNOWS WHAT IS TRULY BEST FOR EACH AND EVERY ONE OF YOU. WOULDN'T YOU AGREE, SELMAR RAYBURNE SL7?

To that point, Selmar had no need to pay attention to Mother's warning. He couldn't think of anyone who'd want items off the list of a lower. But all that was going to change from that day onward. He pressed CONTINUE and scanned his new SL7 list. He noticed how long it had become, eyes quickly spotting what was new. Finer clothes was now an option, even a tuxedo if he wanted one for the upper's *i*-quarterly galas. Nicer home furnishing, genuine leather objects, too. He had the urge to gloat, but as he continued to scan he noticed that what remained was intended to accommodate a life with children – the ones Sheila no longer wanted.

Fighting frustration, he scrolled further and stopped at *Plants, Flowers – Arranged*, something any SL1 could request. Gently, he touched the screen to confirm his choice. A series of beeps was followed by a long pause, and finally a message flashed across the screen.

I'M VERY SORRY, SELMAR, BUT THAT CATEGORY HAS ALREADY BEEN ACCESSED TO ITS LIMIT THIS I-QUARTER. COULD I RECOMMEND A LOVELY SET OF WINE GLASSES? AT SOCIAL STATUS LEVEL SEVEN YOU HAVE ACCESS TO THE FINEST WINES. PERHAPS MY SPECIAL MERLOT, BOTTLED CIRCA ...

He impatiently lifted the bay door on the side of the podium. It was empty. Apparently, during Sheila's recent floral frenzy she had depleted the creds they'd earned for live plants. The podium spit out his access ribbon, and a paper stub confirming delivery of twelve long-stem roses to his home on the first day of the next i-quarter. He crumpled the ticket and dropped it on the floor. Hoping to cancel the order, he pressed firmly on the ABORT key. When he released it, the button popped off, fell to his feet and tinkled against the floor. He kicked it and the ball of paper underneath the podium.

As he left the shop he noticed it had started raining again. An umbrella was also an SL1 item and he considered going back to request one. *No*, he decided, *it's not worth it.* He'd only suffer another disappointment. Instead, he pulled his coat tightly around him, collar wrapped over his head, and ran down Fifty-first Pedway toward home.

The rain continued to drop like needles, even as he stumbled through the front door almost an hour later. He removed his sopping wet coat and hung it carefully over the doorknob. Water ran onto the tile and collected under his feet. He peeled off his shoes and left them there, soles soaking in the small puddle. He heard Sheila in the kitchen making a racket.

"Good evening, everyone," he said, stopping in the middle of the living room to notice the overabundance of week-old flowers. "I apologize for being so late."

"He's gone, Selmar," Sheila said from the kitchen. "He left about ten minutes ago." The clanking of dishes continued.

He could see his bedroom door. It would be so easy to avoid talking to her, needing to fight just to convince her to stick by him. If Dodd was already gone his chances of talking her out of the job were close to none – her decision had been made. But he couldn't ignore the plans they'd made to start a family. Sheila was too important to him to lose her now. The only way to correct the problem was to take small steps. First he'd have to go to her, and apologize for his shortsightedness. He was in this for the long term, and staying together was the only sane solution. "How ... how'd it go?" he asked, walking into the kitchen.

She turned and looked at the floor by his feet. "You're soaking wet."

"Didn't have my umbrella."

"You couldn't stop at a podium shop?" she asked, eyeing the wet footprints he was walked.

"I didn't pass one walking home."

"Your fault for not paying attention to the time." She returned to the counter and continued cleaning.

"I missed the last subshuttle," he said. "It left the terminal early." She was loading dirty dishes into the return bin of the podium. Once she loaded it and closed the lid, Mother converted the contents back into Her fissor material and returned it to storage. Eventually, Mother would reuse what had been the dirty dishes to create something else. Maybe the very arrangement of roses that was due to arrive about five weeks too late. "Did Mr Dodd enjoy dinner?" he asked.

"Very much," she said proudly, as if she'd actually prepared it.

"He didn't want to meet me?"

"When you're a nineteen like Monty you don't have time to wait around for other people."

"*Monty?*" he said. "Since when were you granted first name basis with one of the Seniors?"

"He asked that I consider us equals."

Selmar sat down at the table and slid a vase of zinnias out of the way. "What did you say to him?"

"Selmar, you're leaking everywhere." She knelt, peeled off his drenched socks and stuck them in the return bin with a dirty casserole dish.

"Thank you," he whispered, not sure if she heard him.

"You know exactly what I talked to him about. I already told you."

"Sheila, I'm a seven now. That changes everything." She continued to ignore him. "I'm starting a new job tomorrow."

"So you said. What did Mother assign you to do?"

"Processing in the Criminal Division," he said, "if you can believe it. I'm going to be sending convicted incorps for REMOVAL." She said nothing, but she didn't need to. He already knew what she thought about it – about his entire situation for that matter. "Probably the most terrible thing Mother could've given me."

"You're the one who wanted the promotion so badly," she said, wiping the counter. She tossed the rag in the bin. "I suppose it could've been worse."

"What about *our* hope to see this happen for me?"

"Removal processing–?" she pondered, joining him at the table. "Didn't Jay Vickers do that too, when he was given seven?"

Hearing the name of his best friend sent a chill through his body, but he couldn't figure out why. Jay had always been there for him, the one person who seemed to have all the answers, though their last conversation was strangely absent from his memory. He remembered talking to Jay sometime recently about all this ... Maybe it was her persistence in changing the subject that was making him forget. "I have no intention of dragging Jay's name into this," he said. She still had no response. "I want to talk about starting a family!" There – he'd finally come right out with it.

She refused to look at him, just stared at the puddle of water that continued to accumulate under his bare feet. It was not the reaction he'd expected or hoped for, but she was making it clear enough. Somewhere along the way he'd lost her. She had created other needs, other dreams, other aspirations, and had decided to follow them all on her own. Even after she had promised to stand by him against anything that came their way. Now he'd have to rely solely on Mother, and She was currently holding his life in a perpetual state of oblivion. Mother had succeeded at separating him from the one person that helped define him a whole person. Without Sheila, he felt he would crumble.

She sighed, then turned to face him. "Selmar, Monty needed to know tonight. I had to make the decision without you."

"Can't you change your mind?" he pleaded.

She looked up at him, eyes wide, cheeks flushing. "I don't want to!"

"Don't scream at me!"

"Selmar, I've been very patient, waiting around as long as I could." Her voice had eased some. "A long time ago you promised me that our chances for a family were coming. I trusted you back then, but Mother didn't allow you to follow through with your end of the bargain. And where did that leave me? Waiting for who knows how many i-years while you try to fix something you were born with."

"I can *change* those things about me."

She dropped her elbow to the table and pointed at him. "You're going to be your father's son till the day you die."

He sighed heavily, lowered his head. She was right – as always. "What else can I do?" he asked.

"Nothing, except move on, make the best of what you have."

"Yes, let's do that." Finally, she was recognizing there was hope. They could go on, they could both make a change for the better.

"It's too late for me," she said. "It has been for a long time."

But it wasn't too late. Mother had made him a seven, and now they could put in a request for a progeny pass first thing the next morning. It was their first, best opportunity to set things right again. "There's still so much we can do," he explained. His anxiety felt like a rake in his throat.

"Selmar," her voice had calmed. She placed her hands on top of his. "I've signed on with Monty. This special assignment is important to him, and to me. He says I'm the key he's been searching for. I'm the integral part of his plan. I am the one."

"Why is it more important than us?"

"It'll guarantee me a promotion to eight. It's wonderful news that you moved up, but now you need to let me progress too.

That's why I'm going."

He sunk low in the chair, realizing his legs had fallen asleep; he couldn't feel his feet. "To where?" he asked.

"Selmar, you're not going to ..." She paused, let out a heavy breath, then continued. "I'm going to the Southeast sector. The position requires me to be gone a minimum of one *i*-year. After that, I'll be back."

He said nothing for a moment, simply listened to the faint roar of a plix passing overhead. He couldn't believe she'd agreed to go that far. She hated flying. "What's down there?" he asked curiously.

"Monty is following Mother's suggestion that we collaborate with the primes."

"*Collaborate* ... ?" He was appalled that Mother would even consider it. How could She just ignore more than forty *i*-years of segregation? Mother had turned Her back on those who tried to stifle the Incorporated way of life for good reason – to protect the security and prosperity of those who wanted a better world. And now that Selmar was a part of it all again, he'd be damned if the primes were going to waltz right by him. They didn't deserve Her. "Doesn't Mother realize what She's considering?" he asked. "Mr Dodd of all people should know what'll happen if the primes are let back in now. All this time on their own to think stuff up. I can't even imagine what their minds must be like. They'll poison Mother's thought tank. They probably don't even look like us anymore."

"Monty says it's like looking in a mirror," she said, moving the zinnias back to where they'd been. "They're a reflection of who we used to be he says."

"I can't believe Mother's worried about *me* having children, but She wants to let the primes back in, as if nothing ever happened."

"Mother never expected them to survive this long. They've even prospered. She wants us to find out how."

"Sheer luck," he said sarcastically. Sheila opened her mouth to rebut, but said nothing. "Why're you doing this?" he pleaded, laying his palms flat on the table. "Is this out of spite?"

She continued to shake her head, frustrated. "I'm doing this for me."

"There was a time when we were a family."

"Selmar, that's behind us now." She turned away, her face turning to stone.

"What do you mean *behind?*"

She cleared her throat, then stood from the table, turning her back to him. "I really shouldn't be talking about it. I promised Monty."

"I'm your husband, dammit!" Status level was not going to have a bearing on the secrets they shared, regardless if Dodd was a nineteen or on the council of Senior SL's.

She choked on the words, then finally managed to speak. "My KI is going to be REMOVED."

At first, the words seemed like a dream, reverberating in his ears, making them ring. He tried to shake her cryptic words from his head. "Can you talk slower?" he asked.

She faced him and cleared her throat. "Monty and I are having our KI's taken out when we get to the Southeast sector."

"Oh, please," he laughed, leaning back, nearly falling out of the chair. "Do you know how stupid that sounds?"

Her eyes grew wide. "Don't call me stupid! I really can't stand–"

"Listen to yourself. Mr Dodd's got you under some kind of spell." He stood and paced around the table.

"Look, Selmar, I'm just telling you what Monty said."

"Taking them out is part of the Grand Contribution – it's how we die! Why would you even begin to believe that living through it is possible?"

"We can't connect to Mother once we're there. There're no core nodes in the camp."

"What camp? You mean *in* the prime encampment?"

She shrugged. "Monty says it's all part of Mother's plan. And I believe him."

"Just like when he told you that you're the *one.*" He waved his hands above his head.

She paused as if searching for the perfect response. There were so many right things she could say, but he wasn't expecting to hear any of them. "Stop being so dramatic," she said finally.

"I'm the one trying to be reasonable here." He walked by her and approached the counter podium. He turned it on and requested a cup of coffee. After a few seconds he lifted the door, removed the steaming cup and sipped carefully. Perfect every time, always the same temperature, just a splash of milk, two teaspoons of sugar. The only thing he could ever rely on.

"Why are you pushing me?" she asked. "Will that make it easier for you after I'm gone?"

"I'm on the losing end again," he muttered, still facing the other way.

"There'll be no losers, Selmar. Mother's plan ..." She sighed heavily. "If you could only conceive of the potential."

"Not the kind of conception I was hoping for." He turned toward the wall and took in a mouthful of coffee, burning his tongue. "But I suppose we all have to sleep with the enemy at some point."

"Selmar, I'm sorry we have to leave things like this." There were no words worth speaking. He'd already said everything he had to say. He gulped the last of his coffee. "Are you listening to me?" she asked. A moment of silence passed between them. "I figured as much, darling husband. Well, I'm leaving first thing in the morning. I expect you won't get in my way and make me late. I have a plix to catch and it won't wait for me. I'm not passing up this opportunity."

"I won't bother you," he said, lips still against the mug, voice echoing dully inside. "Not anymore."

Four

Not until dawn broke did Selmar realize he hadn't slept a wink all night. He'd only lain there, eyes wide, staring at the ceiling, thinking endlessly about Sheila's plan to leave him. Mother's project was a mistake, and even to conceive a plan to contact the primes was a crime in itself. Mother would never have tolerated it had an incorp contributed the idea to Her. Radical thinkers and revolutionaries were exactly the types of people he'd be processing in his new job, which made him wonder if that made his assignment necessity and respectable after all. Regardless, there was nothing anyone could do when Mother became the perpetrator. No one could touch Her, no one could reprimand Her, or convince Her that contacting the primes would be fatal to the Unation. Though the opinion of one man didn't matter. Mother wouldn't listen anyway. She always looked out for Herself. But Selmar wondered how he was any different. He was only emulating Mother by doing what was best for himself – making sure Sheila stayed. Time was running out, though. She'd be gone in a few hours, and so would his chances to prove that he was worthy. To do that he needed to show her that Dodd was wrong, dead wrong.

His chron beeped, signaling that his KI was nearly full, and he stifled it before it woke Sheila. He rolled out of bed for the tedious morning ritual, and as he stood the mattress springs squeaked. Sheila stirred under the covers, then sighed. Still asleep. He searched for his slippers by the night stand and, after sliding them on, moved quietly toward the living room. He slid a chair over to the core node mounted on the wall adjacent to the fireplace. The connecting cord had fallen behind the plant stand again and he reached around to find it. Sheila had always asked him to return it to the clip when he was finished, but lying it over the back of the hearth was so much easier, especially since they both had to use it twice a day. He slipped the connector onto his KI port. As Mother made Her way into him, his perception of the room became exaggerated. The walls and floor stretched and twisted, the ceiling lifted away into the sky. He shut his eyes, blotting out his own reality as Mother's presence grew inside him. He heard a soft, androgynous voice between his ears:

Welcome, Selmar. Thank you for connecting with Me today. So much good will come from your thought-contributions. Sharing your thoughts and dream makes everyone's life better.

He lost sight of the conscious sensation of himself and became a small, insignificant part of Her. All his thoughts and ideas from the previous twelve hours had become a part of Her. The memories of Sheila's announcement, his own pathetic reaction, his jealous loathing of Dodd – they meshed with Mother's knowledge. He longed to ask Her advice on his predicament, because he was desperate. To finally hear Her reason for his *i*-years of setbacks and upsets, to discover why She was taking Sheila away, all about the primes. But She wasn't going to tell him, because only Mother knew why She did what She did. One only needed to implicitly believe and trust Her.

Authorization complete. There were zero point zero thalamites of unauthorized memory detected on your KI. I had to erase nothing from your mind and your memories have now become a permanent part of you and Me. Work hard, ponder new ideas, and most of all, enjoy the next twelve hours, Selmar.

He blinked several times and contorted his face, trying to shake off the cold numbness that always set in afterward. He pulled at the cord and it popped off with ease. He draped it over the hearth and mulled his contribution to Mother's thought tank. Nothing but a mind full of worry and regret. Nothing useful. What a waste.

He returned to the bedroom, but stopped short of crawling under the sheets again. Sheila was still asleep, breathing so softly he could barely hear her. Poor, gullible woman. She'd been taken so easily by Dodd's nonsense of having her KI extracted. No one in their right mind would even consider doing that unless they were ready for REMOVAL, to make the Grand Contribution – the final step beyond passing along thoughts and ideas to Mother. For this, She absorbed your entire body. Sheila wasn't *that* crazy. Taking out a KI lead to nothing but sudden death. Sheila knew that. Everyone knew it. Somehow her perception of the truth had become clouded, and surely it was because of Dodd. No matter what anyone else told her, Dodd's answers were always right. But there had to be details he was keeping from her. Dodd must have concocted the KI story as some kind of diversion, to cover up something far worse. Selmar had a right to know the dangers his wife would be in, but Sheila had given him no straight answers. The only solution to saving her from a huge mistake, and saving his own dignity, was to ask Dodd himself. But how do you confront such a powerful man, the one who rescued the world from the brink of disaster? Incorporating an entire planet was an extraordinary accomplishment for one person, nevertheless, the Unation was his doing. Mother wanted everyone to praise Dodd as they would Her. Though at the time, Selmar recalled that some people wouldn't bring themselves to worship either of them – his father for one. Selmar had always refused to share in his father's animosity, but Dodd *had* put the kibosh on his plans for a family. That wasn't worth a single ounce of praise as far as he was concerned, no matter what condition the world was in before Dodd decided to rescue it.

He tiptoed to his closet and dressed quickly. While buttoning his pants, he moved to the living room and activated the vidcon. Quietly, he spoke into the audiophone. "Residential address listings. Dodd, Montgomery SL19." He waited for the machine to complete its search. There was a squeak of mattress springs from the bedroom. He scribbled down the information and slid out the front door just as he heard Sheila crawl out of bed.

He still had two full hours before zero hour, the time everyone was required to report to work. The subshuttles hadn't started the early morning runs from the housing to the labor zone, so he kept up a quick pace toward Dodd's. He felt like he'd walked more in the past day than all of last *i*-quarter, but Mother's travel conveniences only benefited those who followed routine. And proving Sheila wrong was anything but routine.

Dodd's house was still at least another hour away, maybe one and a half, though he couldn't be exactly sure since anyone less desperate would've waited for the subshuttles to start up. But that was too long. He wouldn't make it back in time for Sheila, or for work.

He quickened his step, almost to a trot, knowing there was no way he could be late for the first day of his new assignment. A car – now that was what he needed. But Mother had done away with them shortly after Incorporation, all part of Her plan to re-unify the world. *Who can mingle and prosper in the solitary confines of a car?* He could, that was who. Apparently, the only conveniences that were fine were those She created. All others took a back seat.

Nevertheless, he was determined to go where he needed to, by whatever means necessary, to keep Sheila from making the biggest mistake of her life. Stealing a scout vehicle had even crossed his mind, but that was just on the shy side of crazy – making the Grand Contribution now wouldn't help his cause in the least bit. He wasn't giving in to desperation. Not yet anyway.

He moved faster. Time passed. Zero hour bore down. As the sun made its way over the tops of the smaller buildings, people began to emerge, crowding the pedways. The rain had ended during the night leaving behind an obstacle course of puddles, and the silent crowd moved carefully around the wet spots as if they were more than just water. A handful of loners glanced at him as they passed, turning away quickly when he tried to meet their eyes. Others moved in pairs or threes, talking among themselves, lifting their eyes just long enough to address the others in their group. But they were speaking so softly and only in short quips, as if long, drawn-out responses might give away some secret they'd meant to keep. Often it appeared as if the crowds were talking about him, looking up, pointing furtively, and Selmar tried to read their lips while clumsily dodging the people and the puddles. They, too, must have heard something about him, if not from Dodd then from Mother Herself. But it couldn't have been about Sheila's plans or his lack of progression over the *i*-years. Those who bothered to look did it with glares like the ones he had often given his father.

As Selmar turned to watch a man point and cover his mouth while speaking to a companion, he felt water swirl around his left ankle and into his shoe. He hopped to the edge of the pedway and tugged on the shoe, trying to keep one eye on the man who had been pointing. He and his companion were nowhere to be found. The water around Selmar's foot was like glue; the shoe refused to come off. He pulled, bouncing on one leg, trying carefully not to fall into anyone around him. He gave up and put his foot down, feeling like a spectacle. He expected to see huge vidcons peering down from the buildings around him, recording every move he made. Perhaps they were really there, only they couldn't be seen.

No, that was crazy. What purpose would Mother have for watching? She wasn't going to catch him doing anything out of the ordinary, nothing illegal. He was only interested in finding out the truth about his wife from Dodd. What was the crime in that? But the paranoia intensified, sparked by the thought of the vidcons watching him. Something wasn't right, inside him and out. He felt infected with treason, as if it were wrong for him to pursue the truth. Then he felt his insides change as if an entirely new organ was making itself known to him. And it was leaking poison. What flowed into him was a remnant of a memory that had been buried deep inside that hollow vessel. The taste of day-old blood appeared on his tongue. He felt unclean, as if he hadn't bathed in weeks. The liquid in his shoe no longer felt like water.

The paranoia of being watched had pulled the memory free. It was of his friend, Jay Vickers, the only person in the world who ever took the time to truly understand him. Jay always listened when Sheila wouldn't, and somehow managed to find the right words. His friend had always been loyal and trustworthy. But at that moment Selmar felt that Jay was no better a man than his father, and he couldn't figure why. The poison in his body was playing tricks on him. That had to be wrong – Jay was no coward, and he certainly wasn't a traitor. Nevertheless, the urge to condemn his friend was enveloping Selmar like a stagnant cloud. Three passers-by, a man and two women, stopped and stared curiously. Only then did he realize the contorted expression his face had taken. He flashed a quick smile and walked away, sloshing every other step.

The memory continued to grow as the poison spread. He remembered meeting with Jay recently in some dark, secluded place, a spot near the outer woods, a place he'd never been before. The words from Jay's mouth, and the tone he'd taken, were that of Selmar's father. In his mind he could see the physical words pouring out of Jay, though they were in a language he didn't know and had no chance of ever comprehending. As the words fell to the ground, they liquefied and soaked into Selmar's shoe. Then he knew – he understood, and he wished there was some way to unlearn the treasonous language his mind had just decoded. How could Jay dare to think the same way Selmar's father had?

Selmar was pulled from his dreamy daze by a mechanical whirling noise that pierced the din of the crowd's banter. At first it sounded like a low-flying plix, humming and rumbling from his left, then right, around and around, as if it were casually circling the zone. He hustled through a maze of puddles and bushes toward the other corner of the square. The sound became more familiar – not a plix anymore, but a scout vehicle, one of the big ones used to carry criminals to the REMOVAL bays in a display of humiliation.

He ran to the next block, stopped at the intersection to peer down between the towering buildings, and looked for the armored monster that would muscle its way through anything to find its target. There was nothing to be found anywhere, just people moving around, oblivious to the scouts bearing down on them.

Maybe because none of them could hear it. Only the guilty ones were paranoid enough to hear Mother coming for them.

The words from Jay's mouth, the same ones dampening Selmar's shoe, pleaded for him to run. Selmar swallowed a mouthful of air as he turned, and he ran in the opposite direction of the crushing sound. He had finally gotten the answer he sought. Mother had taken Sheila away from him so She could finally get rid of the real problem – the "Rayburne" problem. This had been Her plan all along.

He tried to move away from the noise, but at every turn he found himself facing it again. All at once, the people in the square lifted and turned their eyes toward him, as if suddenly aware of the crime he'd committed. But he hadn't done anything. He couldn't explain why Mother wanted him. Did he have something beyond knowledge that She couldn't retrieve from his mind? He wasn't ready to give himself to Her. Not in that way.

He turned, thought he saw a younger version of his father in the thickening crowd, and tried to go to him. The crowd got in his way. The noise was becoming louder, deafening.

Finally, the thing emerged from between two buildings at the next corner – an elongated tube-like vehicle, hovering above the pedway, sun reflecting off its silver surface. It was an automobile – a floating one, but a car just the same. It moved around the corner, past Selmar and the crowd that had gathered. The driver's face was obscured behind lightly-tinted glass, waving occasionally with the back of his shadowy hand. A sparkling gold sign hung from the rear quarter panel: WITHOUT MOTHER NECESSITY, WHERE WOULD WE BE?

"Indeed," someone said as the vehicle floated down the pedway. Once it turned the corner several blocks down everyone continued to move again, trance broken. A plague of agitation spread throughout the crowd.

"Mother's brought the automobile back," a young man said.

"Does anyone know what level you have to be to get one?" a woman was asking anyone who would listen.

"I knew I've been saving my creds for a reason," the stout man in front of Selmar let out in a fit of glee. The man pulled an access ribbon out of his wallet and started counting on his fingers as he walked hastily toward a podium shop across the pedway. A crowd had already gathered there.

So few people ever had the urge to request items from Mother so early in the morning. Everyone was always eager to get to work. Earning creds to spend on items like that compelled them not to miss a single day. But this time something more powerful was driving them to line up, an influence over them that Mother sustained with Her innovations. It had nothing to do with what the world needed.

On any other day, Selmar would have also been fighting to squeeze in line at the podium shop, but Jay's voice told him to leave, so he turned and ran as fast as he could in the other direction.

After an hour of running almost non-stop, he finally made it to the Seniors' housing condominiums. He stopped outside the entrance, leaned over and fought to catch his breath. The urge to vomit came and went, but the cramp in his side persisted giving him a limp. He seemed to have sweated out whatever had caused the paranoia. Jay was no longer inside his head, though he wondered what his friend would think about what he was about to do.

He entered the complex. If the listing was right, Dodd's house should have been third on the left. He continued down the small, private drive which disappeared momentarily into a thick wood separating the development from all the others on that side of the zone. Anyone below SL15 wasn't supposed to travel through the grounds unescorted, but he had decided to risk moving through the place alone. The area wasn't actively patrolled all the time, but the Seniors needed their privacy. Being Mother's flesh-and-blood representatives opened them up to a great deal of contact with ... well, with people who had problems that need tending to. Selmar didn't feel that his trespassing came out of disrespect, but rather a desperation brought on by the very man he was seeking. Despair hung over him as he walked deeper into the Seniors' holy ground. The feeling continued to heighten, even now that the paranoia brought on by the rumbles of the floating automobile was gone. Every time he looked over his shoulder he expected to see a scout vehicle right behind him, floating like the car had, except it would hanging there silently, ready to parade him away.

As he broke out of the wooded area, a rumble engulfed the air around him. He glanced up to watch a plix streaking by overhead, its wings fully extended. The monstrosity left behind a thin contrail as it moved southward. Sheila's leaving became all too real again, and he moved his feet faster, despite the biting cramp in his side.

Everything around him was unlike the rest of the Unation – green and lush and perfect, each leaf and tree and shrub meticulously groomed. The grass had been trimmed earlier that morning and the breeze carried to him the smell from the public garden off to his left. If Sheila were with him she would have been in her glory. Nothing she had attempted to grow in their tiny yard compared to the arrangements Mother had provided for these people. She had gone out of Her way to make that place a paradise. *They deserve to live well after all they've done for Her,* was Selmar's first thought ... then he reconsidered. They'd *all* been through a lot. There was no need to exclude anyone.

In the distance two or three separate plots of land had been cordoned off where new building projects were already underway. If even *one* of those were to be another group of luxury suites that would make fifteen new developments this *i*-quarter alone. Mother would have to promote a lot of incorps to fill them. Selmar pictured himself inside one, with Sheila, and one or two of their children of course. He couldn't imagine what he'd do with all that living space. Each room inside must have been the size of his tiny one-bedroom, and he'd heard that these new suites had a podium in nearly every corner. Selmar supposed that uppers needed all the extra room, a place to keep all the things Mother provided for them. He wondered if Sheila would ever want to live in a place like that. It really wasn't her style.

Another plix rushed by overhead, rumbling the ground and breaking his trance. As he watched it disappear over the horizon, another blot of poison seeped into his system, like a virus of burning accusations. Stray words from Jay's language of treason came into him again, though this time it was not a call for him to run but to seek. *Find the man responsible for it all*: the words came to Selmar quicker than before, and with repetitions that made him stop until his equilibrium settled.

But he was doing just that, he was going to the man who had the power to change his life from prosperous to disastrous in the course of a day. He was already following Jay's advice to the letter. What more was there to do?

He stopped in front of the third house on his left, rang the bell twice and waited. No one answered. According to his chron, it was still fifty minutes before zero hour. Dodd couldn't have left for work that early, unless he'd seen Selmar coming and was refusing to answer the door. This time he tried knocking. Dodd should've been expecting Selmar to be knocking on his door. Why should he think that Selmar wouldn't want to talk the man who was sending his wife on some silly crusade? And calling her *the one*, as if Dodd couldn't have chosen anyone for it. Mother should have foreseen that Her plans to change the world – for the worst as far as he was concerned – were going to create contention. If there were sides to choose from, Selmar wondered why everyone was opting for the one he wasn't on.

The door finally opened and an elderly but vibrant man stepped into view. He wore a gold, silk robe with black trim. His silver hair was waxed back off his rough, wrinkled face. Everything Selmar had considered saying to the man turned into a huge jumble of random words. Dodd looked nothing like the vidcon photos he'd seen. He looked up at the man whose face remained stolid and tried to decipher the hodgepodge of remarks stuck in his head.

"What can I do for you?" Dodd asked, half-hiding behind the door casing. He glanced around the yard, no doubt looking for Selmar's missing escort.

"Mr Dodd, I'm Selmar Rayburne," he said, lifting his hand slowly. He stopped for a moment, then extended his hand. Dodd took it and they shook once. "I was looking forward to meeting you last night, sir, but I wasn't able to tear myself away."

"Mr Rayburne." He was still scanning the yard. "Yes, I understand you're a hard worker, so your wife tells me." He paused, then reluctantly turned sideways, inviting Selmar in.

"I thought it'd be a good idea to come speak with you before you leave. You know ... just to rest assured my wife is in good hands." His words marked the beginning of a cordial conversation and it was making him ill. What had happened to the anger he felt the night before? This confrontation wasn't beginning the way he wanted. He forced himself to remember that this man was taking his wife from him, but becoming hostile wasn't easy. It was Dodd's place; it was intimidating him. And there was something wrong with the air; he felt disoriented. For an instant, he had an incredible urge to let out a belly laugh, though he wasn't sure why.

"Sheila's a fine woman," Dodd said.

Exquisite was the only suitable way to describe the living room. As Selmar suspected, it alone was the size of his entire house. The plush gray carpeting gave under his feet as he walked. It felt like a cloud. Works of the Unation's finest artists – before expression outside of thought-contributions became trite and worthless – hung on every wall. Selmar assumed they weren't reproductions at all but originals. He didn't consider fakes part of Dodd's domestic repertoire, or of any Senior's for that matter. They were given what they wanted, all the time, and settled for nothing less than perfection. How else could twelve incorps become so admired by the other ten million?

Dodd moved to the kitchen and he followed. Struggling for Mother's approval was what led him to confront Dodd in the first place. He felt strongly enough that their meeting was going to somehow justify his life of misery and setbacks. Essentially, it had come down to a man-to-man battle over one woman, and he refused to wish that the best one win. The stakes were too damn high for odds.

Selmar walked into the kitchen just in time to see Dodd at the counter covering several small tubes of silver fluid with a white cloth. Dodd was clumsy and slow at hiding what was on the counter, as if he wanted Selmar to see it. Was Sheila going to be some kind of guinea pig for one of Mother's experiments? But he was getting ahead of himself. His focus needed to remain on his predetermined list of questions.

Dodd turned from the counter and in the same sweeping motion grabbed a pot of coffee from the kitchen podium. He poured two cups and handed one to Selmar. "Thank you," he said docilely, not daring to ask for milk or sugar.

"There isn't much more I can tell you that your wife doesn't already know," Dodd said, motioning to a chair. "I can only assume that she's explained the situation."

Selmar sat and quietly sipped at the coffee, forcing himself not to grimace. "She told me enough," he said finally. "But I don't think she understood most of what she was saying." Or maybe she'd purposely kept the details vague. From the time they met, they'd vowed never to keep secrets. Full disclosure. And it was on that promise that he gauged her love for him. So long as there was truth he'd never question his wife's feelings. But it had not come down to a decision over whose love Selmar cherished most. Sheila was his life – but Mother's was the penultimate love. Because from Her one could keep no secrets. "Yes," Selmar said. "Sheila must be confused."

Dodd looked at him inquisitively. "Mr Rayburne, do you have other reasons for coming here? Concerning your promotion perhaps?"

Selmar tried to feign surprise, but realized his act wasn't convincing. Every detail of his life surely had had bearing on Dodd's decision to choose Sheila. No sense in insulting the man's intelligence; he surely knows everything. "I do have one thing I'd like to say," Selmar said. *Here it comes.* "My wife and I have discussed a family for a very long time and you've ..." He stopped short of accusing Dodd of anything. Mother would've considered *contemplating* an accusation insulting enough.

"I'm aware of your previous plans," Dodd said, "but Mother didn't draw your wife's name at random. There is no second choice for this job. Sheila holds the key to our success." He stabbed at the table with his index finger. "She's the key to everything."

"Yes, I recall her saying something like that."

"And I won't stand for her passing up this opportunity, do you understand?" He continued to jam his finger into the tabletop. "My objective is to do what's best for the Unation. This challenge must be faced now, and with determination. Letting everything we've built fall back into ruin is completely unacceptable."

Unbelievable the power Dodd carried in every corner of his person. Underneath that dense texture of wrinkles he sustained a charisma Selmar couldn't possibly challenge. What made him think he could even try to compete? How exhilarating to consider that this man had been in his house the previous night. Selmar failed to fend off the building admiration even though he knew Sheila had been duped by Dodd's persuasive, and convincing, motives.

"D ... don't you realize what Sheila's leaving is going to prevent?" Selmar dug into his pocket and retrieved the promotion slip – luckily, he'd put on the same pants he had worn the previous day. "We're finally able to have children." He rubbed the paper flat with his palm and slid it across the table. Dodd looked down at it, but didn't move to touch it. Instead, he continued to sip from his coffee cup while rubbing the side of his wrinkled face with his free hand. Selmar wanted to continue his plea, mention Sheila's KI story, but figured that would be too much. One thing at a time; go with the obvious.

"Well, this is wonderful, Mr Rayburne," Dodd said in a rather flat tone. "Becoming eligible for a progeny pass is quite a step. This proves you're a dedicated incorp. Of course eligibility doesn't guarantee you'll get the pass. That's an entirely separate matter."

"This promotion means nothing without someone to share it with." He reached for the paper, but Dodd snagged it from his reach. "No disrespect intended, sir, but you're ruining my only chances to ..." He paused to choose his words carefully. "Fulfill my obligations to my marriage. Regardless of Her plans for Sheila, Mother can't be happy about what you're doing to me." Dodd stopped drinking mid-swig, raised his eyebrows.

That was it, he'd just crossed the line. All those things he'd wanted to say to Dodd's face last night were fine, as long as he had kept them to himself. Now, without intending to, he had insulted the man who'd be responsible for his wife's safety, the one person who could make his life worse than his father ever had. After setting his cup on the table, Dodd cleared his throat in a mechanical sort of way, as if preparing for a speech – or maybe a eulogy – and pressed his lips together. He waited a moment before speaking. "Selmar – may I call you Selmar?" Selmar nodded, praying Dodd would get straight to the point this time. "You need to understand my position here," Dodd continued, "in order for you to understand your own. When Mother handed me this project, I was not given a choice." He pointed at Selmar with the same hand that held the mug. "Therefore, you don't have one either. Once you come to terms with that, this whole separation will seem so much easier."

"I'm not asking for a lot."

Dodd shook his head. "If you could understand where this is going to lead, you would see that I, too, am asking very little." His voice had changed, he was no longer talking to Selmar as a nineteen, or any status level for that matter. For the moment, Dodd had given up his status that brimmed with power and influence. He was just a man, explaining something that was, to him, very important. "Selmar, the last thing I wanted to do was to squelch your plans for a family. I know how important it is for you – for the future of the Unation, as well. But your sacrifice will be remembered for generations to come once Sheila and I complete what we're setting out to do, believe me."

Imagine that, he thought, *a Rayburne remembered for i-years for something good.*

"Selmar, your sacrifice will change you in ways you couldn't possibly imagine. Mother won't know what hit Her." Dodd cracked a smile for the first time.

The man had power, and he seemed sincere enough. Maybe Dodd would suggest giving him a promotion where he could live in a place like this. Just think of the reactions from everyone at the office, the ones worthy of inviting over for drinks or dinner. They'd ask where he lived. He'd tell them. They'd raise their eyebrows, too impressed or jealous to comment. When they would arrive he'd show them around, detail the history behind the piece of art he had hanging on the wall, tell them it was still worth a great deal even if Mother didn't think so. They would all forget who his father was. They would all love him.

Of course, none of that really mattered though without Sheila. She was the only part that made him complete.

"She's leaving me," Selmar said, immediately ashamed of his immature tone. "How can Mother reward something like that?"

"That won't be an issue," Dodd said, his influential SL19 voice returning.

He assumed the conversation with Dodd was at an end when Dodd removed the coffee pot and mugs from the table and placed them in the return bin, then stood over Selmar with his hands on his hips. Dodd's pursed lips were speaking silent words of his appreciation for him stopping by and wishing him the best of luck with the future. The fixed stare that quickly caught Selmar's attention was all but showing him to the door.

But he didn't want to go just yet, he needed to ask a thousand more questions, the ones Sheila had no answers for. In the back of his mind he sorted through his conversation with Dodd, searching desperately for a drop of consolation, disappointed to find none. He only managed to uncover a new fear. Sheila would certainly return to him, but with an entirely new and heightened frustration at her husband's slow and useless progression. That was still going to be a problem, even an *i*-year from then. She had been so tolerant to that point, but leaving would only prove to her that she didn't need him anymore. If that was to be the case, he thought he'd be better off having his own KI torn out and spare himself anymore suffering.

As Selmar walked out of the Senior complex, he quickly felt contemptuous of his stupid, desperate actions. A reprimand for his unannounced visit with Dodd was undoubtedly going into his permanent incorp record. Now Mother would have one more reason to continue repressing him and Sheila would have another excuse never to come back. Regardless of his recent promotion he still felt cheated. Pity for his own situation was quickly replacing the worry he had for Sheila. He'd been waiting for the break everyone told him would be coming. *Mother's got good things planned for you*, his superiors would say, and he believed them. So what other choice was there but to rely on hope? And he had tried so hard, but still he'd managed to set himself apart as an outcast, just like his father. Though his father had worked a lifetime at it; Selmar had managed to bottom out in a matter of half a day.

How did Jay manage so well? Their friendship had stretched over a lifetime, working through their juv periods side by side, becoming incorps together. From early on they strove to live such similar lives – their secret vow to each other – hoping that both of them would advance through the status levels together and not be separated by the barriers that always grew between uppers and lowers. He and Jay never wanted to have to pretend they weren't friends, or be forced to live in zones where the other was not permitted to visit without an escort. So they each worked as hard as the other, equally dedicating their lives to Mother, but Jay still managed to move up much faster.

Jay and Ramie's first child had arrived shortly after Jay became a seven, six *i*-years before. Sheila wanted to give them a party to congratulate them on their success. She said the first child was always reason enough to celebrate. Mother had a different outlook on a couple who brought a child into the Unation. It was no reason to party. Mother rewarded the couple generously for their gift, and the Vickers had been no exception. Mother had given them their new house and a longer item list to make living easier. Jay received his new assignment and promised Selmar he'd still visit his side of the building, when he could afford the time.

At the party, Selmar avoided mingling. Jay had obviously noticed the somber look on his face as Ramie circulated with their daughter. Jay led him by the hand into the study, wanting to know what was troubling him. Selmar felt like leaning on his friend's shoulder and crying, but he couldn't bring himself to do it this time, so he told Jay straight out how frustrated he'd become, unaware of what lay ahead. Just another six *i*-years of misery and heartache. Jay took his hand, shook it warmly, like a real friend should, and reassured him. *Mother's got great things planned for you,* his friend told him. Then Jay hugged him. He'd always been the stronger one. Good ol' Jay. The only person who ever really understood him, the one friend that would listen.

Replaying the memories of Jay caused the small black organ to dump poison into his body again. The paranoia didn't make its grand entrance this time, rather a thin thread of guilt appeared in its place, unraveling his anger at Jay's success. Selmar knew that the envy he had for his friend would some day wear on him, and he took in a deep breath, held it, and waited for the feeling to dry up and wither. But it wouldn't, and the poison brought with it a stronger truth that Jay had betrayed him somehow. This time Selmar could remember that Jay had given him something and he hadn't wanted it. But Jay wouldn't listen, he had simply continued to talk, and in his mind Selmar could see the manifestation of words running from Jay's mouth again. *Mother's got great things planned for you*: he saw the words fall from his friends lips and run down, staining the front of his shirt.

Selmar stopped walking and shut his eyes before dizziness overtook him. *The guilt and envy are causing this,* he reassured himself. He tried desperately not to let the blame inside, but he'd always been his own best accomplice. Talking with Jay was the only thing that ever helped. He was always there for him, and at that moment Selmar needed a friend more than ever.

Selmar used the key Jay had given him to unlock the front door. "Jay?" he called out. "Ramie? Anyone home?" He stepped through the foyer and into the living room. All the furniture had been moved around again, all part of Ramie's tendency toward extreme fits of boredom. But this time the furniture had been moved hastily; it was crooked. Scattered across the floor were old issues of the *Incorporated*, the Unation's *i*-quarterly magazine. The collection, which Jay had hacked to pieces, was part of his fascination with conspiracy theories. Selmar had always laughed at Jay's hobby, and Jay sometimes laughed too, writing off the fiction he was creating. But right then, the whole idea did didn't seem so crazy.

Their kitchen was clean – now that was unheard of. The house looked lived in, but not *lately*. He began to wonder if Jay and Ramie had deserted him as well. "Jay," he tried to yell and whisper at the same time. "Ramie? I let myself in. I was hoping we could talk." He tried to relax his tense shoulders. He had forced the image of Jay's regurgitated words from his mind, but still faced a wall of anxiety about the possibility of progressing the rest of his life alone.

He moved through the other rooms and found no one. Puzzled, he returned to the living room and leaned his back against the hearth of the fireplace. This was no time for Jay not to be there for him. He sighed heavily, pressing his fingers into his temples. Without answers soon, his mind was sure to turn to clay and his fingertips would sink right in. Jay and Ramie had obviously left for work already. But that didn't mean anything; he had snuck into Jay's labor sector before, he could do it again. All he needed to do was to mingle with the moving crowds. After a moment, he glanced at his chron. Dammit, twenty minutes until zero hour. That wasn't nearly enough time to talk things out with Jay *and* make it to work.

He bounded for the door and tripped on the edge of the hearth, nearly falling into the couch before regaining his balance. After dodging the mess of magazines lying in the middle of the floor, he grabbed the doorknob, then pulled his hand away quickly. The handle was damp and sticky. He looked at his palm and saw the blood. He didn't think he'd fallen into anything sharp but maybe he'd cut it on the brick of the hearth. Turning his hand over he saw streaks of blood covering the sleeve of his shirt. He went back through the living room, taking care not to slide across the magazines again. Looking closely at the hearth, he moved his head down slowly until the angle of the light was perfect – the red brick was covered with a glassy liquid. Portions had clumped together forming small globs. He touched the hearth again. The blood was thick and drying; sections had already started to crack like weathered skin. He stumbled back, then began frantically to move furniture. The couch, the recliner, the tables – all had been used to hide dark red stains. He got to his knees and pressed his hands into the carpet. The fibers clung to his skin. Taking Sheila hadn't been enough for Mother. She wanted to take everything away until his life was empty. He lifted his hand and stared at the dark, congealing blood clinging to him. The memories of Jay's last words reverted back into indecipherable babble. The stains on his shirt didn't look like the words that had been falling from Jay's mouth; it looked like nothing more than wet paint.

He ran most of the way home, avoiding the subshuttles since he looked like he'd just killed someone. He couldn't help but think that in some odd, indirect way he had. Jay and Ramie were taken because of him, when all he wanted was for Sheila to stay.

It wasn't long before his chron rang out – zero hour. He was officially late for work, but that didn't matter as long as he could get back home in time to stop Sheila from leaving. She was sure to listen to reason once she learned about Jay and Ramie. If he had pushed Mother's buttons enough to take the Vickers from him then he imagined there was nothing to stop Her from ensuring Sheila conveniently disappeared too.

He tripped and fell, leaving red handprints on the concrete. It took him more than a minute to catch his breath, then he pushed himself up and kept going. He quickened his pace again and continued along the empty pedways as everyone else in the Unation was settling down to work. He had made sure he was never late for work in his life, but his refusal to report for his first day didn't bother him in the least. The promotion to seven meant nothing.

He made it home in about half the time it took him to get to Dodd's. Even before he had the front door open, he called out for Sheila, voice wavering. He searched each room, but as he feared, Sheila was already gone. She hadn't left a note, just her itinerary which was still on the table. He snatched up the paper and headed for the vidcon. Once he found the plix's code he hurriedly repeated the sequence of numbers into the machine, and it rang back: *in flight*. While staring at the caked, dried blood on his hands, he prayed Sheila made it to the plixport safely, and at the same time he forced himself not to consider what she was likely flying into. Part of him had wanted nothing to do with her after admitting she'd changed her mind about a family. But that was before he'd discovered how eagerly Mother was taking from him everything he had, and everyone he knew. Now all he had left was Mother. If She ever left him, he thought he would surely cease to exist. For an instant, he felt he'd entered the bizarre, illegitimate world of the primes – and had finally recognized the difference between the two.

He accessed the reservation system through the vidcon and checked the afternoon flights to the Southeast sector. All of them were booked solid except one that would layover in the Southwest sector for nearly three hours. That would have to do. As he slid his ribbon into the scanner, he wondered if Sheila was going to believe him about Jay and Ramie. Likely she'd just turn away, furious that he dared to follow her – and even worse, to make up a story about the deaths of their friends. He'd tell her anything to bring her back into this stagnant life she claimed to have.

Suddenly, the vidcon buzzed loudly. A soft voice spoke from the unit's audiophone: *Selmar Rayburne, you're still at home, and it is one past zero hour. You of all people should be aware of how this appears. I am not requiring an explanation of your actions. I am simply revoking your promotion and suspending your cred account for the remainder of the i-quarter, limiting your requests to food only. Please report back to your old office immediately.*

The vidcon went silent.

He sunk slowly into the recliner. Losing his status phased him little, the promotion didn't mean a thing, but freezing his cred account ensured he'd never find Sheila in time. The Southeast sector suddenly seemed a million miles away. Desperation continued to eat at him from the inside; sharp, stinging pains flared in his chest and arms. He fought for a satisfying breath. Mother had given him the ultimate push and at that moment he sensed he was so close to the precipice that a stiff breeze could send him plunging into the gorge, the one he'd been staring into whenever he closed his eyes.

Disregarding the blood, he pressed his hands to his face. He was a lower again, and likely would be until his Grand Contribution. But until that time he vowed he would start to think and act like a lower, one with no hopes or ambitions of moving up, one whose faith in Mother never existed in the first place, because he had nothing left to strive for, nothing to look forward to. He had become stagnant, and that was worse than death.

He glanced up at the mantle on the far wall and stared at Sheila's genuine crystal dove with an olive branch in its beak. It was one of the rarities that Mother offered in extremely limited quantities, and specialty items like that were always in demand by those who couldn't possess them. Since his cred account was dry, all he'd need to do was find the one person who'd be willing to pay enough to cover the cost of a flight.

He took a towel from the bathroom and carefully wrapped the dove. After hastily washing the blood from his face and hands, he put on a jacket to cover his soiled shirt and left to wander the zone.

He avoided the areas heavily patrolled by the scouts. Being spotted alone on the pedways during a work day was a seizable offense, and for all he knew the entire zone had been alerted to his insubordination. He could just imagine what Mother might have told the scouts about him – *consider him dangerous, a murderer, a thief.* No one would pretend to be his friend. All of them would start treating him as one of Mother's fallen. If he hadn't been made to suffer he wouldn't even be here, roaming the empty pedways, clutching a crystal dove as if it were the last thing in the world of any value. But it was worth *something*. This was going to get him to Sheila, and then he'd bring her home.

He had been alone on the pedways for several hours, patiently awaiting midday when the crowds would pour out of the office buildings. Then he'd find someone who'd be willing to pay for his rare find.

He waited and wandered. Eventually, Mother's tower horns blared over the labor zone. People emerged from the buildings to stretch their muscles, eat lunch at one of the podium restaurants. As the people mingled around him, filling their faces with hot food and cold drinks, his stomach began to churn. He walked by some people and started to remove the dove, ready to demand their best offer, but suddenly felt frightened that the invisible surveillance vidcons were watching him, so he moved on. He hugged the crystal dove closer to him as the pedways became more and more crowded, people bumping into him as he passed along, his eyes roving the buildings for the telltale recording equipment. He didn't feel guilty about actually selling a portion of Mother, even if it was a crime. After all, there was enough of Her to go around. Everything around him was made of Mother's fissor – the plants, the buildings, the clothes on his back, whatever She had created for them. But the statue was too small to worry about, too insignificant. She shouldn't care if selling it would lead to his own happiness. That was Her responsibility to him.

He forced his way through a group of people that had gathered outside a podium shop. Several of them were huddled around one man in a dark green suit who had just stepped out of a floating car, rubbing his coat sleeve on the hood and smiling as the others gawked and raised their eyebrows. They took turns patting him on the back. Selmar walked by the man, looking into his hauntingly distant eyes, as if he was from a completely different world. Selmar suspected that if the man opened his mouth and spoke, the words would be foreign, though only to him. The rest of the people would gather and laugh, understanding every word. He hugged the dove tighter until he feared it would crack then moved on. These people had no use for what he had.

The crowd stepped around him in random patterns, driven by some force that refused to exert its energy on him too. He felt weaker, and couldn't help bumping into several of them. Then the midday tone blew again – the fifteen minute lunch break was over – and everyone scurried frantically toward their office buildings. Selmar moved quickly, hoping to find the perfect person who'd want to buy his jewel. He didn't feel a part of them anymore. Mother's signal no longer instilled him with that robotic desire to obey Her demands to return to work. He wondered if these people passing by him were actually part of some KI-induced hallucination. He walked through the crowd, slightly hunched, arms wrapped around the bundle, still petrified that the vidcons were watching him.

Then a man in the distance turned his head and his features stood out from the all others. His face twisted and contorted, as if he too were still conscious and aware of the spell the crowd was under. Selmar lowered his head and tried to move with the crowd, hoping the man didn't realize he hadn't been touched by Mother's charm. Selmar furtively glanced at the man. It was Jay – and he was moving in and out of the people much like Selmar was trying to move, stepping by everyone, fighting to keep balance, heading for a very different place. Selmar followed as Jay moved swiftly through the crowd. He was so relieved his friend was still alive. Mother had been very convincing about Jay's death. What a power She had over the real world.

"Jay!" Selmar yelled, turning the corner onto Thirty-eighth Pedway. He dodged between people moving in the other direction. Selmar couldn't see him anymore. He walked two more blocks, closely watching the people hoping to find Jay moving among them. Then he saw Jay disappear behind a door on the bottom floor of a building just ahead. As he approached, he recognized the neon sign hanging in the window flashing green and red. It was the podium shop, the same one he'd used the previous night. He stopped in front to glance at his reflection in the mirrored glass. He could see right through himself, and the eyes he saw in his head were not his own. He stepped away from the glass and cracked the door to the shop, peeking in before he entered. The curtains around two of the podiums were drawn. A breeze crept by him causing the curtains to wave and wrap themselves around the bodies behind them. Jay had seemed so anxious to access a podium. Perhaps he was trying to escape from Mother, too. He imagined that his friend was in the same predicament as himself because of ... whatever the memories were, Selmar could not remember right then. But Jay knew something. Something important.

A hand crept out from behind one of the curtains and it flew open. A tall, middle-aged man stepped back into the podium, startled. He tucked something deep into his coat pocket, then gave a polite nod and left quickly without a word. The other curtain was still drawn. Selmar took several steps toward it pausing between each. He desperately needed to talk to Jay. He wanted to tell him about Sheila, Dodd, and what he'd found in Jay's house.

"Jay," he whispered. "It's me, Selmar."

Silence. The curtain didn't move. The two feet remained stationary.

"Jay, I was afraid that something–" he paused. Now that was strange – he couldn't hear the podium running. Other than the faint breathing of the person behind the curtain, the room was completely quiet.

"Sorry to bother you," he said, and turned to leave.

Behind him, the rings of the curtain squeaked across the metal rod and hands grabbed him by scruff of the neck. He dropped the dove and heard it smash against the floor just as something pinched the back of his neck. It was on his KI and seeping into his head. As if his entire life had been compressed into a single moment, his mind became filled with a thousand images, and the ominous descent of darkness soon followed.

Five

The morning after Dolan returned to Earth, he dutifully followed his orders and called the number Susan had given him. As the telephone began to ring he tensed, readying himself for the voice that was sure to be amazingly familiar and thoroughly painful to listen to. With every passing second he wanted nothing more than to hang up and tell Theman that the mission to contact Susan Reil was a failure. Surely there were other people Dolan could befriend. But choosing Susan, he determined, was Mother's plan – to implement the ultimate test of his loyalty. So he decided he'd take Her test, play by Her rules, just to prove that he was still worthy of his status level twelve.

Not that on Earth it made a bit of difference.

"The C. A. U. S.," a squeaky voice said. "Can I help you?"

He took a deep breath and held it. The game was afoot. "Susan Reil, please," he said.

"She's quite busy right now."

"This is Patrick Dolan. If you check with her you'll find she's expecting my call."

The line clicked, then a moment later someone picked up again. He swallowed hard and closed his eyes waiting for the venom of Maggie's voice to strike him, but this time she wasn't there. "Patrick?" It was Susan; just Susan, no Maggie. Had he only imagined that she'd sounded like Maggie? The feelings he was expecting to well up in him never came. He was having a conversation with a virtual stranger, nothing more. This was all Mother's doing. She certainly had a great deal of control over this world She'd created, and apparently influencing Susan was no exception. Her voice was completely different, but Dolan could still recognize it. And it was sweet. "Patrick, are you there?" she said.

"Susan, I'm so glad to speak to you." He supposed he should have considered exactly what he was going to say *before* he called. "Thank you for getting in touch."

She seemed genuinely enthusiastic, and that calmed him some. Though he was still worried that at some point he might slip and reveal something she shouldn't know. For a brief moment he wondered what Mother would do if he actually did tell her. "I want to know more about your plans," he said, stammering a bit. "I'd like to help out if I can."

"That's really great, we need all the help we can get. A group of us are getting together for the council meeting on Tuesday. Can you be there?"

"Yes, I will." He was still expecting the Maggie in her to surface, when her voice would change and he'd be talking to his wife again. He heard Susan flipping pages and talking to herself about appointments and luncheons. Mother was right for taking Maggie's quirks from Susan, otherwise he didn't think he'd make it another day knowing she was here and he couldn't have her.

"My last meeting that day is at 5:30. I'll meet you at city hall say ... 6:15? That will give me time to get you up to speed."

"Fine. I'll see you then." He paused for a moment not sure if it was impolite of him to end the conversation. "Goodbye," he said finally.

"See you in a couple days," she said. "Thank you for calling, Patrick. It means a lot to me."

After cradling the receiver he sank into the dining room chair. For a single day, he'd had Maggie back and now she was dead again. He wondered why Mother would have placed the likeness of Maggie in Susan to begin with. Over the *i*-years he had learned not to think about his wife, or the pain he'd experienced when she died. How clever he thought he was being by using his assignment on Earth to mask that hurt. But Mother knew what he was doing – She knew more about him that he did. He couldn't even keep his thoughts of staying here away from Her.

It was obvious Mother did him a favor by resurrecting Maggie. And by taking her away again, he finally realized he'd never given himself a chance to miss her. But now it was too late. He couldn't even remember what it was like to hold her. He had lost her forever, he had allowed himself to forget too much. The person he was when she had died burst open inside him, swelling his chest and throat. He couldn't breathe. Then, giving in to the pain he had ignored for so long, he laid his head on the table, folded his arms around himself and cried.

He awoke the next morning, still sitting at the dining room table, back stiff and sleeves still damp, but sensing a happiness he hadn't known in a long time. What had been locked inside him since Maggie's death was no longer there. He had cried for the loss of her memory, and he wasn't overwhelmed anymore with the urge to run away or bury himself in his work. He had gone for too long allowing his unending need to please Mother to overshadow the gaping hole Maggie had left in him. Now that he'd finally laid what little of Maggie there was in him to rest, he could think of absolutely nothing in the Unation worth going back to – except his obligation to Mother. The piece of Her in his neck assured he always remain loyal. And as long as he had his KI, serving Her was what he lived for.

He spent the following two days preparing for his first social interaction with the people of Earth. Knowing that casual mannerisms were the key to his success, he spent a good portion of the time observing people. In the mornings he would walk downtown, occasionally stopping to eavesdrop on a conversation, pretending to be gazing at the river or into a storefront window. At one point, a few days before, he moved on during the midst of a conversation, worried that the elderly women would find it odd that he'd spent fifteen minutes staring at an old chair in the antique shop.

He still had a good amount of money left over so he decided to eat breakfast at a little place called The Corner Café. The food was good, but the conversations were better. People everywhere were talking with a carefree attitude and little concern for those who might be listening. And the talk was unlike anything he had ever heard before. These people were proud that they lived for themselves, working to sustain only them and their families. The nuances of the couples in the restaurant suggested to him that desire alone must drive them to lovemaking, an act that, on Earth, must have been a very private event.

Incorps could do nothing without Mother's knowledge, no one worked without Her reaping some benefit from it, and most of all, She was an integral part of sex – even orgasms weren't possible without Her involvement. Mother was the hub of all activity in the Unation. It was the basis of living, of survival. It was who they were, who *he* was, and it would always be that way. Dolan gave in to his envy and left without finishing his food.

"Everyone," Susan stood at the head of the meeting table, "This is Patrick Dolan. He's going to be joining us in a volunteer support role." Dolan smiled and glanced around the table, nodding politely as he'd seen someone in the restaurant do. A surge of paranoia ran through him, worried again that his KI was showing. As the group eyed him, he resisted the growing nervous tick of constantly matting his hair. "Patrick," Susan continued. "This is Janice Stoddard, she's in charge of fund-raising. Brent Smith, he keeps all the councilmen and media apprised of our doings. And Jason Bachman here plays lawyer when he needs to." The group laughed, and Dolan gave a small chuckle to help him fit in.

"I'm really new to all this," Dolan said. "Sorry if some things seem strange to me."

"Don't worry too much about it, Patrick," Janice Stoddard said, moving her hands as she spoke. She leaned into the table, pushing it forward a couple inches with her heavy body. "There ain't much to it, and besides no one here knows what the hell they're doing anyway."

Everyone laughed again. Dolan relaxed in his chair slightly.

"So, Patrick," Bachman the lawyer said, "what do you do for a living?"

How could this question have come so soon? Though spending two days observing people had prepared him for this. No one in the Unation would ever ask the status level of someone they'd just met. But he knew of these people's obsession with asking about other's work. Here it wasn't considered offensive.

He gathered his half-truthful answer. "I'm in collections." He waited for a reaction, but none came. Had he worded it wrong? Maybe they didn't know what he was talking about. He feared he'd given himself away with his first words. Now they knew he was a stranger and didn't belong among them.

"Getting people to pay," Bachman said finally, "is one of the hardest things to do." He turned to the others. "If anyone should know." He turned his thumb to himself.

"What do you know about getting money out of people?" Janice Stoddard said wryly.

Again, they all laughed. Dolan had no idea what they were talking about, but joined in anyway. He hoped that was the end of the questions, at least about his job.

Susan stood and turned to her three associates. "It's getting kind of late for a full-length prep session. Why don't you folks head down to city hall now. I'll stay here and brief Patrick on what we've been doing."

Janice snickered, then winked at Dolan. "We understand, dear," she said to Susan. "Let's go you two," talking to Bachman and to Brent Smith who hadn't spoken a word the entire time. "Ms Reil needs to get down to her *business*."

"*Janice*," Susan gasped and lowered her head, blushing. That gesture reminded him of Maggie, but it wasn't Mother's doing this time. He was sure it was just coincidence. But that, and the way she chewed on her lower lip, had certainly caught his attention.

The meeting with the city council had gone just as Susan planned, but regardless of her repeating that over and over again, Dolan had understood almost none of it. In fact, the entire time he was petrified to be casually mingling with so many people. He hid in the back of the room most of the time, listening in on conversations.

The meeting had remained orderly, people spoke in turn and were very respectful of the decisions made by the council. Considering these people's independence, Dolan never expected to see such courtesy. All those he'd dealt with over the *i*-years had not acted this way; they had all been so self-absorbed. No doubt a product of living alone in your mind. As he sat at the kitchen table staring at the way mechanism, he wished he knew what that felt like. But instead of brooding over it he concentrated on how to sustain his and Susan's conversation when they met for coffee in less than an hour. After agreeing to get together he worried about Mother and Theman. To what extent did they want him to become involved? Even after only two days he'd met so many new people suitable for Mother's study. She was going to be pleased with his refined selection process, bringing Her those that would consistently teach Her something new. His job suddenly seemed less ... haphazard.

But this evening was about more than work. Susan intrigued him in a way Mother could never comprehend, no matter how many people from this world She studied and probed. He wondered if he'd be able to convince Mother, if it ever came to it, that Susan was not right for candidacy. There were others that could suit Her needs better. So many others.

He recalled the thought-contribution he just gave to Mother. He had provided Her with the richest supply of information about Earth ever. What he had observed at the council meeting, everyone he'd met there, was now a part of Her. While crossing back, he made sure to avoid Theman, hoping to prolong the inevitable, but knew that sooner or later Theman would come to him with a list of names. He hoped Susan would not be on it.

He looked at his watch. Susan was now five minutes late and

Dolan began to wonder if she *did* mind driving all the way back to Garrison, even though she'd said it wasn't a problem. He couldn't allow anyone to ride in the front of his own car because of the tracking equipment under the dashboard. He went outside and waited for her at the end of the driveway, hoping he hadn't already tainted their relationship because of broken etiquette. Unfortunately, arranging transportation was not part of any conversation he'd heard at breakfast that morning. Mother would be very disappointed at yet another failure, and he'd never forgive himself for allowing this opportunity to pass, no matter how difficult it was to mingle with these people. Mother wasn't going to give him a second chance.

An odd sense of relief washed over him as he saw her approach. The car squeaked and knocked as it stopped, and she leaned over to unlock his door.

"Were you beginning to worry?" she asked.

"I didn't doubt you for a second," he said, getting in. Her car was much nicer than his own, though the instruments on the dash weren't nearly as elaborate.

"Are you hungry," she asked, "or just in the mood for a drink?"

"No food," he said. He had a handful of memory caps to watch later, and a big meal was the last thing he needed.

Their trip was brief and silent for the most part. Susan tried to make small talk, but Dolan often felt trapped being in such a confined space with her and could only come up with one word answers.

Susan parked in front of The Corner Café and he got out quickly to make sure he got to the entrance first. Holding doors wasn't a gesture unique to this world. "After you," he said. She smiled and walked past him.

"You want to find us a seat?" Susan asked. "I'll order."

"That'd be nice," he said nervously, hoping to keep the door close just in case their conversation became more than Mother would want. Trampling someone to get out was not his idea of a quick getaway. He reached into his pocket and handed her three of the "five" bills. Besides breakfast the previous day, he'd only used money for cigarettes, gasoline, coffee cakes and root beer. The price of anything completely eluded him.

Susan glanced at the bills, them up at him. "How much coffee do you want?" she chuckled.

"Can you ask them if they have root beer?"

"I doubt they do," she said. "How about a latte?"

"I'll have what you have." He pointed to a table by the window, and very close to the door.

Susan nodded, then moved in behind the people already waiting at the counter. Dolan sat and watched as Susan ordered their drinks, pretending to stretch, but in fact checking his KI. Joining Earth's society – rather than skirting its edges – had brought with it more worry than he was used to. A split second of inattention could ruin it all. Why hadn't Mother bothered to prepare him for this whole new level of paranoia? He wanted a real explanation for Mother's change in his assignment, trying to find more than just Her superficial reasons. She had wanted him closer to them, and so far he hadn't felt anything terribly adverse ... so far. It *had* helped him bury Maggie, and for that he'd always be grateful. To Susan, not Mother.

Susan approached the table with a steaming cup in each hand. For a moment he didn't dare say anything, fearing she'd know every detail about him the second he opened his mouth. But that was no way to begin the evening. He tried to relax and instill the same confidence in himself that Mother obviously had. This is not going to be a problem. Small talk was no different here than it was back home. Though, in his mind, the word "home" was fairly ambiguous.

Susan sat down across from him and began sipping. "This is really nice," she said.

"Yes," he said, taking another sample of the latte. "It's very interesting."

She snickered. "No, I mean this. You and I. This feels different, I feel like I can be candid."

Dolan nodded, knowing that being candid was the last thing on *his* mind.

"The way I act at work is so unlike me. There are always people around and I'm trying to make an impression. I hate needing to be fake. Having to sell yourself to get what you want." She paused to take a sip from her cup. "I hope you don't think that's how I really am."

"No, I don't think that."

"The council meeting is a perfect example. I wasn't being myself when I addressed them. God, I wanted so badly to tell them what I really thought about the rezoning efforts, but it's not about me, it's about selling an idea. I hate how it gives people such a false impression."

"You're secret is safe with me." He reached for his neck, feigning another stretch.

"It's frustrating sometimes, because I've always been so honest with everyone." She leaned against the back of her chair, genuinely disturbed. "I hate needing to violate my principles to stand up for what I believe in. No matter what I do, I'm always struggling against something I can't see, and constantly wondering why."

"I've been living that, too," he said, hoping his next thought-contribution to Mother wouldn't reveal this part of the conversation.

"I'm sorry, Patrick. That's not what I hoped to talk about." She leaned into the table and looked up into his face. "Okay, so you mentioned the other day about your work, but I can't remember what it was."

Better off that way, he thought.

"Oh, now I remember," she exclaimed. "A collection agency. You track down people with bad debts?"

He grunted, nodded and left it at that. Before she could continue he grabbed his mug and drank slowly, hiding his eyes behind it. Remaining purposefully vague was the only way to keep his story consistent. He set the cup down, empty, wondering what he was going to hide behind if she asked another question. "So tell me, do you do this often?" he asked, determined to change the subject.

Susan coughed up a mouthful of her drink, then wiped her face with a napkin. "Do *this* often?" She pointed to the both of them. "Ask men I hardly know out for coffee?"

"I was just ... curious." And desperate to steer the conversation away from himself. Or at least his *real* self.

She pressed her fingers to her lips. Her cheeks flushed. "Oh my God, are you married?"

"I was. But my wife died." The admission flowed out of him easily. He had Mother to thank for that. He turned to the window and watched an elderly couple walk by slowly, the woman holding tightly to the man's arm as she worked her feet.

"Patrick, I'm sorry. That was unfeeling of me. I never meant to –"

"It was a long time ago." He turned back to her. Her face was still red with embarrassment. "I've been able to put it all behind me."

An uncomfortable silence passed slowly between them. Susan finished her drink while he fidgeted with a small piece of torn fabric on the arm of his chair.

"I feel awful for bringing it up in the first place," she said finally.

"Really, it's okay. I've moved on." He touched the back of his neck. "There's so much I've missed during the twelve *i* ..." he bit down on his tongue to stop himself, then continued, "twelve years since she died. I've been running and I've allowed so many opportunities to pass by." He thought of everything he might have had by staying in the Unation and facing Maggie's death. He'd likely have another wife, more children. Mother would have provided him with a good home and a respectable career. Everything an incorp would want, except the self-determination – that would only come from staying here.

The air suddenly became dense and humid as if the room had shifted into an entirely different place. Susan turned toward him, her limbs edging along with mechanical movements. "Let me ask you this," she said inquisitively, her voice distant and hollow. "What type of person are you crossing over for, Patrick?"

Her words were electrified. The calmness of her tone robbed him of all the energy he'd been using to make sure his true identity went unnoticed. Though, however hard he had tried was not enough. At some point during the evening, or over the previous three days, she had figured him out, and had played along until this moment when she knew he'd be vulnerable. His relative distance to the exit, no matter how close he was, became obscured. There was no other alternative but to play along. "What do you mean by that?" he said, nearly choking. He forced himself not to blink and watched her intently. The light in the room shifted instantaneously from dim to bright. Outside, the dull red automobile that had just passed a moment earlier suddenly reappeared. Everyone in the room slipped back to positions they had been in just seconds before. The mug Susan had placed on the table was in her hands again, as if she had willed it to vanish and reappear under her lips. He knew exactly what had just happened, because he'd seen them all the time on the Unation when he was younger – a folding loop from inside a vidcon program.

"What type of person are you looking for, Patrick?" She spoke in the same nonchalant tone as before, though the voice had returned to normal.

He didn't answer, waiting in anticipation for another folding loop. Mother was indeed watching him after all. But could it have been that he never left the Unation in the first place? It was almost inconceivable to think that Mother had placed him inside this elaborate vidcon program for the past twelve *i*-years. He wondered if he had been crossing over at all, or if his life here had been taking place solely inside a box on someone's desk. He felt like a germ under the light of a microscope – Mother's only genuine candidate, but to what end? Calling Her on the bluff now wasn't going to solve anything, so he remained calm, at least externally, and continued to play along.

"Patrick," Susan said, her head tilted slightly. "Are you okay? You look as if you've just seen a ghost."

"Yes. Yes, I'm all right." He repositioned himself in the chair. "I'm sorry, I just thought of something I needed to take care of. I didn't mean to ignore you."

"That's all right. As long as it's not the coffee or my conversation. If you're planning to be around me, you'll have to ready yourself for a lot of both."

Mother was keeping the program running. Good. "What did you ask me again?" trying to remain very interested.

"Type of person. What type of person are you looking for? You know: demure, stay-at-home, socialites ... comatose? Which is it?"

"You mean ... women?"

"Well." She blushed a little again and cracked a smile. "Yeah."

"I don't know really, I never think about it much. My work essentially forces me to separate myself from people like–" He stopped himself from saying *you*. "– People, in general."

"You're not separating yourself now. So why me?" Susan seemed genuinely curious. Maybe the program wasn't as predetermined as he originally thought. That was certainly a strange angle for Mother to take.

"Your eyes," he whispered.

She furrowed her brow. "My *eyes?*"

He thought of what Mother would most like to hear. "They show you to be a trustworthy person."

"Is that important to you?"

"More than you can imagine. There're things about my world that not everyone is meant to know."

"You mean, 'your work'?"

He nodded, and continued to play along. "But occasionally I have an urge to disregard all that. I start to burn with the desire to tell my secrets."

"Sounds exciting."

"Even if it will put everything I know at risk, everything I've worked my whole life to accomplish."

"Your job must mean so much to you."

"Yes, but at some point losing it all doesn't sound too bad, especially when it's been in vain. You know, when you wake up one day and find out that the past twelve years have been nothing but a sham." She looked at him with her mouth hanging open slightly, saying nothing. "Do you see what I'm talking about?"

"Yeah, I'm pretty sure I understand."

She obviously didn't, which worried him. Couldn't Mother figure out what he was talking about? Didn't She realize he was onto Her? He decided not to blow it and continued playing along, seeing how far She'd let him go. They sat quietly for several moments. Dolan scanned the room hoping to catch a glimpse of another folding loop, no matter how small, just some other telltale sign that Mother was really behind all this. But he noticed nothing out of the ordinary. The cars sped by outside, the people glided by inside, Susan raised and lowered her coffee mug with quaint, uninterrupted motions. Her face had become oddly indifferent, as if she *had* understood what he'd just explained, and was upset that he wasn't confiding in her. He didn't think Susan would really care to hear what he had to say. His speech was meant more for Mother than her. And anyway, Susan was only a projection inside a vidcon program. It didn't matter what she thought.

"So then, Patrick," she said, staring out the window. "Since your work forces you to stay so ... independent, have you ever considered quitting to live a more normal ..." She paused. "Sorry, I didn't mean that exactly. Your life isn't abnormal. I mean –"

"I know what you're getting at. Yes, I've considered it, but it's not that easy. I can't just change my job on a whim. I need to be promoted into a new one, which doesn't always coincide with my personal aspirations. But you learn over time to incorporate it into your life."

"You're a fascinating and dedicated man, Patrick Dolan."

"I'm glad you think so." And that went for Mother as well. He sighed heavily and leaned back in his chair, clasping his hands behind his head, ready to bring this electronic farce to another level. "Actually, Susan, I have been considering resigning altogether. You know, one of those risky, life-altering decisions. I have a large supply of money stashed away."

"Have you thought about where you'd go?"

"I might settle here, I like this area. Before that, though, I'll take a vacation. Travel the world." He studied Susan closely. Her facial expression didn't change, at least not in a way that Mother should have reacted to that statement. Susan still looked disappointed rather than outraged. Mother was disguising Herself well. "Where would you go? Wait, don't tell me. You look like a South Pacific kind of guy. Fiji, maybe?"

He had no idea where Fiji was. "Yeah, that sounds like a place for me." He smiled at Her – not at Susan this time, but at Mother, and She reciprocated through Susan. Mother was controlling Susan's image quite well. Though her features seemed genuine, Mother was behind those eyes he had called trustworthy.

"Would you like to get going?" Mother suggested through Susan.

"I'll leave here whenever you're ready." She stood and he followed. He wondered how this performance stacked up against his others during Her prolonged experiment. His recorded life likely consumed a entire vidcon library stack at that point. Twelve *i*-years of actions and reactions all cataloged in chronological order – for what purpose he had no idea, but he was still determined to find out. It seemed an awful waste to create an entire world for one man.

Mother's projection of Susan slyly took hold of his arm as they left the café. She momentarily leaned her head against his shoulder. He never would have expected Mother's physical projection to be so affectionate, or beautiful. Until that time, he had always thought of Her as an untouchable entity, existing in every corner of the Unation. Her omnipotence seemed too vast to funnel into a single projection. That was why Theman existed, to represent Her in a form that everyone could comprehend, whereby securing their faith. But Mother had duped Dolan into believing in a world that didn't exist outside of a program. How did She expect him to retain his trust in Her with that? But that, too, was another answer worth waiting for. If he broke away from Her now, he may never discover the truth. He would stay with Her – he had been patient for this long.

Susan's lingering touch was starting to affect the most sensual parts of his body. With a deceitful expression of contentment, he looked down into Susan's eyes. The two-tone blue in them revealed that Susan wasn't alone behind them. Mother had manifested Herself in Susan's image. The only thing She was missing was a knowledge implant, but why would Mother need one anyway? She *was* knowledge.

She drove him home in awkward silence. Mother's secret exploits of Dolan were, by Unation standards, unethical, but he convinced himself that his reactions to Her tests over the *i*-years had in some way benefited the people of his world. But why the physical manifestation? Her intellectual stimulation came from the millions of thought-contributions. Could it have been sexuality? She should have no need to explore the realm of procreation where She was already part of every intimate moment that occurred between couples. Without Her involvement it was impossible for a woman to conceive. No, She wasn't interested in childbearing – the Unation was Her offspring. But the allure he had felt as She touched him was unmistakable nevertheless.

"I had a wonderful time tonight," Mother finally said. "I'm glad I finally got through to the Patrick I *didn't* know."

"Happy with what you found?" Of course She was. Mother's always pleased.

"I'm very pleased," She mused.

Feeling a physical attraction to Mother was beyond his immediate comprehension. Yes, Her image was undeniably real to him, and quite beautiful. He leaned across the seat and kissed Her softly on the cheek. Her warm, supple skin seemed surprisingly alive and real, though he knew better. "Good night," he said.

"See you soon," She said, and drove away.

She was apparently allowing Her secret field test to continue into the next day, and he agreed to let it. The car sputtered off around the corner and out of sight. Only the buzzing yellow streetlamp remained to shed any light on the gray, formless surroundings. He tried to focus his eyes on the things around him. The hedges, the apartment building, the lamp post, the car – they all appeared as if he could move his hand right through them. She was very clever, but not enough to fool him forever. He had begun to see right through Her elaborate, staged projection. It had taken him a long time, but he had finally beaten Her.

Now he wanted to know why – why had She kept him inside this illusion called Earth, pretending to take its inhabitants to Her? He wished Mother would return and explain Her reasoning to him, to put his mind at ease. But he realized that relying on Mother wasn't the answer. He needed to continue playing along until She was willing to reveal Herself. He needed to pretend he didn't know.

And to remember that She was always watching.

He turned and quickly climbed the stairs to his apartment. The best thing to do was to continue on schedule. He had ten new memory caps to watch. And he still needed to collect the three children and bring them to Her. He'd keep doing whatever She asked.

Yes, that was what She'd want – to continue playing.

The first four memory caps slid on and off with ease. The pictures inside his head were not as harsh as the three from his previous set. These recordings were certainly not as sharp or vivid. He had not awoken in the bathroom, or on the porch holding the way mechanism over the railing.

One by one, he brought the rest of the children into his head. The fifth, then the sixth, wasting no time going from one to the next. The seventh and the eight. Each juvenile that entered his head was surrounded by blackness and filth, every one of them destitute. A foul, stagnant odor overran his olfactory senses each time he connected a new cap, remaining with him as he returned to his own mind.

The ninth. He looked at his watch. Only twenty minutes had passed since the first cap, though he felt as if he'd been sitting at the table for hours.

Distant black images and rancid odors filled his head for the tenth and final time. That was fine with him, because he'd had enough for one night. He would continue playing Mother's game in the morning.

After the cap expired, his mind emptied and became his own again, but being alone suddenly frightened him, as if it were the most unusual feeling he'd ever experienced. So many voices inside his head, and now they'd all gone silent. He felt that no matter where he turned there would always be someone behind him waiting to slip back into his mind, and send him to a death that was never meant for him, not here.

An overwhelming loss of sensation spread throughout his face and neck, then into his torso and extremities, splintering his body into tiny pieces. He tried to stand up, but couldn't muster the strength to move his numbing feet and legs. The floor suddenly became narrow, as if everything in the room, maybe the whole building, perhaps the entire world, had become a fine wire. His arms grasped for balance. The thumping in his chest became louder, almost deafening. After a time the noise moved outside his body to the tall, thin door in front of him. Something was outside entreating entrance into his head. It called out for him. He recognized Mother's voice and Susan's body, and he longed for both of Them. He extended his arms and waited. Now he could see Her, Mother and Susan as one, across the twisted room. And he walked to Her carefully; She still looked so beautiful. Their bodies moved through the opaque air, then fused. They danced together, melded embrace, across the fine line floor until they lost their balance. Their soft feather fall was broken, caught by a bed of clouds. He kissed Her again and again, because that was what Her eyes and lips said to do. The thick asphalt air enveloped them both as She reached through the skin above his beating heart with Her fiery fingertips.

Six

It was still dark outside when Dolan awoke, relieved to find that his mind was still his own. Ten consecutive memory caps had pulled him to an edge he'd never seen before. But with the illusion of calm and stability that rushed through him after the first few, it had been tempting to push on. So he did, more than he ever had in the past, well beyond Mother's limit. She wouldn't have been very happy about the risk he'd taken. Even if this world was all a projection, his death within it would still be very damn real.

But Mother had come to him – that was right, he remembered it distinctly. She appeared after the last cap expired, when his awkward, mental condition had peaked. What a mess he must have looked like to Her, though She hadn't voiced a disapproval of his foolish move. She'd just wanted Her experiment in curiosity to jump to the next level. He had no qualms. It seemed like the next logical step, for both of their agendas. Hopefully, whatever Mother had learned somehow benefited the Unation, because for him, their night together had debunked his reasons for distrusting Her. It had left him surprisingly content, no longer compelled to ask Her *why* anything.

"What are you grinning at?" a whisper floated out of the darkness.

He sat up and opened his eyes, fighting to focus regardless of the sudden bout of dizziness. "Who's there? Mother?"

A face moved toward him, faintly visible in the dim light of early morning. It was Susan. Her faint image became more concrete as his eyes adjusted. She touched him softly. "Who else would it be?" Her voice was her own; Mother was no longer in her. "I'm sorry I woke you so early," she said, still whispering. "I have a meeting this morning and I need to go home and shower first."

She leaned into his lips, and he retreated. "Did you ... ?" he started, pausing to focus on her eyes. "Were you ... ?" Mother had been inside her, he was sure of it. But now the projection was lacking any sign that She's been behind the affection. The previous day had convinced him that Mother was leading to some kind of end, entering the program when the vidcon simulation had become so obvious. But now She had retreated, leaving him alone in Her make-believe world, and again with no explanation. Had Mother intervened just to cover up the folding loop? If so, it hadn't worked. He still knew this was all a sham.

"I can wait as long as you can," he said, hoping at least Mother could still hear him through Susan's image.

"You okay?" Susan placed her warm hand against his cheek. "You're not still dreaming?"

"Are you alone?" He moved his hand in front of her eyes. Still no Mother.

"Patrick, wake up," she said, patting his cheek.

"I am." He turned and put his feet on the floor.

"What's the matter?" she asked, then recoiled slightly. "You're not already regretting last night?"

"The complete opposite." He moved in and wrapped his arms around her. Her skin was silk, very much like he remembered. While he held her, memories of the Unation dissolved into nothing more than a thousand broken fragments. That was what he wanted, that was all he dreamt about. *If this were only genuine,* he thought. *Please, Mother.*

"At first I felt strange about coming back," she explained, her cheek pressed firmly against his shoulder, "but I felt so comfortable with you. I didn't want the night to be over. I still don't."

"Thank you," he whispered in her ear.

"Don't thank me for expressing my feelings."

"I meant for helping me clear my head," he said. "I was wrong.

Everything is so different this morning."

"Different *how?*" She pulled away, an inquisitive expression on her face. "That you got what you wanted, now you're changing your mind?"

"Yes, I've reconsidered." He was ready to accept that Mother was manipulating him. But that was all right; that was Her purpose. And in the meantime he would live his life as it was meant to be. To love another woman, and to have her love back. The place where it happened didn't matter to him. How had he lived so long ignoring these feelings, the ones that would've closed the gap Maggie had left behind? "I'm seeing things very differently," he added.

She turned, covering her breasts with her arms. "I can't believe I opened myself up to this," she said through tiny sobs. "I've got to go." She started to dress.

"It's hard for you to understand," Dolan said, "I can't explain it all to you." If she could know of the life he was really living. He wished for once he could enter her head the same way he brought others into his. Then she'd understand, and they could be together.

"Don't even try to explain it to me, Patrick." She buttoned her shirt and carried her shoes out with her.

He threw the blankets into a ball at the end of the bed. This time he'd let himself go too far. There was a good reason why Mother forbade him to become intimate with a person from this world. He'd always assumed it was because Earth had been created out of Mother's imagination, but Her reasoning went far beyond that. Free will controlled the emotional lives of these people, he'd seen that now. They had no equivalent of Mother to arrange couples, to guide the emotional growth of two people whom She declared perfect for each other. He damned himself for thinking he could find himself another companion, another lover. Having been gone so long, he'd forgotten how to rely on Mother. Instead, he led himself to believe Susan *was* Mother.

He hoped She'd been watching anyway. *Roll the vidcon program,* he thought. *Study me all you want.* Mother would never learn what it was like to hold another person. She'd never understand.

Dolan didn't think there'd be room in the trunk for the third candidate, Michelle Brenahan. The "sleeping" bodies of Justin Marcotte and Jeremy Baines were taking up most of the room. He stared at the two boys, desperately wanting to give them nicknames, like all the others, but couldn't bring himself to do it anymore. The boys would simply be "the boys". He'd just have to call the girl what everyone else called her – Missy.

He measured up the remaining space. A copy of the police report said Missy weighed one hundred twenty pounds, but she could have easily lied about it. It didn't really matter; he'd have to make room. Returning with only two of them was out of the question, so he set out to pick up her up. The sooner he finished and brought them to Mother, the sooner he could return and straighten out the mess he'd made with Susan that morning. And he didn't want help or guidance from Mother on what he needed to do. Besides, She was not a part of it, and he preferred it that way.

He drove south on Route 125, taking the last exit before leaving Garrison. Missy lived on Emery Street. The location monitor on the dash displayed a detailed grid map of the town. As he pressed the east and north keys on the pad, aerial shots of several neighborhoods and downtown blocks flashed across the screen. Grid 7-E revealed a small cluster of streets separated by the main highway running through the center of town. Emery Street was to the left. He adjusted the CNS tracker until he detected Missy's signal. On the display, a tiny, blue light moved quickly along Emery Street and off the edge of the screen. It was Missy, and she was moving way too fast to be on foot. No doubt she was in a car. As he turned onto Rumney Street, two blocks away, he flicked the tracker over to automatic. The monitor changed grid maps, following the blue light as it moved off the screen. Being unfamiliar with the area, he was having a hard time following the pip as it zigzagged across several side streets. The location monitor changed grids so fast he barely had time to read it before it switched. After finding the nearest street sign, he realized he'd taken two wrong turns and was heading in the opposite direction. He watched the blue light zip onto Highway 101 just a short distance away. He jammed on the brake and slid across a patch of sand, then backed up into a driveway where an elderly man was washing his car. Without turning, but keeping sight of the old man in the rearview, he pulled away, clipping the fence, watching the man shake his fist and spray the back of Dolan's car with the hose. Dolan waved an apology, hoping the man would accept it – he needed no more attention from the police.

Traffic on the highway was thick. Cars everywhere, too many people to be witness. The setting sun created a glare that made it hard to see. He sped up, trying to catch the vehicle that had disappeared from the monitor. Fifteen minutes had passed before the red pip of his own car entered the same grid map as the blue. At that point, he was going seventy-five, still barely gaining on her. She was in an awful hurry to go somewhere ... unless she was running from something.

Not this time, he told himself. No second guessing, and no assumptions. She simply wasn't going to get away from him. There was too much at stake.

From inside the pouch of his briefcase his chron beeped. His KI was nearly full. He glanced at his watch, then dug for the chron as he fought to stay in his lane. The countdown had started, and he absolutely did not want it to reach zero. He accelerated, passing cars like they weren't moving at all.

All three candidates – he needed all three of them. Theman's threat was sincere enough, and if this assignment wasn't done correctly, there was no way he'd be coming back. Whatever it took, he was going to get her. And hopefully he'd accomplish it before his KI started to shut down.

The location monitor beeped a caution signal – he was getting close. Most of the traffic had taken other exits leaving the road deserted. The sun had finally disappeared behind the hills, and he could see just ahead of him the taillights of a lone vehicle. The monitor flashed the remaining distance – less than a mile away, but it seemed there was an entire continent standing between them. He sped up even more. Eighty, ninety. The rear lights drew closer. Suddenly the car was engulfed by the shadow of the hills, leaving two red eyes staring back at him. The monitor buzzed again. *Use extreme caution.* He switched it off. Moving closer to Missy's car, he noticed it had something strapped to the roof. Impossible that the authorities would have allowed the girl to leave, not after what she'd done to that family.

He moved even closer to the vehicle, just enough to see the faint silhouettes of two people through the rear window: one driving, one in back. His engine was screaming; he'd never pushed it so hard. He moved in closer. The girl was going back with him, one way or another. This collection needed to be over quickly, and if it had to get a little messy like the last one, then so be it. His chron beeped again, ticking away toward zero. Then he braked hard, slowing to match the other car's speed, not believing what he saw on its roof.

He fell back and followed, contemplating is own death as he stared at the rack of blue lights mounted on the police car. He didn't want to do anything he'd regret, but he had no other choice. He had to take her back. There were no other options.

And without another thought, he stomped down on the gas.

The first hit was only a nudge, rocking the car back a bit. They were both driving too fast to force the police car off the road and risk killing the girl. Though he also didn't want to invoke a chase, giving the cop too much time to call for backup, or reason to use deadly force without a second thought. He accelerated again, slamming into it this time, denting the police car's rear fender and shattering the taillight. Then he pressed hard on the brakes and came to a stop on the shoulder. The bait had been set, just enough of a lure. He'd wait there for the cop to come to him.

The police car had pulled off a short distance ahead. The emergency lights came on, blinding Dolan for a moment with winks of pulsing blue. The cop backed up quickly, skidding to a halt in the sand, sending up a cloud of dust. Dolan put on his best drunk and stumbled out of the car, falling to the ground for that touch of authenticity. Out of the corner of his eye, he saw the cop slam the door and give a frustrated shrug, arms rising into the air. "You goddamn drunk. Get on your feet," he said as he approached. Dolan struggled to stand, using the car door as leverage. He looked up and gave a twisted, inebriated grin, then launched himself at the cop.

The cop backed a half step, causing Dolan to reach a little further than he expected. They fell to the ground. Dolan smacked his head on the brass buckle of the cop's gun belt. The cop's legs twitched furiously as he tried to get out from underneath. Dolan held on tighter, dragged a short distance through the dirt before the cop swung at him. The punch grazed his chin, the unspent energy twisting the cop's body around. Dolan was left facing the cop's half holstered gun. He grabbed and pulled. It slid out with ease. Another punch landed square on the side of Dolan's head, then another, four, five. But they were halfhearted. Dolan tried to stand, genuinely punch-drunk now. The cop grabbed his wrists and they both moved to their feet.

The gun went off, straight into the air. For a brief moment, the action seemed to stop as they both looked at each other in disbelief, then the struggle resumed. The fight had become a wrestling match, even on both sides as they circled around in a stalemate. The gun went off again and again. A round went into the sand of the shoulder, another shattered a window in the police car. The cop finally lurched forward and tried to kick Dolan's feet from under him. Dolan side stepped, twisted around and shuddered as the gun went off for the last time. He felt hot liquid spray his face, enter his mouth. The cop fell backwards. Dolan went with him. Dolan lay there, white-knuckling the gun until his breathing slowed, and the cop's breathing stopped.

Dolan was floating, somewhere outside his body, watching himself roll the lifeless body to the edge of the road, arms flopping as if they were stuffed with dead leaves. The police car's tailpipe spewed exhaust into his face, but it had no smell. In fact, he couldn't smell anything. He could only see – the cloud of smoke, the hypnotic flashing blue of the police car's strobe lights, the crushed fender of the cruiser stained with streaks of red paint from his own car, the hole in the dead cop's neck pouring blood onto the ground. Where the bullet had come out looked like raw meat.

Dolan slipped in the sand, falling to his knees and across the body. A rush of air was forced out of the body and into Dolan's face. His sense of smell had returned. The cop's breath reeked like a morbid mixture of onions. It mixed with engine exhaust, spent gunpowder, burnt flesh. Dolan looked down at his wide-eyed, cement expression, recognizing the face for the first time. It was the cocky young one that had been at his house. Theberge. *We're going to be keeping an eye on you.* And Dolan knew the young man had meant it.

He shivered uncontrollably. He'd never wanted to hurt any of these people, especially the ones Mother hadn't fingered for collection. That had become his personal vow, his special secret to himself. But Mother had forced this upon him, turning him into a killer to serve Her purpose.

Now he had a even larger secret to keep. He never wanted it to be more true, that Mother was right in saying She'd created this place. That what he'd been doing here – what he'd just done – would have no consequences in the end. At least not in this world anyway.

His chron ticked away. No time to plan a reasonable solution, even if there was one. He was thankful they'd entered a deserted area, no towns, no witnesses, just trees for miles and miles.

Then headlights broke the horizon. Up ahead.

We're keeping an eye on you ...

He stared at the two pinpricks of light coming at him. If the young man had followed proper procedure he would have told the other officers where he was, that he his car had been hit. Dolan slid through the dirt toward the front of the police car. The radio inside was screaming. "Garrison 304 ... advise your status." A pause. "Theberge, repeat your location." Then another voice came on, one Dolan recognized. "Delvechio to dispatch. I've spotted him up ahead on Mitchner Road. I'll advise." And then, in the distance, the two pinpricks of light started flashing blue.

Dolan scooped Theberge's gun and the empty shells off the ground and tossed it over the guard rail. Dolan flung open the back door of the police car, shards of glass falling at his feet. It was only then he remembered the girl was inside, and saw that the stray bullet hadn't only broken the window. Missy was slumped over lying in a pool of her own blood. He dragged her out, watching the lights in the distance grow brighter, larger. Bright blue, winking in and out. The police radio squawked, "I need backup here, notify state ... " Dolan didn't wait to hear the rest.

He wasn't going to fight for space in the trunk of his car. He pushed Missy into the back seat, jumped in, and with his headlights off, spun the car around and watched as the blue lights started to shrink away until there was nothing behind him but darkness.

He felt as if both of his worlds had deserted him, unhappy, unsatisfied, disgusted with what he had just done. Even desperation didn't seem to suit the cause, after the fact anyway. But he'd done it for both of them, Mother and Susan, though neither would care to hear an explanation. It wouldn't have been acceptable to either of them.

He'd parked the car in the dark corner of the driveway and waited. He could hear his chron ticking like a bomb with a hidden timer. His mind began to clear. He reached up to rub his eyes and recoiled at the excruciating pain in his right arm. He clawed at his sleeve and discovered that he too had been shot. The bullet had only grazed him but the pain was still intense. Then he remembered he wasn't the only one bleeding, and in one motion he turned and climbed over the seat, turning Missy on her side. The stray bullet had gone through the meat of her shoulder and out her back. He could see pieces of her shoulder blade sticking out through the fabric of her sweater. With his arm on fire, he pulled his shirt off and pressed it against the wounds. His chron chirped. The cotton t-shirt became soaked. They both had too little time.

He hastily scooped the boys from the trunk one at a time and carried them into the house. He had to bite down hard on his tongue to keep from screaming. He returned to the car for Missy, but hesitated before picking her up. Normally, he would have given her a sleeper, but it was impossible to judge her body's reaction because of the gunshot. She was far worse off than the woman whose head he'd cracked open on the tar. He hoisted her up, knees buckling, hoping she wouldn't regain consciousness. On his way up the stairs the clot on his arm tore open and blood began to ooze again.

He set Missy down on the dining room table and lifted the edge of the t-shirt. Blood had soaked the entire neck of her sweater and part of the sleeve. Her pants were torn, probably from the broken glass, and one of her shoes was missing. What a fucking mess. Returning her like that was going to provoke more questions than he wanted to face, but his chron wasn't slowing, still counting down the seconds. His KI was about to expire. He took a clean cloth from the kitchen and pressed it on her shoulder. His chron chirped again, only two minutes on his KI. She'd have to go as is.

He connected three pair of crossover goggles to the way mechanism, placed one on each of the boys lying on the floor beside the table. He activated the goggles and listened carefully for the eyelid retractors to engage.

The towel he'd placed on Missy's shoulder was soaked already, but as long as she stayed out, and didn't move, she'd be fine – he hoped. If she wasn't alive when he delivered her to Mother, he wouldn't need to bother emptying his KI. Mother would just take it out of him.

He fastened goggles onto her, plugged the cord into the way mechanism and a third readout appeared on the monitor. Good, she was still alive. But as if switching on the goggles had revived her, she groaned and struggled to sit up, clutching her wounded shoulder. She spasmed with pain and managed to slide her legs off the edge of the table, dangling like knives over the body of the boy, Jeremy. Thick streams of blood ran down her fingers as she squeezed the towel. Dolan scrambled for his sleeper case, couldn't find it, then realized he'd left it in the car. Trying not to step on the boys, he circled around the table and eased her back down. She didn't resist.

"My eyes," she half coughed, half screamed, pulling at the goggles.

"Don't," he snapped. "You'll hurt yourself. No need to worry, you'll be all right. You've had an accident." He reached across the table and punched the activation code into the way mechanism. His wound spat blood as he tried to avoid her lunge. With his bum arm he held her down, with the other he snatched up the cord and connected it to his KI. The machine's warm-up took an eternity. It whirled, beeped, and paused, then finally the glass orbs crept into the air. Mother's dust spun inside them and the room began to melt away.

Missy's screams turned from rage to sheer terror, sending him into a panicked frenzy to quiet her. Because she wasn't "sleeping", the link they shared with the way mechanism was bringing them together, each conscious of what the other was thinking and seeing. In his second sight, he could see only the blackness inside her goggles. She, on the other hand, was looking down on herself as he forced her against the table, her own face staring back, contorted with fear. He closed his eyes, ending her horrific view of what was happening.

The ripples created by the swirling dust in the orbs passed through him and he became disoriented, losing his balance. He fell back, hitting his bloody arm on the metal chair. Spots of red landed in his eyes, fire wormed its way through his torso. The fading floor of his dining room seared the palms of his hands. He opened his eyes just in time to see Missy roll her body toward the edge of the table and fall on top of one of the boys.

The heavy door of the gray crossover room swung open and Henry Douglas entered, his face washed with panic. He started toward Dolan, turned to the girl, then stopped. Dolan wasn't surprised by his reaction. Internal security scouts weren't good for much beyond intimidation. But expert field tactics weren't a necessity right then. Dolan simply couldn't afford for this girl to die, especially after getting her this far. "Don't just stand there staring. Help her up," Dolan ordered, hoping to coerce him to move.

Douglas fumbled for the transmitter on his hip, missing it with every attempt. "Um .·. I'll call for help."

Somehow, Missy had managed to remove the goggles. Blood was running out of the corners of her eyes. "Help her now!" Dolan tried to stand and fell back against the wall as a wave of nausea overtook him. Thick blood from his reopened wound ran the length of his arm.

Douglas stood frozen over the girl for several moments before finally picking her up. She didn't resist – the fall apparently had knocked her out again. Douglas placed her gently on the table and managed to grab his transmitter. He paused and turned to Dolan. "Should ... who do I call?"

The girl was sure to die if this moron continued with his fit of confusion, and Mother certainly wouldn't send any blame his way. Dolan would eat it all. Still unable to stand, Dolan held out his hand as he slid down again, back against the wall. Douglas shakily handed the transmitter to him. "No, Douglas, help me up," he commanded. Douglas pulled him to his feet and Dolan took the transmitter away from him. "Come here," he said to Douglas, then signaled for the med-techs.

"What ... what do you want me to do?" Douglas asked timidly.

"You're going to have to get your hands dirty." He took Douglas's arm and had him press down against the bloody towel covering Missy's wound. Douglas started to resist, but there was no way Dolan was going to allow him to walk away. Dolan needed all the help he could get, particularly then. And maybe by showing incredible concern for the girl's safety Mother would go easy on him. Of course, that was a long shot. He doubted any of this would make a difference in the world. But right then saving the girl mattered to him.

His arm went numb and his KI bit into him. His chron belched out a tone. Zero. What other choice did he have but to leave Douglas's side? He had no choice but to trust this guy with his life. He moved to the core node on the wall, fumbled for the cord and turned to check on Douglas. Hands covered with blood, Douglas stood fast, grimacing and looking away as if he were a firsthand witness to Dolan's inevitable execution.

Dolan leaned against the wall outside the crossover room as the med-techs brought Missy out on a gurney. "I'm surprised she's alive," one of them muttered as they passed. Dolan looked at him and said nothing. He could think of several other reactions he might hear, particularly when Theman and Mother found out. Of course it was too late to prepare them with a well-devised scenario before telling them – they had discovered the truth the moment he connected. The two had most likely convened already and discussed the bleak plans of Dolan's future.

Let it include her, he thought. He wanted to see Susan again in the worst way, to set things right. But that wasn't going to happen, either way. Mother would surely sentence him for REMOVAL if the girl died. And if she survived, Mother would do something far worse – bring him home for good. He glanced around at the synthetic corridor and the automated movements of the people passing by. He realized it was his first time stepping out of the crossover room since he left for Earth. There was nothing exciting about it. None of it seemed real.

The med-tech who had cleaned and bandaged Dolan's arm approached from the secured area at the end of the hall. The man had changed into an operating gown that hung to the floor, and his cloth boots poked out from underneath as he stepped. Streaks of blood stained the front, partially covering the faint impression of the Unation's emblem on the breast.

"Mr Dolan," the med-tech said in a concerned tone. "Can we speak?" He glanced sidelong at Douglas.

Dolan turned to Douglas and nodded. "Could you give us a few minutes?"

Without a word, and in a sort of amateur drill formation, Douglas snatched up his rifle, placed it on his shoulder and marched down the hall. He stopped and waited near the elevator door.

"How's the arm?" the med-tech asked.

Dolan tried to lift it and winced. "Still hurts like hell."

"Here." The med-tech held up a KI cap. "I've been told to give you this."

"What is it?" he asked. It looked very much like a memory cap, and the last thing he wanted was someone else inside his head. He tried to hand it back to the med-tech who waved it off.

"It's a pain cap. Restricted at your status level, but let's just say someone felt it necessary to prescribe one to you."

Unavailable at twelve or not, he had always been familiar with Mother's creations. Even an SL1 knew what they'd be eligible for when they became a fifteen. Knowing what was to come encouraged people to work harder for Her, to gain promotions, to acquire those rewards. He had never heard of a pain cap before. How far had this world progressed in twelve *i*-years? How far behind had Mother planned to leave him? "I don't understand," he said. The med-tech took his hand and led Dolan's fingers to his KI, then snapped it into place. Dolan waited several anxious moments, but nothing happened.

"Give it time," the med-tech said, then walked away toward the secure area. Douglas snapped to attention as the med-tech strolled by. Before turning the corner at the end of the hall, the med-tech lifted his right arm and clenched his hand into a fist several times. Dolan reluctantly did the same, waving back – if that *was* a wave. As Dolan lowered his arm he felt the pain vanish. He touched the bandage softly, then squeezed it increasingly harder, feeling nothing. He leaned back against the wall. With the pain in his body masked by Mother's technology, he wondered if he'd feel Mother ripping the KI out of him before tasting the blood.

Douglas marched back down the hall, snapping the rifle off his shoulder and resting the butt on the floor. He turned his head to

Dolan. "Anything wrong, sir?"

"No," he answered quickly. "Couldn't be better, Mr Douglas."

"I've been advised that the gathering crew's on the way up for the other two."

That meant Theman would be contacting him very soon. What was he or Mother going to say about this complete mess? He had failed Her in the worst way. Dolan certainly couldn't lie, saying he was in any way forced to shoot the officer. Theman would only revert back to Dolan's thought-contribution to find the truth, leaving Dolan empty-handed and begging for his KI. Although, if he explained to Theman how his KI was about to expire when he killed the officer, he and Mother might agree that those were desperate enough measures.

He tried to shake off the worry, knowing he hadn't killed an incorp. How tragic could the shooting have been in a world that existed inside a vidcon program? Fatal mistake; game over; reset the machine and send him back. Except he didn't want the *entire* world set back to zero. When it came to Susan, he'd rather pick up where he left off than start all over again.

The door at the opposite end of the hall swung open and three burly men in gray smocks started walking toward him. The first man, Philip Tuft, stopped in front of him and stared, saying nothing. The other two continued past and into the crossover room. Maybe Mother was saving Her reprimanding for later. Apparently a barrage of ridicule was coming first in the form of Philip Tuft's sarcastic attitude. Just what he didn't need right then. Tuft squinted, examined the bandage on Dolan's arm. "Bit of a scrape this time, eh Patrick?" Philip Tuft laughed.

"A bit," he said sternly, refusing to look away. "And don't call me that."

"In the shits again," Tuft commented to Douglas. "Don't worry, Dolan. The next batch might be a little easier. Maybe Mother'll send you after a handful of whiny little girls? You partial to that?"

"She shouldn't skimp on my account."

Tuft leaned into Dolan's face. "If She listens to me, your next time won't come!" He grinned, then entered the crossover room.

"Tuft!" Dolan called.

The brawny man stuck his head out of the room, his brow furrowed. "What?"

"Next time I return," Dolan leaned toward him and whispered, "I'll bring you back something real nice. How about a pretty plant? You partial to that?"

Tuft stepped back into the hall. "Fucking plant. You losing your mind over there, Dolan? Or you just been leaving pieces of it behind? The Seniors are going to have a field day with this little mishap."

Dolan pressed tongue against cheek. Discussing the Senior SL's was something he wished to avoid. Dealing with Theman was one thing. He was a projection, Mother's voice, Her rational mediator. But there was one thing Theman didn't have that kept him safely separated from the illogical wrath of the Seniors: an ego.

"Take my advice, Patrick. Stop falling for shit over there," Tuft reentered the crossover room. "Like that little toy you brought back with a bullet hole in her. Better hope she doesn't die."

Dolan took a deep breath and held it. No response was the best one, especially in Tuft's case. He'd already pushed Tuft further than he wanted to. Best just to wait for him to leave, then quietly retreat and wait for Theman. The last thing Dolan wanted was more surprises.

"Sir, I hate to bother you again, but there's a message coming through," Douglas said, pointing at his transmitter. He changed his voice to a soft whisper. "The Seniors are ordering you to a debriefing."

"Great," he muttered, lowered his head and wrapped his hand over the back of his neck.

The Senior SL's didn't call for meetings unless there had been a breach of Unation security, or anything worse. He'd heard rumors of how they conducted themselves – illogically, manipulatively – but he never expected to be a part of their assembly. Facing

Mother's jury was, oddly enough, the first of many steps through Her inquisitions. Each of the seven Seniors had struggled to reach the last rung on the SL ladder, achieving greatness in the eyes of the world, having completed the quest sought by everyone else. Maybe that would work to his advantage. Maybe they'd be sympathetic once they realized what he'd been through, everything he'd given to the Unation by being on Earth. But that wouldn't change the blame; he knew the fault was entirely his own.

He rode a surprisingly unchanged elevator to the 201st floor and followed a curiously familiar hallway to the very end. There was already a small, laminated sign posted on the door: "Dolan, Patrick SL12 – Private Meeting in Progress. Do Not Disturb". He knocked softly and when no response came he entered.

The room was extremely disproportionate – fifteen feet wide at most, but almost as long as any hallway in the building. A row of conference tables lined the side walls which were covered with framed images. All were simple, ordinary objects: a picture of a podium, a vidcon, an access ribbon, even a pre-implanted KI. He quickly recognized these things, and that eased a small portion of him. At least the fundamental parts of the world hadn't changed.

The familiar flag of the Unation hung between every third picture. They were all made of a silky, light blue material which he'd never seen before, though the insignia was still very much the same. It still displayed the seven incorporated continents encompassed by stalks of grain on either side, which had been Mother's way of signifying the simple, wholesome unity She brought to the world. But he didn't feel that doctrine represented him anymore, the ideal wasn't his to relish. He had traveled beyond the world where one's own limits were accessible and subjective. On Earth, unity was a conscious choice, not just a way of life.

He walked down to the far end and sat in the chair that faced a stretch of tables. Off to one side, a vidcon whirled to life and began projecting pictures on the wall. The photos were of common, everyday people living and working in the Unation: a busy podium shop; a scout on patrol; a med-tech in a surgical bay preparing to remove a KI. Business as usual had continued while he was gone, except he saw a noticeable change in the people flashing before him. Their expressions displayed the happiness that Mother guaranteed them, but their eyes told a different story. They were all hollow – he couldn't see anything inside them.

The vidcon displayed objects next – a podium, a KI, an access ribbon. Then, to little surprise, a picture appeared of an item he didn't recognize. A simple, round metallic canister equipped with long, stringy connections that looked like KI fittings, but he couldn't be sure. He studied it closely until the image vanished, then the vidcon turned itself off.

The tall door against the back wall opened and six people entered – four men and two women, all dressed in black. Their faces were staunch. For a moment Dolan lost his will to breathe. There were so many things this group might suggest he do, too many wrong answers he might give them. And what would their questions be? Would they even speak the same language anymore? He could see the same changes in their eyes, but with them it didn't end there – the way the group walked, the way they dressed, was frighteningly different. He prayed that mercy was still common practice.

The Seniors stopped behind the table, sat, and began reviewing a stack of folders, likely Dolan's entire Earth experience funneled down into one long, detailed vidcon report. None of them would acknowledge his presence while they shuffled papers. There had always been seven Seniors at any one time, but only six were there. He wasn't about to ask why and he'd be damned if he could figure out who was missing. After so long, he couldn't remember names anyway.

At some point he realized he'd started to breath again. After nearly ten minutes, when the group had finished quietly discussing and reviewing his entire life boiled down to nothing more than ink on paper, the man to Dolan's far right stood. He handed his pile of folders to the woman next to him, then turned and looked at Dolan for the first time.

"Good afternoon, Mr Dolan," the man said.

"Afternoon, sir," he replied, nearly choking.

"This isn't going to be a formal inquiry as you may have been expecting, considering the recent events. Think of it as a simple question and answer session."

"Will Theman be joining me at any point?" He couldn't recall a time that he'd wanted Theman with him more than right then.

"No," the man said. "He's ... preoccupied with other matters. Don't worry, you'll need no representation. We'll make sure Mother gets a full and impartial report." He smiled smugly. "We're here to help you, Mr Dolan."

Each person at the table began scrawling something across a piece of paper and passed them along to the man standing – no doubt he was the one in charge. "Very good," he muttered to his associates. "Mr Dolan, a decision has been made by this panel, but before anything can commence we'll need to ask you several questions. Are you prepared for that?"

It depended on what he meant by *decision* ... "Sure," he said. "I'm ready."

The man turned the vidcon toward Dolan and activated it. "This session will be recorded," he announced. "We, the available staff of Seniors, are here during this third *i*-quarter of this fortieth *i*-year of Incorporation with Mr Patrick Dolan, SL12. Let the session begin now."

As he sat, the blonde woman next to him stood. "First of all, Mr Dolan, what is your relation to the injured female who crossed back with you from Earth?" she asked, as if reciting it from the paper in her hand.

"The female was one of the three candidates I'd been assigned to collect." He hoped he wasn't going to be reiterating facts they should have already known. Listening to it all over again was going be very irritating.

She took her seat and the next man stood. "Was her injury inflicted by you?" he asked in an extremely soft tone.

"No, it wasn't."

The next person, a woman with auburn hair, cleared her throat as she rose. "How then did she sustain such a life threatening injury?"

He could see in the woman's eyes that she already had the answer. "She was inadvertently wounded by a weapon before crossing back."

"Her eye injuries resulted from removing activated goggles, didn't they?" she continued.

He could only nod.

"Could you speak up, for the recording," she said, smiling politely.

"Yes," he said, leaning forward slightly.

"You didn't issue her a sleeper?"

"She'd been shot."

The woman sat. "You should know," said the man with a bushy beard, remaining seated, "that the use of weapons during a collection is strictly prohibited."

"Yes, I do," he answered sternly.

"Then kindly explain the circumstances."

The papers in front of them surely had answers to all their questions. He was bound to contradict himself, whether intentionally or not. Why were they delaying the inevitable outcome?

"Mr Dolan, we're waiting." The man stroked his beard.

He inhaled slowly and spoke in one breath. "Before I could collect her, she had been taken into custody by a law enforcement officer. During the collection, we struggled, the officer and I. He shot at me, obviously feeling that both his and the candidate's lives were in danger. The bullet struck her in the shoulder, but not before hitting my arm."

"Yes, we can all see the bandage," the man at the other end of the table said as he stood. "Does it hurt?"

Dolan hesitated. Was that anger or sarcasm? He had the papers right there in front of him, so the man knew he wasn't lying. All the same, Dolan needed to keep in mind that this Senior obviously had some predisposition to challenge everything he said. No embellishments or diversions – just give them the simple truth. "It hurt's a little," he lied, not knowing why. The pain cap was working fine. The man sat down, staring at him without blinking, as if he knew better.

"So," the blonde woman said, "you'd classify this as a simple miscalculation – an accident?"

That was not the word he would have chosen. "Well ... yes."

"How have you been feeling lately, Patrick?" asked the man in charge. He didn't stand this time.

"Fine."

"Any problems or difficulties during your recent crossovers?" asked the auburn-haired woman.

Don't hold back, he told himself, *the truth is in front of them.* "I did actually see something kind of strange the other day while I was over there."

"Elaborate," she snapped.

"I saw ... or rather *thought* I saw, my nephew, Jacob Dolan." After what had happened over the previous twelve hours, divulging that could do no harm.

"That would be Patrick Jacob Dolan?" she asked, reviewing a sheet.

"Jacob ... Dolan," he corrected her.

"How could you have possibly seen him?" asked the bearded man.

"I don't know, really ... he went through REMOVAL a while back."

The man at the other end, the angry one, stood up quickly. "You say this was *days* ago and you're not reporting it till now?"

The man in charge motioned for him to sit down. "Mr Dolan, you know the procedure for reporting an incursion. What was the reason you broke protocol?"

"Because I believe now that it wasn't him." And why should it matter to them? It was all nothing more than a vidcon hallucination. But he wasn't about to let them on to Her game, and likely be charged with insubordination, too.

"Answer the question," the angry man said.

He needed to keep reminding himself that the Seniors already knew everything. They were just searching for truthfulness, continuity in his story. But he had no idea what really took place at that construction site. How could he have logically explained what he saw? *It's beyond that now,* he thought. They weren't interested in his interpretation of the events, just in the reason why he avoided reporting it. All part of Her plan. "I became preoccupied with an assignment change."

"So, due to your need to focus efforts on the new assignment, time was of the essence," said the soft-spoken man, as if encouraging his statement as truth.

"Therefore, there was no time to file a proper report, is that correct, Mr Dolan?" the blonde woman followed up.

He didn't dare disagree – not now. "Yes, you're absolutely right," he said.

The angry man exhaled heavily and folded arms.

The man in charge stood again. "Is that all, Patrick?" he asked.

There were the cigarettes, the gas station man, the coffee shop, and–

"Yes," he said. "I believe that was it."

"Good, let's move on," he said, sitting back down.

The Seniors seemed interested in only reaffirming that Dolan was still convinced of Earth's existence. Perhaps they didn't know, and to divulge Mother's secret now would only break him down, ruin the remainder of his career – or so they thought. He wasn't about to admit now that he was onto them. *Let it go,* he told himself, *and they'll quietly send me back.*

The bearded man slid back his chair and crossed his legs. "Mr Dolan, if for some reason we gave you the ability to crossover and stay there for ... say ... a week, *without* contact. Describe to us your reaction."

Caution flag. This was the real test of character. "Well, besides going mad from not connecting, I'd say I'd be ... reluctant – somewhat reluctant." The panel remained quiet. After a moment, the angry man sprung from his chair, activated a second vidcon and approached the image it cast on the wall. "Mr Dolan, tell us what this object is."

"It's called a microwave oven," he said without hesitation. "It's used to cook food."

"Really?" The man's snide, accusatory tone made Dolan sink further into his chair. "Well, I can't say I've ever actually seen one, let alone had the chance to use one. I guess Mother's missing out on a wonderful creation, isn't she?" He pressed a button and the image changed. "And do you know what *this* is?" There it was again, that metallic canister he'd seen earlier. The angry man continued without giving him a chance to respond. "You can't remember, can you, Mr Dolan? Something that Mother has made available to us for a long time." He turned off the vidcon and sat down. "You certainly *should* remember ... but, for some reason you just don't know."

"I can't say that I recall what that is, no," Dolan said almost in a whisper. "But I have been away for some time and –"

The man in charge stood. "Mr Dolan, we all understand you've been through quite a bit as our first crossover agent. Twelve *i*-years *is* an extremely long time, but you've been more productive than we could have ever imagined. In fact, you've exceeded Mother's expectations, and She's very grateful."

"Thank you, sir." He would have been more appreciative with an explanation.

"That's why we've come to a unanimous decision –" He paused as the angry man grunted and folded his arms again. " – To promote you to SL13."

Dolan wasn't sure he'd heard the man right. He'd nearly killed one of Mother's candidates ... and for that She was awarding him with a promotion? He couldn't argue with being given a new status level, but he knew that moving up meant ... "Please tell me I'm staying on assignment," he said.

"We think a change is best," the auburn-haired woman said.

"Nothing ... permanent," the man in charge said. "Think of your new job as temporary."

"How temporary – ?" The sooner he could get back, the better.

The soft-spoken man interrupted. "Patrick, there's an infinite number of secrets for you to discover, but all in due time."

"You're a thirteen now," the auburn-haired woman followed up quickly. "It's time to start thinking about your future."

"Face it, Dolan," the angry man snapped. "You're not getting any younger, and your work is starting to affect you." He looked

down the table at his colleagues. "At least one of us can see that."
The man in charge continued.

"After the recent course of events we feel you should take a break. Reestablish yourself, become familiar again with your true surroundings." He paused then smiled. "Welcome back to the Unation."

Dolan struggled to remember what it had felt like to hold Susan earlier that morning, but couldn't. The only sensation he could muster was a sense that she wasn't real, as if nothing had ever really happened. He tried again to dissolve his memories of this place like he had when he held Susan, but those of Earth faded instead. He hoped he could get back before they were gone completely. Game over; reset the machine. He looked at the vidcon on the desk. Was that the one he'd lived in?

"What do you want me to do?" he asked.

"We need your expertise in the real world, Patrick," said the blonde woman.

"We need you to locate someone who's turned up missing," said the man in charge.

The auburn-haired woman broke in. "This is vitally important to the Unation."

"You'll need to fly to the Southeast sector," the blonde woman added.

"We're all counting on you, Patrick," said one of the men.

"And when you're done with that, you'll return to work," said one of women.

"Then you are sending me back?" he broke in anxiously.

"All in good time," said the man in charge.

"Who will I be looking for?"

"The seventh Senior," grunted the angry man, voice still thick with sarcasm. He pointed to the empty chair. "Don't tell me you've forgotten about his majesty, Montgomery Dodd?"

Seven

Food came to Selmar like clockwork. And by carving a notch in the soft clay of the cell wall when each meal arrived, he figured out that he'd been held captive for nearly three days. He longed to look into the sun. The insignificant window near the edge of the ceiling had been painted over. The walls were crumbling, the floor was pitted. Harsh light from an unshaded bulb was his only means of seeing anything inside the damp, deteriorating room. The light burned ceaselessly, making his incarceration seem like one endless day. His captors still hadn't allowed him to connect to the core and his KI was full. Not since the morning Sheila left had he contributed a single thought to Mother. As he huddled in the corner, his mind agonized over the erasure of recent memories from his KI. One way or another the KI had to make room for new ones. As each minute passed, he sensed tiny pieces of his mind chip away and fall to the floor. He tried to control his KI, speaking out loud the thoughts that circled around in his head, but they still managed to escape him. It was only a matter of time before any notion of the previous three days vanished forever. All that he'd done for Sheila, everything he'd seen in Jay's house – only vague, insignificant shadows remained. He could still remember being captured, but had already forgotten what he was doing at the time. Starting his selfish quest over again frightened him – searching for the truth behind Dodd's job offer, struggling to accept Sheila's departure, rediscovering whatever had been in Jay's house.

The corner he stayed in managed to remain dry despite the

water seeping through spots of the sagging ceiling. The air in the room became chilled again, and his body shook. Mother's podium ducts were somewhere very close by. The familiar thrumming filled his ears, not allowing him much sleep, as masses of fissor sped through the cooled tubes to someone's podium. Each time an incorp requested an item, a glob of fissor would pass by, leaching more heat from the room, and from him. Maybe the small portion of Her happening by right then was going to be transformed into a hot meal for some hungry juv, or building materials for another new housing complex that he wouldn't be living in. It was probably a floating vehicle on its way to the home of a well-to-do upper who'd use it as a conversation piece. As if people had no better way to use their creds.

He lifted his knees closer to his chin and pulled the damp blanket tighter. Sheila would've been so embarrassed if she knew of his situation. But she wasn't here, she'd never know – unless the same vidcon surveillance that had monitored his actions outside was recording in here, too. Out of the corner of his eyes he furtively scanned the walls. They were bare, or at least that was how Mother wanted them to appear.

Pain came. He squeezed his eyes shut and fell over onto the damp floor as fire consumed him deep inside. The heat in his neck, painful, spreading itself through his head and back. Memories gone with each blink, his KI obliterating pieces of the previous three days. The choppy segments that remained were starting to make less sense. Day one was a jigsaw puzzle cut into a hundred pieces, he had no clue to its solution.

Then his KI brought itself to consciousness. Heedless of his own need for air, the thing expanded and contracted, as if it were breathing on its own.

The long stretch of pain finally subsided and he lifted himself up out of the small puddle of water. The blanket was drenched now. Notches in the wall next to head – he felt a dull recognition of their importance, but that was all.

Damn Mother and Her cruel methods of protecting Herself. Why the torture? She only needed to take whatever knowledge he wasn't supposed to have. A simple, routine method for helping incorps retain their focus. *Just take away the thoughts and ideas I don't need!* he thought.

Visiting Dodd – what a bad idea. And the conversation was in pieces, almost gone. *Mother, Your lessons are persuasive, but I won't budge. My head will empty, but whatever truth you seek will stay. It won't stop haunting me.* He saw blood on his shirt and frantically checked himself for the wounds, puzzled to find none.

A familiar metal clang, the narrow opening at the bottom of his cell door lifted. Feeding time. His mouth watered. As before, a grimy hand slid a tray of food through the slot, then retreated. Only darkness on the other side. He pushed the tray, reached out to the other side. "Hey," shouting into the opening. "I want out, here!" Faint ghost of a person of the other side, it floated in circles, then left him. All alone again.

Only the meal was there – cheese sandwich, apple, milk. No thanks; not eating another bite, ever. Making death a conscious choice.

The rain, seeping through in constant streams. It's time to leave this misery behind again, moving back into the better days by shutting out the room, stop looking at this depressing sight. So eyes closed tight.

Water still falling, but now on the pedway, on the way home to Sheila. That night's a permanent memory; it sure isn't going anywhere. Dinner's waiting, Dodd and Sheila, too. Running along the pedway toward home, faster and faster, rain coming down harder, oppressive. The memory is intense, but different this time. Raining harder, streets dirtier and awkward. Not the right neighborhood. Regardless, home is close and a stern talk with Dodd in front of Sheila will change everything. The cell will vanished, change to the bedroom, Sheila fast asleep, just like the morning she left. But be careful, not time to look yet. First, this memory must go on.

Pedways and houses still changing, shape and distances skewed, all the more unfamiliar. Remembering even more now, very comforting. Walking through the rain, but something is there this time. The presence is trying to grab hold, not physically though. It's an illicit thought out of nowhere, the kind that made Mother quite upset. It's circling the edge of awareness, refusing to show itself. Forget about it. Push on. Though, still, nothing is right. Buildings half the size, they had once touched the sky. Rain clouds, now dots of moisture on the night. Scouts on every corner, too, talking softly. Their glares unnerving, but that doesn't mean run. They're looking for that, hoping for it.

The illicit thought has found flesh, biting down, refusing to let go. No choice but to make an escape. Damn the scouts and their roving eyes.

The thing is pushing venom below skin, mixing with blood. The poison is making memories surface, same ones Mother has been erasing. They're evil ones, wrong to consider. How dare the mind make up such foolish lies like that. No one would ever think of deserting Mother.

The thing vanishes, but its venom's still deep, heading for the brain, showing off the secret it uncovers.

Clarity struck like a hammer. Selmar opened his eyes upon his damp cell.

Jay's secret ... all along it was his thought I've been suffering for!

And Jay had been killed because of it. It was so clear now. Jay had found a secret way to escape Mother, and he was going to abandon the Unation.

Jay, beg aloud for Her mercy, just this once.

But his rising voice fell silent. There were no apologies. She wouldn't hear of it.

A clank that made the saliva flow again, and the cell became brilliant, water still running from above. Mother was coming for his REMOVAL.

The end of it all, yes, I welcome the end.

A spot of pressure on his shoulder turned into a tight fist. Now on all the extremities, and what a strange sensation to be floating motionless above the floor. People – five, six, seven, ten. Who could count them all? They moved too quickly.

Cruel hands. I expect nothing different. Defying Her, acting on my own, for myself. For my wife. Jay did the same, and look what happened to him!

Now on a soft dry bed, so much better than the unforgiving floor, wet and pocked. Hands on his body, but soft and caressing. Caring for the maladies.

Jay, don't tell me what you think about. There is nothing I want to know about leaving Her behind. I will forget. I will force myself to forget.

A burst of memories leaving his head at unimaginable speeds – finally, they found a way out of his KI.

Bless you, Mother!

Eight

Selmar's mind was his own again, the pressure relieved, though he'd been left with an unsolvable puzzle in his head. But a solution didn't matter anymore, because he was content with what little he still retained of the previous three days. It suited him. There was so little need for concern anymore – Mother was going to take care of him in time.

Someone spoke, telling him to open his eyes so they could have a look inside. But he didn't want to let them in, or allow the secret to come out. He was content remaining alone, holding in the venom until Mother came for him. Nevertheless, this person insisted, it was all for his own good. The pressure on his shoulders vanished and reappeared on his face. Forcing their way in – how dare they. He tried so hard to keep everyone out this time, fearing the venom would escape, contaminating someone else. Jay had already died, why should others suffer over the secret buried in his brain? But they forced his eyes open anyway, and the contamination of the rest of the world would begin. Mother wasn't going to be pleased.

People leaned over him – six, seven, eight, still no idea how many. Bodies covered in long, white gowns, faces plastered with papier mâché masks, tiny slits for eyes. The one standing over him, tall woman, golden hair flowing from behind her disguise, bent over and looked into his eyes. Her mask had a peaceful expression. She held a light, making bright orange spots that blotted out everything for a moment. He expected the light to draw out the poison and destroy it, but no such luck. Then she spoke. "We made it just in time." This was to the others, but the lips of her mask did not move. That didn't matter, though. The group had obviously worn them to hide their lips – nevertheless, he heard, and understood clearly.

He, too, tried to speak without moving his lips, transforming his face into a mask just like theirs. *I know what you want*, he said silently, *but it's not worth dying for.*

"Mr Rayburne, can you speak to me?" The woman's voice again. "You're with friends."

He listened to the others speak in turn, announcing they'd found nothing out of the ordinary. In gestures of trust and good faith everyone removed their masks. How awful, each of them suffered from such weary symptoms he'd never seen before. Mother would never allow an incorp to appear so wan. Only the faces of primes looked so haggard. He looked into each one's face again. The primes must have taken him. But why? The venom was never meant for them.

A sting, and he watched a curious tube of silver liquid disappear into his arm. He supposed this was an initiation ritual, or even worse – what if the Grand Contribution didn't mean rejoining Mother as an ethereal collection of fissor, but excommunication into a life of eternal shame as a prime? A lifetime of hard work and determination – all in vain. How pathetic.

But he was in no mood to examine his life now, the silver was spreading itself through his body, filling the holes in his mind with memories of others. A tranquil conversation began with the ten, twenty, thirty, an infinite number of people, all flowing into his head. Each and every one of them had an elaborate story to tell, and he listened carefully to each, though he soon realized none of these people were from the place he had called his home.

The silver moved deeper. Missing portions of the previous days returned, sliding into place until the puzzle was complete, then the segments fused themselves together. They weren't going anywhere ever again. He was able to recall why he'd been so desperate to confront Dodd, and how much Sheila meant. Feelings he'd missed dearly. He also remembered the death of his friend, and that he could have lived without.

The silver touched his core. A new truth settled upon him, one that debunked everything he'd ever believed in. He was *aware* – for now he knew that's what it meant to recognize Her lies.

Very soon this will all be over, a voice said. The woman above him, but her real lips weren't moving. *Don't regret the past, Selmar, and don't turn your back on the future. Look inside yourself and you'll see that it is you, not Sheila. You are the key. You can unite us all.*

He blinked and opened his eyes onto a different place, surrounded by Mother's technology – high walls with core nodes and podiums. Useless junk. The woman was there with him, and she leaned over, slipping something onto his KI. He watched her mouth the words, *this is how we travel,* but he was already aware of that, and then the room faded away. He was soon surrounded by a pool of pure knowledge and absolute thought. He was moving through Mother, and She had no idea he was there.

Nine

Dolan woke up early the next morning convinced he'd been the victim of a bad dream. The sun had yet to rise and he couldn't see a thing, but the bed was certainly his own. The sheets, the blankets, the pillow – they all had a familiar feel that suggested he was back on Earth where he belonged. There was nothing he wanted more than to find Susan lying next to him. She would be cozy and content, wanting to sleep until the morning light came, and he'd wait until then to tell her about the nightmare he'd had. All about how he'd been taken to a strange, oppressive world, not allowed to return, and how he'd felt about never seeing her again. Never having the chance to work out their differences, or to touch her. He reached out, but she wasn't there. Maybe she was already gone. After noticing how soundly he'd been sleeping, she had decided not to disturb him. That was kind of her, but he wished he'd had a chance to mention his feelings about their first night together. That would have meant a great deal.

He rolled out of bed, anticipating the floor to be cold. And it was. His slippers were where he'd left them next to the stand. Through the dark he moved to the bathroom, not needing to feel his way. The door was where he expected it to be. He turned the light on, and everything was exactly as he left it. Razor, toothbrush, towels – all in their places. Mother hadn't sent anyone here to search for evidence to use against him. Nothing in the apartment could give away his true identity, or rather his *old* identity. No one on Earth would ever know where he was really from, unless he chose to tell them. And Mother couldn't stop him if he chose not to let Her. The only option She ever had was to trust him. *And does She?* he wondered. All that he'd seen during the previous two days left him wondering which side of the rift was real. Nevertheless, he was still here. He was free again to roam Earth, a world that essentially belonged to him, and if he chose Susan as his traveling companion, then so be it.

In the mirror he examined the bandage on his arm. There was no blood soaking through, which meant it was healing. And it still hurt, unlike in the dream. That was all good. If the gunshot was real, then so was his memory of collecting and delivering the three candidates to Mother. He was on schedule.

He moved to the kitchen, and by the soft glow of lights outside the window, poured himself a glass of root beer and drank it slowly. It was smooth and creamy, and he thought about making a trip to the store later to buy another bottle. Maybe a pack of cigarettes, too – just because he could. There was no one on Earth who could stop him.

After removing a coffee cake from its plastic wrapper he placed it in the microwave and turned it on. The outside street lights winked out in preparation for dawn. He moved to the window and found himself staring into the face of a building that hadn't been there the day before. He was surprised that the builders on Earth could put up a structure almost as fast as Mother. This was the kind of development Susan had been fighting. She'd said nothing would ever be the same once the deep-pocket, big business types took complete control, and they always move in overnight. She was right – this one had done just that.

He heard the microwave ding, but first moved to the other window to see what else was happening to his home, only to find the soft field of tall grass had been replaced by a fragment of the other world – tall buildings, pedways, and the flag of the Unation flying high above it all.

He had expected nothing less. No matter how much he tried to avoid mixing the two worlds together, they were both a part of him. He'd just have to get used to living in a mental unification of both. But the illusion was incredibly authentic. He was surprised at the detail his mind had retained after such a long time. It almost made him miss it. Almost.

He turned to retrieve his coffee cake from the microwave and found a podium in its place. The machine towered over him, resting on its legs as if ready to pounce on anyone who approached. The illusion was beginning to seem less like a fabrication of his mind. He didn't dare move for fear of finding something else that had crept out of his old world into the new. He wondered if a time would come when he wouldn't be able to tell the difference between the two. Surely there would, and the day was likely to come very soon.

Something signaled to him from the living room with a screeching tone that made the skin around his KI tingle. He moved slowly, pausing between each step. The noise came again, more ferociously this time. He peeked around the corner, scanned the room in the shallow light, then stared at the end table. That's where it was, he could still hear the noise. He slid his hand up the wall, feeling for the switch, but stopped short of turning it on. *Ignore it,* he thought. *It'll go away quietly.* But he turned the light on anyway, and saw a vidcon on the table. It signaled again, queuing an incoming call. He found his finger hovered over the answer button. Perhaps by willing his mind to imagine the caller as Susan he could end his obsession with a world that he'd rather leave behind.

He activated the vidcon and it projected an image into the center of the room. As the shape focused, layers of his elaborate delusion melted away until he was left with nothing except the concrete memories of his return to the Unation and his meeting with the Seniors. One of them stood wavering in front of him; the image was as hazy as Dolan's recollection of Susan's face.

"Oversleep?" the Senior asked, arms folded across his chest. It was the angry man, and he was still upset. "We're all waiting for you." Dolan thought he could hear the buzz of the podium in the kitchen. The walls had taken on a gray hue, darker than he remembered from the apartment on Earth. Everything around him had been constructed by Mother, made from Her fissor, and She hadn't missed a single detail. Even the week's worth of dirty clothes in the corner. Was this to make him feel more at home, or to reinforce a more permanent state of confusion? Mother probably figured that a person left constantly guessing would never discover the truth, even if they were staring it in the face. "I, for one, seriously oppose this whole idea of sending *you*," the angry man continued. "But Mother's got some kind of fondness for you that I don't share."

"I wasn't expecting any of this," Dolan said. His worse fear had been proven – Earth had never really existed, except in Mother's mind. She'd merely let him out of his cage.

"It's all a surprise to us as well, but regardless, we need to find out what happened to Mr Dodd. Either you're up to the challenge, or we'll convince Her to find someone else who is."

"You're not really leaving me with any choice. If I refuse, my career's over."

"Correction," the angry man said. "*Mother* isn't giving you a choice. I've come up with plenty of options, but we're only human. I suggest you move. There's an escort waiting outside your door to take you downstairs. You'll be debriefing a replacement for the crossover assignment before you leave."

"You never said anything about sending someone in my place." It wasn't a jealousy thing, just a matter of principle. Why was She going to allow another person to enter that dreamworld of Hers? But he didn't want to ask. It was better to play along with the lie than to be REMOVED because of the truth.

"Mother demanded the collections continue, and no one questions Her." His voice was losing some of its resilience. "Not even us."

"No one will ever know Earth better than me." *Not even Mother*, added in silence.

"The only thing I want to hear from you is that you're on your way," the man said sternly.

"I plan to come down shortly before zero hour if that's –"

"You've got fifteen minutes," the man barked, and the vidcon went dead.

Alongside the silent vidcon was the pain cap and an old, half-drunk glass of root beer. Resting against the glass he noticed several large pieces of torn paper, black lines and colored blotches on each. He spread them out over the bed and tried to piece together his sketches. He moved the segments around, but none of them made sense. The pictures had become distorted. Finally, he wadded them and tossed them over his shoulder into the bedside trash can. The paper hit the floor; the bin wasn't there anymore.

He sat down on the bed and waited for the room to stop changing, wishing someone would put him out of his misery.

The cool air in the crossover room sent a chill through Dolan's body. But he wouldn't be warded away by the temperature or the gray walls. He'd been in the room countless times and never before had the room's oppressiveness driven him away. He wasn't about to start now.

He sat and waited for his replacement, who was later than he had been. A thick, metal spring was poking through the rough fabric of the chair and sticking into thigh. Even the very chair he'd occupied more than a thousand times was trying to reject him.

He leaned his head back, closed his eyes and tried to clear his head of the mess Mother had left behind. He didn't want to imagine himself on Earth, or picture himself walking with Susan and nervously allowing her to touch his arm like she did in the coffee shop. Mother had brought him back home, taken him out of the dream. His life as an incorp had resumed, and now all he wanted was to pick up the pieces of himself that were strewn behind him. But each piece was too heavy to lift. As incomplete as he was, he'd have to move on without them. But that wasn't such a bad thing. After all, Susan had helped him shed the burden he had carried for Maggie. Those pieces had fallen off quite easily and he gratefully buried them deep on Earth, no matter how unreal the place was. That world had changed his life, altered the person he'd been, so to him it existed, it always would. But he could not hide inside what he'd left behind this time, ignoring his loss until it became infectious and diseased. He knew he needed to bury Susan alongside Maggie, the final step to restoring his life with his one true love: Mother. He had to accept Her love again, regardless if She had exiled him for twelve *i*-years. Allowing Her the freedom of control was part of who he was.

"You could pass for catatonic." The unexpected voice startled him. He opened his eyes and turned to see Philip Tuft closing the door. Tuft adjusted his tie and glared at him with the same arrogant expression he'd worn earlier. In fact, the man seemed to always have the same idiotic lines in his face. Pathetic excuse for a smile.

"I'm not in the mood, Tuft," he said. "What do you want?"

"Your job," he said. "But, looks like I already got it."

"*You're* my replacement?"

"Why is it so difficult to imagine?" Tuft said. "Theman recommended me to Mother because of my flawless record." Dolan could see Tuft pressing his tongue against the inside of his cheek.

"You're the perfect man for the job," he said, leaning back in the chair.

"I've been after this for a long time. Ha! Finally slipped it from under your nose, and now," he took a seat, "you're gonna sit here and teach me everything you know."

Obviously She hadn't informed his replacement what to expect, and Dolan surely wasn't going to. Let Tuft find out for himself. "So I should shake your hand for getting me promoted?" Dolan asked, deciding to play along.

"Please, you flatter me." Tuft snickered in jest like a child, then became deadly serious in almost the same instant. "I want details, and then I'll be on my way."

Dolan leaned back and folded his arms, hoping for some kind of insight into Tuft's iron ego. He was going to fit right in. "What do you want to know?"

"I want you to tell me about the people. What are they like?"

"What kind of crazy question is that?"

"Oh no," Tuft said, reaching across and poking him in the

chest, "I'm not the crazy one, not me pal. I haven't been over there for twelve *i*-years yet. I can't even imagine what it must be like to live over there. It must be like owning your own world. Am I right, Patrick? Boy, I may not want to come back. Maybe I won't." He cracked a sly grin and winked.

Dolan stared at him, speechless. He knew that Philip Tuft was getting ready to enter a world where he could be a king if he tried hard enough. And Tuft wanted that more than anything – Dolan could see it in his eyes. "Moving speech," Dolan said, trying to lighten Tuft's earnestness. "So, where would you like me to start?"

"Well, Patrick, I'd really like to hear how *that* happened." Tuft pointed at the bandage on his arm. "So I might avoid similar ... complications."

"Stuff it, *Philip*," Dolan barked. Mother made the Earth experience as true to life as She could, but Tuft would have to discover on his own that dying was just as real there as it was here. "I'm not here to play games with you or do show and tell. Let's get serious."

"I am serious. You of all people should know that while I'm over there my main concern is safety. Look at what happened to you yesterday. That little piece of meat you brought back with the bullet in her shoulder."

She was fake, he told himself, *a vidcon projection*. But from a place deadly enough to either of them. Though he wasn't going to let Tuft in on that secret.

"That should've been proof enough," Tuft continued. "Your so-called safety protocols went to shit a long time ago. Whoever did that to you was out for a kill. So spill it. Were you trying to off them, too?"

"That's not even an issue." Talking about it made it seem so real, like the murder had actually happened. Despite the cap, he thought he felt pain in his arm.

"Oh, but it is," Tuft said, "because killing is not our business."

Dolan leaned back in the chair again, wanting to push Tuft just a little further. "Do *you* know why Mother sends us in?"

"Don't talk down to me, dammit! Every single person in the Unation has a job to do. And everyone depends on the other to do it right. But you ... you were different, because you went away. The secret place that no one was supposed to know about. What you were bringing back changed the Unation more than anyone'll ever know. I can't believe that for twelve *i*-years so much of this world depended solely on you. Scary fucking thought, isn't it?" Dolan refused to answer, because he knew Tuft was right. Except Mother wasn't using the candidates as food for Her thoughts. *He* had always been Her main dish. "Well, that's over now," Tuft continued. "End of an era. Out with the old, in with the new. Now it's time for all of you to depend on *me.*" He poked himself hard with his thumb.

Dolan cringed and tried to mask his facial contortions by rubbing his palms across his unshaven face. It seemed too late to do anything about Tuft. Whatever results Mother would derive from watching this man were sure to be catastrophic. The Unation would never be the same. "That, my friend, is an even scarier thought," Dolan muttered.

"Ain't it, though?" Tuft said through a grin.

Zero hour was approaching as Dolan left Tuft to go on his merry way to Earth. Dolan didn't have the heart, or the inclination, to tell Tuft what he was getting into. If anyone deserved to become the next pawn in Mother's game, it was Tuft; then he might realize what it was like to return as a stranger to an even stranger land.

He moved through the lobby toward the outside and his heart began to race. He hoped the world would welcome him with a thousand familiar sights. Even though he hadn't seen the light of day in the Unation for some time, he hoped, or rather prayed, that not a single moment had gone by without him.

But that had been too much to ask. He let the door swing close behind him. The hustling commuters, the encroaching buildings, even the blue-green sky – what little could be seen between the high-rises – were as alien to him as Earth had been at his first crossover. He stepped to the side to let people pass. They wore clothes he'd never seen before; pants and skirts made of a glossy material that changed colors as they moved. Some wore suit jackets made of random pieces of fabric all carefully pasted over their outfits. Many wore strange metal rings on top of their heads, a loose wire looping around the neck, attached to the KI. Their faces were artificially placid. No one took notice that he wasn't coming along as they rushed feverishly through the automatic doors and into the buildings. Only he was aware that his destination was a different place than theirs. Shamefully, he realized that was the one and only thing that *hadn't* changed over the *i*-years. He was always going where no one else was, leaving behind the one life he wished to keep, or return to. He wanted to be normal again, to live an unsuspecting life among all the other incorps, live and work each day merely to earn his creds, to acquire the things Mother offered that would help him live well. The simple things.

But he knew better, having transcended that desire to simply work and spend the creds on Her rewards. Mother had put him in a world where those who wanted to could make a difference. Susan had shown him how to do that. He'd had a taste of the freedom to think for himself only to have it taken from him. He wanted it back but Mother would never hear of it, because She was still in control. She always had been.

He made his way through the thinning crowd along the pedways, following signs to the subshuttle station. He stopped three different people for directions who sent him in the opposite direction each time, but not before looking him up and down. He must have appeared old-fashioned to them, his clothes, his demeanor. Unless they were seeing something more. Something that gave away the *Earth* in him.

He finally found the subshuttle station. The all-too-familiar zero hour tone signaled and the few people left in the station suddenly began to pace, as if instinctively they were expecting a reprimand for not being at work. Dolan assumed they, too, were excused from reporting to their offices so they could travel. Though they had homes to come back to. He felt useless, a drifter – a temporary assignment was no consolation. No job meant having no meaning. And when the assignment was over, and he had no idea what would come after. To have no direction – that was the worst experience of his life.

He stopped walking. Even the steps he was taking seemed pointless. Where was he going if not back to Earth? What was he striving to become? Weren't these things Mother should have been considering for him? He began to wonder if his life had meaning even before the Earth program. But he overlooked his doubt, knowing his life before Earth had revolved around Maggie. He had purpose then. While they were together, she had given him everything he needed to be happy. Susan had been no different. After losing both of them, Mother alone was surely no substitute. She could never be enough.

Once Dolan figured out how to use the new access ribbon, he paid for his ticket at the podium stands and took a seat in the very back of the subshuttle car. After some time the doors slammed shut and the car lurched forward, carrying him and the rest of the jittery people to the plixport. The newer, sleeker shuttle car sped along the tracks. Nothing in the Unation – at least at the time before he left – had ever traveled so fast. The rattling of the windows and the whining of the wheels against the track pierced his ears and at times made it hard to breathe. The view outside became indistinguishable blurs of green and brown, as if Mother wanted to keep him from seeing how much She'd actually changed the world. But he didn't want to be kept in the dark. He was back and he deserved to know. Mother owed him that much.

Within minutes the subshuttle slid into a tunnel and came to a screeching halt underneath a huge sign pointing to the entrance of the plixport. As the travelers got off the subshuttle, each was handed a metal box. A loudspeaker told them to follow their mechanical escort to their gate. Dolan set his on the ground and stood back. The oblong, insect-like metal can on wheels tugged on his pant leg with its tweezers and then rolled away. Mother must have programmed one for each traveler. She had started keeping track of every person, where they were going, where they'd been. Stretching Her influence just a little further.

He followed the tin can escort along a corridor plastered with signs. The language looked foreign at first, but he soon deciphered the words on some and wondered why Mother would go out of Her way to actually advertise Her new items. Granted She had so many to choose from, and Her list by then had, no doubt, grown enormously, but why push the rewards onto those who willfully worked to obtain them? Who was She trying to convince?

The small can on wheels approached him and tugged on his pants, encouraging him to move along. He followed as the machine sped off, continuing to study the advertisements on the wall. He'd seen variations of Mother's new items on Earth. She'd created something called a psiphone – a portable telephone with a KI attachment allowing people to converse with each other from absolutely anywhere. That must have been what those people in the square were wearing on their heads, the same ones who had looked so withdrawn. Another ad – Mother had brought back the car, but nothing like the old ones he'd seen on Earth. These could float, allowing people the freedom to drive where they wished, or so Mother boasted. What had become of the world he had left behind? This Unation had been altered into a fast-paced frenzy of conveniences, still controlled by Mother, but no longer driven by the dreams and ideas of the people who thought-contributed to Her every day. It seemed they all simply existed as slivers of tarnished metals buried under a huge pile of rubble. They were all suffocating.

At the gate entrance, the tiny escort pointed its tweezers at the line of passengers forming along the back wall, then it turned and sped away, no doubt to report to Mother that Dolan was at the terminal. He was alone again, wishing the mechanical escort had stayed with him. So far, that little piece of tin was the only thing that even came close to acknowledging his situation – simply by recognizing that he existed, or even mattered.

Following the others, Dolan moved to the end of the line and waited as the scout by the gate's entrance gave the once-over to each of the boarding passengers. Dolan watched carefully as the scout measured an old man's cephalic index with a handheld scanner, then passed some other small device over his frail body. The elongated, metal box let out a scream as it passed across the old man's left hip. The scout dug through the his pocket, confiscated whatever he had in there and took him away by the back of the arm. Another scout promptly appeared to resume the check-in. The old man was weeping as he and the scout disappeared around the corner.

"Check your pockets people," the new scout announced. "Unauthorized items can't leave the sector. We should all know that by now."

The couple in front of Dolan spoke softly to each other, then when the scout turned to process the next person in line, they snuck away clinging tightly to each other. Dolan felt inside his pockets. The Seniors never mentioned anything about not removing things from the sector. He pulled out his access ribbon and two soft sticks of root beer flavored gum. For all he knew, the old man could have been taken away for something as simple as that. In his back pocket Dolan found a wrinkled sheet of paper with Mr Dodd's last known whereabouts. No one was supposed to know that Dodd was missing, or that Dolan was looking for him. What would the scout think if he saw Dodd's name on the paper? He considered sneaking away as the young couple had just done, but the line continued to move forward and the scout was sure to see him leave. Then he'd have to explain his failure to the Seniors, and Mother. Though She should've been used to that by now.

He crept closer, stuffing the paper deep into his pocket. When it was his turn the scout measured his index and passed the metal wand up and down. It didn't scream, and Dolan silently let out a sigh of relief as he handed his access ribbon to the scout. He wondered again what the old man had been carrying, but wasn't about to ask. He simply waited for the young man to hand back the access ribbon and then went on his way toward the gate entrance.

A vidcon-projected attendant escorted him down the aisle of the plix. The image stood over him and wouldn't leave until he was securely in his seat. It didn't even bother to ask if he wanted anything to drink. *You have such an ego, Mother,* he thought, but for some reason he felt so alone in the awareness of it. The rest of them hadn't been through the Earth program; to them, ego had no meaning. He had seen too much having gone there – the rest of the Unation would always know less than he did.

Though, maybe that made them the lucky ones.

The plix rumbled to life, a chugging noise filled the cabin, one of a hundred unfamiliar sounds. He looked out the window and watched the wings extend. The projected attendant demonstrated how to position one's arms and legs in the seat correctly to avoid broken bones or other injuries when the strapless seat belt was activated – whatever that was. Dolan followed the instructions meticulously and waited with his teeth clenched and eyes pressed tightly closed. After a moment he heard a distinctive tone over the drone of the engines. The attendant informed everyone to take a deep breath and relax. He could only manage the first. The seat became warm under his body. He sunk slowly into the soft cushion, as if some huge magnet was pulling him down. The weighty sensation stole his breath away. He guessed this was nothing different from the REMOVAL bays, the overwhelming feeling of helplessness. He didn't like knowing that this was what his nephew had gone through, all because of his mistake.

Once they were in the air, he eventually relaxed. He eased the pressure from his eyelids, dozed off, and dreamt in fragments about Susan and Maggie – how they were still alive, yet both in different worlds than his. Susan had slipped away like turning off a light bulb, living somewhere inside the tiny specks of Mother's dust that controlled the way mechanism. Maggie, on the other hand, was somewhere across the Unation, her body returned to fissor and reused. He envisioned she had become a bouquet of roses. He bought them from a podium shop and kept them in a vase, but they died before he could wake himself up.

He opened his eyes upon a woman across the row having a vomiting fit. An attendant was hovering in the aisle trying to comfort her by simulating rubbing her back with a transparent hand while the woman threw up into a tube that disappeared into the floor. He turned away, refusing to watch the pathetic display of affection. Mother was so detached, even in Her sympathy.

The plix rocked as it landed and the strapless seat belt kept him pinned until they came to a complete stop. The thrumming of the engines persisted in his ears. Once he was allowed to, he lifted his head and shook it, trying to silence the noise, but that only made it worse. He rode the elevator with several other head shaking passengers to the exit where a scout was waiting. A line quickly formed again on the back wall and each person proceeded to go through a security check, all part of Mother's bizarre welcome to the Southeast sector. Dolan fell in at the back of the line. Everyone around him appeared just as nervous this time as before. He began to mimic the quirky expressions and mannerisms of the man in front of him in order to remain unnoticed.

Before long a plixport attendant wheeled in a platform carrying the tin can escorts. Dolan glanced at the wooden skid looking for his. One by one, the attendant placed the little machines on the floor and each sped off to the person they'd been assigned to chaperon. Their demeanor lightened as the mechanical friend joined them in line. Dolan felt curiously relieved when his rolled up and tugged on his leg as if to say hello. *A little bit of Mother that anyone can relate to,* he thought, but nevertheless appreciated the companionship.

After clearing security again, he followed his escort down long stretches of corridor that, as shown by the signs, would lead him to the subshuttle station. Then a clicking sound that reverberated through the corridors stopped the crowded plixport dead in its tracks. He paused one step short of crushing his escort. The machine waited while Dolan desperately tried to emulate the motionless crowd in any way he could. Whatever it took not to stand out.

"Your attention please," the speaker blared, echoing throughout the plixport. It was a strange variation of Mother's voice. It was final – nothing in the Unation had gone unchanged.

At once, the crowd looked to the ceiling. Dolan did the same. "Southeast sector general delivery has a priority message for Patrick Dolan SL13. Would Patrick Dolan please report to the nearest mail console."

He cowered slightly and glanced around, fearing everyone was looking at him. They all knew what he was doing there. The word was out, and in no time the entire Unation would know that Dodd was missing. That would be a failure worse than any he'd made on Earth. He thought again of the murdered officer and the way the bullet tore away part of the young man's neck. That was nothing in comparison.

The escort pulled at his leg and pointed to the left. He followed it. Maybe the message was from Mother, telling him the girl he'd brought back had died. That he need not continue with the assignment because he was too much of a risk to the safety of the Unation, the *real* people. But there was too much at stake to stop now. He had to find Dodd in order to prove to himself that he could still fit in. He needed to belong, learn to fit in again, like he'd done on Earth.

The escort led him to a mail console in a small private cubicle near the entrance to the last gate. Beside that was a podium, already running. Someone had obviously forgot to shut it off. He used his access ribbon to retrieve the message as the instructions told him to do. The escort waited attentively by his feet, chirping and buzzing, turning in circles, keeping itself occupied. He waited for his letter. Finally, a mail tube slid into the delivery pouch. He removed it, took out the letter and read:

> *Patrick,*
> *Bring him to me. Use the floatie in G45. We're all counting on*
> *you.*
> *M.D.*

He flipped the paper over – blank. Then he furtively peaked around the curtain. No one in sight, which was a first since he left that morning. The note had to have been an elaborate joke. Dodd was supposed to be missing, and no one was supposed to know, so why the note with his initials on it? And who was *him*?

"Are you the one?" he asked his mechanical escort. "Am I supposed to bring you somewhere?"

The thing whirled and beeped in its digital-speak, sounding out the words *not me*, Dolan plainly understanding it. Then the activated podium suddenly began spitting up tiny droplets of pink slop. Dolan stepped back as the floor of the cubicle became saturated with the quivering jelly globs. The escort slid under the curtain, beeping in surprise as the podium continued to leak. Dolan recognized the stuff collecting by his feet – it was fissor material in its raw stages. But he hadn't requested anything. There had to be something wrong with the thing. He backed away as far as he could, realizing he had cornered himself, the accumulating mound of fissor resting between him and the curtain. Had the angry Senior finally convinced the rest of them that he was a real threat? What a deceitful way to trap him into a Grand Contribution, without an official REMOVAL hearing.

He readied himself to leap over it, but the pile of fissor began to take form. It slowly grew limbs and hair. The texture on its surface tightened, becoming imperfect, turning to skin. He expected the figure to take on the likeness of the officer he'd killed, bits of his neck still missing. This was another part of Earth that he'd carried back in his mind. He didn't want to spend the rest of his life fighting off hallucinations more real and intense than those he'd suffered on Earth.

The body continued to form, features defining themselves. Thankfully, he didn't recognize this person. It was no one he'd taken from Earth, or had killed and left behind.

After a short time, the man finally opened his mouth and took a deep breath. He stayed on the floor, naked, eyes shut. Dolan bent over, looking carefully for the man's KI, not wanting to touch him. He had one. This man was no vidcon-produced image. He was of the Unation, and for some reason Dodd wanted him, if that had been Dodd who sent the letter. There seemed to be a depth to this assignment that the other Seniors weren't aware of. But, regardless of the fact that Dodd was missing, he too was a Senior, and Dolan's only job was to follow their orders, not to question their own personal motives. That was Mother's job.

He helped the man sit up as he fought his disorientation. And with every right. If this person had been born from the fissor then this world would be as strange to him as it was to Dolan. But the man's eyes were telling a very different story. He knew of things that Dolan didn't, as if being inside Mother had revealed new truths, had shown him a world he never knew existed. Dolan had seen that same look before in his own bathroom mirror, but that life had proved itself to be a lie.

The escort re-entered the cubicle chirping wildly. "Clothes," Dolan said. "Good idea." He slid his ribbon into the podium, then sized up the man for some pants and a shirt. After the clothes arrived, Dolan helped him dress. The man could stand, but had a great deal of trouble walking a straight line. His eyes moved around, almost independently of each other. Dolan pointed to the escort and motioned to the man to keep his eyes on it.

"G45," Dolan said to the escort, looking again at Dodd's note. "That mean anything to you?"

The machine chirped in the affirmative and rolled away slowly. The man followed it. Dolan walked right behind, catching him when his body began to sway.

The escort led them to G45, which turned out to be a location code to an endless row of the tubular floating vehicles. As they approached, the escort pointed to their floatie and called out to Dolan in a fit of electronic exclamations. It moved underneath the floatie, turned its beady eyes back in their silvery sockets and stared. Dolan could see his own reflection in the glossy finish, too. The curves of the smooth body made him look very wide and pale in the face, as if the vehicle were just another of Mother's newest items mocking his ignorance. Not this time, though. He was ready to defeat anything that tried to keep him from surviving in the only place he had left.

Dolan motioned for the man to sit against the wall of the next stall. He scanned the lot to make sure no one was watching before he attempted to get in the floatie. After some hard searching for a handle he managed to open the door, then crawled into the front seat. The instrument panel was unlike anything he'd ever seen, even more elaborate than his car on Earth. He waited several minutes, sitting quietly as other people walked by, crawling into their own vehicles and floating away. None of them took notice of his companion still sitting in the adjacent stall, head bobbing as he continued to fall in and out of consciousness. Many of the floatie's readouts were gauged in units that meant nothing to him, switches marked with words in a different language entirely, separate from the signs in the plixport. He searched for a key, or something that would start the engine of the thing – if it even had an engine. Frustrated, he began pressing buttons on the navigator's control panel, hoping that one would tell it to get going. The navigator chimed. "Destination arrival – three hours. I hope you're enjoying your trip." He sat back and waited, but still nothing happened. After trying a few more switches and a handful of buttons, he noticed a small lever by his left knee slightly resembled an oversized key. He reached out and turned it. The floatie roared to life, but soon began to shake as the navigator piped up again. "Calibration mode – please keep clear of the floatie." He reached for the handle, but couldn't get the door open in time. He grabbed onto the soft edges of the forward control panel as the floatie began to rock back and forth, then side to side. The magnetic field that no doubt kept the thing afloat pulled at him the same way the strapless seat belt had on the plix. His left arm was pulled forward then behind him as his chron followed the wake of the field. He contorted his body as much as possible to keep his arm from breaking.

The thing continued to rock as the navigator called out: "Port adjustment complete." After his arm was freed he managed to open the door. He tried to step out, but the ground moved in and out of sight making him lose his balance. He landed flat on his stomach, air rushing out of him. The floatie dropped onto the concrete pad. Underneath it he could see the small tweezers of the escort waving frantically, then it went limp. He lay there laboring for a satisfying breath, able to fend off the humiliation, but not the remorse he felt for the helpless machine. He had no business being back in the Unation, pretending he'd never left. Before long he'd have to beg Mother for a demotion, to return to his old assignment, because he just couldn't live this way.

Ten

There wasn't much else to do but try to sleep while the floatie cruised along, but the navigator kept waking Dolan by announcing that their trip was going to take several more hours. Even with that, he still couldn't figure out where the floatie might be taking them. Still, nothing looked familiar. Even the landscape had been altered severely. The ground itself had been scraped and cut by something he had yet to see – no doubt more of Mother's machines used to manipulate the world. The rectangular gouges looked like enormous graves ready for thousands of dead, a ritual he'd only seen on Earth. To his left in the distance were the populated zones of the Southeast sector, congested groups of silver and black high-rises sticking out of the otherwise barren horizon, the structures disappearing into the clouds.

He turned to his companion, still unconscious. A few times Dolan checked to make sure he was still alive, still real. He was, and he seemed normal. Dolan leaned back and closed his eyes, hoping to doze a bit before something else in the floatie had a chance to sound off and wake him. But he couldn't clear his mind. It raced with bizarre scenarios of what Mr Dodd had planned for him and this man, whatever was next on Mother's list of cruel experiments: *Place each of them in a world all alone, watch as they suffer from withdrawal and loneliness, remove all the air so they can't even find comfort in the sound of each other's voice.*

It was safe to say that he wasn't the only one Mother had subjected to Her "culture shock" tests, for Dolan could find no other way to describe what was happening to him. This man, too, could have been a pawn in a completely different equation, and now Dodd was going to evaluate the results.

Dolan's mind wandered; he felt his limbs became soft as he drifted off. Then his body jumped, startled by the bitter whine of metal against metal. He looked behind them at the twisted scrap protruding from the ground. It was certainly large enough that *he* could have avoided it – if the machine would just let him drive.

His companion grunted in a hoarse voice and turned painfully to Dolan.

"Glad to see you're still with me," Dolan said. "Is everything working okay?"

His companion glanced down, examined himself and nodded as if to say he seemed to be intact – two arms, two legs, one torso, and a head to sense it all. Dolan could hear something odd in the man's breathing, hints of a dull panic, as if his insides had been reassembled in the wrong order. The man turned back to Dolan and tried to open his mouth to answer, but gave up and nodded instead.

"Are you sure you're all right, Mr ... ?"

"Selmar ... Rayburne SL7. Six. Oh, I don't know anymore."

"Patrick Dolan, SL ... " He paused, then shook his head. "Just Dolan." It took a moment for his companion to raise his hand, but they eventually shook. "Mr Dodd asked me to see you to him. I'm a friend."

Selmar blinked. "Mother doesn't need to know that Dodd's alive," he said after a moment. "Let's keep that between you and me."

Dolan turned away and gazed out the window again at the barren nothingness. Could the Unation have come so far that destinies have options? No, Mother wouldn't allow such free will to occur, although right at that moment, he couldn't see a single shred of evidence that She even existed. Even the buildings in the distance were gone, replaced by a blank, lonely horizon.

Selmar turned to him. "Where are we being taken?"

"I wish I knew," he said. "To Mr Dodd, I trust. I was thinking, though, that maybe you could persuade him better than me."

"Of what?"

Dolan re-positioned himself in the seat, trying to cross his legs, then gave up. "To come back. Mother thinks he's missing."

"My wife is with him ... but it's me Dodd wants. That's why he's waiting."

"Why this secrecy? Doesn't anyone answer to Mother any-more?"

"I thought you might already know." Selmar looked at him curiously. "You haven't been shown the truth of this world. I can tell by your eyes, you're not *aware*."

"I've seen too much to know what's real anymore." Dolan turned to stare out the window again. "I don't recognize any of this. It's not the same." The enormous gouges in the land became larger and more frequent. Occasionally, the floatie seemed to turn toward one of the sandy rifts as if it wanted to send the two of them plunging down, a place they would remain out of sight forever, but the floatie skirted the edge, giving Dolan a frightening view of the empty grave.

"What did She do to you?" Selmar asked.

"Sent me away long enough for the world to change. And I can't see the benefits."

"I've been shown how this world used to exist, in the time before Incorporation. The reason we live like this is all so simple now." Selmar paused, then added softly as if to himself, "My father fought against this for me." His head lowered and he scratched his temple, purposely covering his eyes. "For me."

"Did I miss the day that we gave up our way with Mother?"

"No, that day is today." Selmar looked up, staying focused on the road ahead. "You know of the movement against Mother some time back."

"And the primes are still paying for it."

"The resistance is still alive. The people behind it have made me *aware* of what they know." He turned to Dolan. His eyes still had that resilience, stronger than ever. Like the people on Earth. "Think back, Dolan. Can you really remember anything about this place before Incorporation?"

"I hadn't been born yet," he said apprehensively.

"But your prepmaster told you stories, and your parents. You went through the conditioning. Mother wanted everybody to know our history verbatim. But She concocted most of it, changed the rest, and made us believe it." Selmar poked at his KI. "We were all told the primes didn't want to be part of Her. So She exiled them, but not before forcing us all to forget what really happened. She rewrote our past."

"I remember our past very clearly."

"But some of the primes started to remember how it all really began, because She had no control over their thoughts."

"How *what* began? Mother has always existed, She incorporated the Unation –"

"That's what She wants us to believe, but we were all like the primes at one time. Living, thinking, creating for ourselves. I never believed living without Mother could be so satisfying, till now."

Dolan recalled that the Earth simulation had tricked him into believing the same thing. Was She planning to infect the entire Unation with a false sense of prosperity? Was that the purpose of Earth? He saw his own delusional fate in Selmar's wide-eyed expression.

"And after Mother was created," Selmar continued, "some people wanted to leave before they were caught up in Her Unation. They didn't want to be part of a homogenized pool of thoughts and ideas. She thought She was giving the rest of us paradise – providing whatever we wanted, unlimited material wealth, so long as we worked hard enough to pay for it."

Dolan shifted uncomfortably in his seat. The longer Selmar spoke, the more surreal his surroundings became. For a moment he thought the floatie had zoomed past a ghostly replica of his old apartment, then a gas station, a sign flashing: *Mick & Herb's*. The stale taste of tobacco coated his tongue. He was afraid if Selmar kept up the chatter, he'd begin to think he was still inside the vidcon, the program continuing to play itself out. Maybe he'd actually been born inside one, having spent his entire life controlled by projected lights, his world changing as quickly as the person outside could switch a program disk.

Selmar rambled on. "Now the primes are fighting to reveal the truth. They want us all to know how She's been using us as slaves and –"

"Do you know how absurd you sound?" Dolan interrupted. "How would Mother benefit from enslaving us? I mean, for me to consider myself a pawn in some experiment is one thing –"

"She wants us to believe that we're –"

Dolan cut him off and continued. "But to accuse Her of manipulating our minds and our past –"

"No!" Selmar bounced in the seat, hitting his head on the roof. "I know the truth. I know how it is. I know about the primes, I know about the old past, and I know about Her crimes against the people of Earth!"

Dolan's world collapsed back into his head with a profound sense of reality. It was like waking from a dream to find that you were never really asleep in the first place. He suddenly felt extremely fatigued as he ran his fingers through his hair. The apartment, Susan's face, the deathly expression of the officer as he fell to the ground – the images came rushing back to him. "It's all real?" he muttered, a half question. The night with Susan, the way she felt against his skin, his need to reconcile after she left. He still wanted her back, he deserved another chance.

"Of course it's real," Selmar said brusquely. "Mother was conceived there."

"Mother ... came from Earth?" He could barely get the words out, finding it impossible to imagine that She was derived from a place where people instinctively rejected the concepts Mother embraced.

"You're familiar with the place," Selmar said.

Dolan could only stare at him silently, waiting to hear more. "I was there," he stammered, "for a very long time. Mother sent me."

"What was it like?" Selmar asked in a highly curious tone.

"Dirty," he whispered, staring into his lap. "And green. Too many people, laughing quite often, dying ... murdering, cheating, and making love to each other all the time."

"I understand that once they die their bodies are honored as symbols of their lives. That's wonderful."

"Tell me how She got here," Dolan asked, turning back to the window. There was nothing but an ocean of craters on either side.

"Mr Dodd can explain it better. He's known all along."

Dolan stared out the window silently for a several minutes. "I don't suppose you know what those are?" he asked finally, breaking the silence. He pointed at the holes in the ground. The setting sun was casting a reddish tint in the sky over the lips of the chasms. They looked like bleeding wounds.

"Mother's been running out of fissor trying to provide for us," Selmar said. "She's been using the ground itself just to keep up."

A short time later – what seemed an eternity to Dolan – the floatie approached an enormous length of twisted metal fence that separated the Wick prime encampment from the rest of the Unation. It was the first camp he'd ever laid eyes on. He'd been told many *i*-years before that the structure had been built by Mother to keep the primes in, but after what Selmar had told him, he wondered who really wanted to keep whom out.

The gate was at least four stories high, creeping spots of rust clung to the exposed girders and several windows in the watch towers were broken. In the incorp sectors, nothing was in such disarray, but the neglect here was likely intentional, to ease the primes' sense of autonomy that existed with the other side, the Unation's side. They simply didn't want to be a part of it.

Dolan noticed several building-size trenches had been dug along the edges of the fence, but on the inside the land was pristine. There were even some natural sprigs of green scattered here and there. Primes were walking around in the grassy areas. Two young children were tossing a red ball back and forth. A small group of men congregated around a table covered with food. They stopped talking and stared as the floatie came to a halt right in front of them. Two of them were smoking cigarettes and Dolan's mouth began to water. One spit into the grass before turning back to his companions.

"I don't like being this close," Dolan said as the engine eased slowly into a silence.

"No one does," Selmar replied. "But that will change."

Dolan didn't want to move until Selmar did, and stayed seated even after the door opened. "What about the scouts in the towers? They don't bother the primes?"

"The scouts are theirs," Selmar said, stepping from the floatie. "To keep *us* out."

He and Selmar were met at the gate by a burly prime scout in haphazard garb. He growled at them before reaching his open hand through the thick metal bars. Selmar handed the man his ribbon. Dolan followed suit. The scout looked at Dolan suspiciously, and again at the security ribbon. He didn't know what the ribbon was going to do for him; actually, he didn't know if Dodd was leading him into some kind of trap by giving him access to a prime camp in the first place. Dodd could have been the one who fed Selmar the information about Earth. But Selmar was the least of his worries right now. The scout knew they were both incorps, and the scout – a stone wall of a man – could have easily broken them both in half if he really wanted to. Although, if this guy had some real grudge against Mother, they'd both be dead already.

"This doesn't look like the usual ribbon," the scout said.

"How do you know what a usual one looks like?" replied Dolan, unaware of how rude he sounded until he said it.

The scout only looked at him, unwavering. "Wait here." The giant turned and re-entered the bunker doorway to the left.

"Some of them haven't been made *aware*," Selmar whispered. "Don't hold that against them, please."

Dolan looked around, glancing through the thick branches of the trees to the grassy acre. He could only see the primes lounging and playing carelessly in the pale light of the fading sun. There were no men with the guns, though he had no doubt they were somewhere, fixed on the both of them, ready to kill if they needed to.

The scout stepped out of the bunker and handed the ribbon back through the bars. The man looked thoroughly frustrated, as if he were about to do something against his better judgment. Dolan wondered if that meant needing to kill them or allowing them to pass.

"Your names have been confirmed. You can go, but let me tell you something. A lot of us don't like the idea of having so many of you Mother lovers in here at the same time. You're all a bunch of greedy, brainwashed assholes to us." The scout struck the butt of his rifle against the wall of the bunker, then disappeared inside. "You'll have to walk. Your pretty little car stays here. And careful who you chose to call your friends!" The man laughed and small group of others joined in. Dolan looked back at the floatie, then to Selmar. Dolan matted his hair down over the back of his neck, protecting his identity as he always had, but Selmar wasn't as well-equipped. His KI stood out like a boil. They stood silently, listening to the scouts snickering occasionally, and waited for the gate to open.

The further they moved into the camp, the more Dolan wondered how the primes had survived for so long on their own. Few buildings remained, and those that were standing desperately needed to be repaired. Broken windows, dimpled roofs that caught the weather, people wearing clothes that were torn and stained unnatural colors of dirt and grime. Their faces were pallid, and those they passed were all very young. There was only one tree in the entire village and that too was dying, hanging limp and struggling for the last touch of light as the sun dipped below the horizon.

At least on Earth, people had access to the resources they needed to stay alive, but Mother wasn't even giving the primes the simplest of necessities. She was hoarding it all for those who supported Her way of living. Though maybe *support* wasn't the right word. Maintain – that was more like it. Incorps maintained Her, She maintained them. And the primes were finally ready to break the vicious circle. If Selmar really held the key, Dolan decided the man was worth his weight in creds. If it meant changing the anguish he saw in the primes' faces, Dolan was prepared to defy Mother, even at the risk of becoming one of these miserable people. The world outside the gate wasn't his own. These people were more like those of Earth than any incorp he'd ever known.

"They all seem so indifferent to us," Selmar said.

Dolan nodded in agreement, thinking how *i*-years of conditioning by Mother had made him loathe the primes. These people were supposed to be lazy, rebellious, and lacking any kind of intelligible, independent thought. Yet they'd survived – and prospered, to a degree. Mother made sure that fear and disgust kept the truth from being known. The primes had nothing of Hers, and in time, would prove that they were far better off because of it.

They continued deeper into the camp, closer to a populated area. The people began to pour out of the buildings onto the edges of the dirt streets. Word was certainly spreading that a couple more incorps had made way into the camp, and Dolan wondered if Selmar's story would ease any of their increasingly hostile glances. If Selmar was aware of what was truly going on, shouldn't most of these people also know? Along each side of the street was a string of dilapidated buildings, people lining up in front as if everything they owned could be found hidden underneath the leaky roofs.

A trio, two men and a woman, evil expressions cramping Dolan's stride, moved from the steps of a fire-gutted building. Dolan kept them in the corner of his eye, but Selmar wasn't as discreet. Dolan gave him a nudge but it was too late – Selmar had turned three times now.

"*Wait* just one teeny minute there," one of the men yelled. He rubbed his hand slowly over his bald head. "What's that I see? Some kind of bumpy thing sticking out your neck? You got some kind of disease or something? Don't lie now." The group stopped in front of Dolan and Selmar. The bald man turned to the others. The woman had a road map of scars over her face and the second man was a behemoth, nearly twice the size of any of them. "You two see it?" the bald man asked his companions.

"Yep," the behemoth said, working his fists.

"Yep," the woman said. She was running her fingers through the grooves on her cheek.

The bald man put his hand down his pants and adjusted his crotch. "Nobody makes a delivery here without coming through us first. I don't care what you got for us."

"We're meeting someone," Selmar explained. "We didn't bring supplies with us this time."

Dolan took a step to his right, closer to Selmar, just in case the three decided to take one of them instead of whatever supplies they were expecting.

"None of you slave freaks supposed to come here unless you're bringing us stuff," the woman said.

"I want new sneakers," the behemoth muttered.

The three moved closer and Dolan and Selmar matched their steps in the opposite direction. Selmar looked at each one of them, then turned to Dolan. He could tell by the look in Selmar's eyes that he'd been stricken with dumb fear. No doubt a physical confrontation would be as dangerous as ... well, as dangerous as trying to walk away. And the trio wasn't going to let that happen.

"We were promised a whole bunch of new things over a month ago," said the bald man. "We're still waiting, my well-dressed friends." The trio started sizing up his and Selmar's clothes, even though there wasn't a chance they'd fit into any of them.

"You have to understand," Dolan began, trying now to wedge himself between Selmar and the bald man with little success. "Whatever you're waiting for isn't far behind."

Selmar raised his eyes to Dolan as if to indicate that saying too much would only sink them even deeper. Maybe in his awareness Selmar knew better than to underestimate the people who'd spent a lifetime thinking for themselves. After all, they were the only ones who could have freely devised a plan to rid the world of Mother Necessity, at least without Her knowing.

"My friend here has something," Selmar said, telling Dolan to hush with a quick look, "for a man in the camp. One like us who's also here to help."

"I do?" Dolan whispered.

"Give it to us," the bald man said, grinning. *"We'll* make sure your friend gets it. Won't we?"

"Yep," the woman said.

"Yep," the behemoth mimicked.

Dolan glared at Selmar, then watched the trio cautiously. To think he trusted Selmar this far and now he was turning on him.

"It doesn't work that way," Selmar said. "You should know better."

The three moved in even closer. There was nowhere else to go besides back, and Dolan tried to persuade Selmar to shut his mouth with a firm elbow. The bald man was close enough now that Dolan could see faint liver spots on the man's skin. He even smelled sick – a sour, rusty odor.

"Can I have his sneakers?" the behemoth mumbled.

The bald man reached for Dolan's arm and managed to grab his wrist. His grip was crushing. Dolan moved back, expecting to step on Selmar, but he wasn't there. Dolan resisted, but there was no chance of breaking the bald man's grip. The woman leapt on Dolan, knocking him to the ground. As he fought to pull the woman off with his only free hand, he could see Selmar running down through the center of the camp, the behemoth quietly watching him escape.

"This is all wrong!" Dolan bellowed as the woman jumped on his chest and tore at his clothing. The bald man knelt beside Dolan's head and forcibly turned it, shoving his nose into the dirt.

"This will be payment enough for being late with the shipment," the bald man said, and dug his fingers into the back of Dolan's neck. He felt the man's fingernails pierce his skin, but it didn't hurt until the pain cap popped off – an instant reminder that he'd forgotten it was there. Dolan felt someone pulling at his feet and managed to see the behemoth lifting his legs in the air and untying his shoes. The woman started scratching his chest, trying to remove his shirt. The bald man had let go of his head and was examining the cap as if considering it for his prize instead. He'd lost focus in the struggle, so Dolan found the strength to kick the behemoth in the mouth and toss the woman to the side. After first tripping over his shoelaces, then breaking the grip of the woman furiously grabbing at his ankles while spitting out dirt, Dolan made it to his feet and scurried in the same direction as Selmar. Behind him he could hear the soft, quick patters of the woman and the laborious tromping of the behemoth as they chased after him. The bald man called out to let him go, and the incessant panting of his pursuers faded as he dashed further down the road to an area that was less dense with structures and more cluttered with mounds of trash and filth. He clasped the back of his neck, relieved to feel that his KI was still intact, though the skin around it was bleeding.

He fell to his knees in the dirt, panting, then coughing out the dust that went down his throat. So close to killing, or being killed. For a second time – it almost happened again. How little he had really remembered about the shooting until that moment, or how little he had wanted to remember. But the horror came back, as warm as the young cop's slippery blood on his hands. He hadn't meant to kill the boy, really he hadn't. He only wanted the girl, Mother wanted the girl. Mother ...

He had killed for Her.

And now on Earth – a place that truly existed – he was a murderer. Even if he wanted to go back, the crime he'd committed would follow him like the dreams he'd carried back and forth. He would never sleep knowing what he'd done to the boy, what he had been doing to all of them.

He heard footsteps again, someone running toward him. The corner he had turned led him to a dead end. He was surrounded by mounds of junk – or a trove of fissor for Mother, depending on how one looked at it. Selmar was nowhere to be seen, though Dolan was sure he had run this way. "They could have killed me," Dolan said. He glanced through the garbage searching for his counterpart. "I was protecting you."

"What's in my head is of no consequence if I can't be with my wife." Selmar's voice came from every direction.

"We all need to face our demons," Dolan said.

"Mine is inside me, hiding, and only Dodd knows what to do with it." Dolan heard sobbing. "Every time I try to think about it I feel like I'm losing my mind."

"If your wife is here, she'll want to help you." Dolan paused. "I want to help you."

"I don't know if anyone should. You don't understand what we'll be leaving behind."

Dolan ducked behind a pile of old tires, hearing the three primes approaching. He waited until they passed. "You won't have to leave anyone behind. Not your wife, not anybody."

Selmar stepped out from behind a stack of empty cardboard boxes marked HAZARDOUS MATERIAL. He brushed the dirt from his pants. "It's Mother I'm worried about. She'll do whatever it takes to make sure we don't abandon Her."

"You sound like me," Dolan said, "before I had reason to resist."

Eleven

Selmar knew where to go in the Wick camp to find Sheila; he was *aware* of that, too. He followed the dry river along its sandy edge and counted the buildings that passed on his left. He swung open the doors of the fifth one and entered, Dolan following close behind. The inside had been well maintained – hallways and rooms with sturdy doors, intact walls and freshly-painted ceilings. Had Selmar not known better, he'd have thought he was back in the sector, on his quiet sojourn to work, preparing to spend one more day performing for his life, instead of simply living it.

The main corridor narrowed, split into two, and Selmar heard Sheila's voice softly filling the air around his head. It was much sweeter than he ever remembered, like the way he felt the first time she spoke to him. Mother had been generous by coupling him with Sheila, but Her kindness mattered little now. He'd managed to rejoin her all on his own.

He followed her voice, stopping occasionally to make sure he wasn't putting distance between him and her words. His entire journey had not seemed so urgent as it did right at that moment. His *awareness* was riding a distant second to his desire just to hold Sheila for a very, very long time. The rest of the world would have to wait until he and his wife had shared themselves with each other. Only then could the world move on. Only then would he be sure.

Her voice reached its zenith in front of some double doors marked by a slip of paper bearing his and Dolan's initials, eloquent handwriting entreating them to come in. Selmar just wanted to stand and listen for a bit longer. Her tone was massaging the stiffness from his neck, but before her soothing inflections could finish working his tired muscles Dolan cut in and opened the right side door.

There she was, across the long room, wearing her hair tied up just as he liked it. He hoped he'd never forget the smiling curves of her face as she turned and held him in her gaze. Nothing else in the room mattered; if there had been anything standing between them he was certain he'd pass right through it. When he touched her hands, only then did he know for sure that the loving woman he had hoped to find was standing right there, waiting. He readied himself to say I'm sorry, but she told him how unnecessary it was with a simple flick of her eyelashes. She didn't need to apologize either, for anything, and he lowered his eyes as she moved in and wrapped her arms over his shoulders. He could feel right through her skin that she'd been made *aware* of everything, too, and she was as ready to help the world to move on, to let them to live and think in quiet solitude.

She led him by the hand into the next room. It had been a long time since he'd seen such emotion in her eyes, and for once he didn't need to ask what she was thinking or how she was feeling. He didn't need to engage her in a battle of words. Expressions and glances were saying everything at that moment. Soft, young eyes – twenty i-years gone, were now suddenly back again. They told a story, everything was clear. She wanted to spend the rest of her life with him, and with him alone. And she wanted a baby inside her. There would be no more interference from Mother. A new life for the two of them was to begin that day.

His hand in hers, they moved to the far side of the room where a skeleton of metal bars and wires had been constructed around a singular leather reclining seat. With a flick of a switch she turned the contraption on. In any other circumstance, the machine would have brought a sour taste to his throat since it looked so Mother-made, cold and unyielding. But under Sheila's manipulation the metal beamed warmly and seemed to sigh under her touch, the same way he did when she turned and began to undo his pants. The buttons of her blouse seemed to vanish between his fingers.

The chair inside stretched itself flat, creating a make-shift bed. He lifted her gently, maneuvering her through the metal crossfingers into the heart of the device, then joined her. A cord for their KI's awaited each and they joined with each other in a way that only Mother could have before. He felt as if he hadn't touched her skin in *i*-years, but his fingers still found her beautiful imperfections quite instinctively. As their bodies met, he could sense the machine reassuring them both that it was okay, that it would act in Mother's stead. They no longer needed Her permission.

Twelve

The woman was unmistakably Sheila. Dolan watched as she led Selmar gently by the hand to the opposite door. Selmar had described her quite accurately. She was absolutely beautiful – wide, knowing eyes, sharply cut chin. The body language she developed as Selmar walked in, the way they looked at each other – as if for the first time – made Dolan fear that Mother had at some point eliminated love altogether, only to have it rekindled by these two. From out of nowhere, an adolescent desire had returned to envelop them.

Selmar and Sheila disappeared through the door, and he watched with a bit of jealousy. He recalled wanting to feel that same way the first time he met Susan, even the morning after they made love. But the feelings wouldn't come. Mother was holding him back against his will. She'd robbed him of the love he had for Maggie, and of the chance to feel love for another person again. That opportunity had come and gone, but unlike the feelings for his wife that he'd been forced to bury, She was not going to trick him into sacrificing the person he'd become. Twelve *i*years was too long to just throw away. One way or another he was going to let Susan know he loved her.

"Patrick," came a voice from behind. Dolan turned and stared into the face of the man that everyone longed to emulate, though the experience wasn't as exciting as he expected it to be. There was nothing electrifying about him. He seemed no more a man than Dolan, but also no more an incorp. By appearances, he still belonged to Mother. Dodd was dressed as a nineteen should. It was more in his eyes – a knowledge that had been induced, but it was there just the same. And he'd seen that same awareness before in Selmar. They both knew how Mother got here from Earth, and what Dolan had really been doing there. All Dolan wanted was to go back.

"You look ill," Dodd continued. "Is there anything I can get for you, Patrick?"

"I'm fine, but I prefer 'Dolan'," he murmured. "If you don't mind, sir."

"Very well."

"My nephew's name was also Patrick," he explained. "Patrick Jacob Dolan. Mother REMOVED him because of a mistake I ... " He shrugged, forgetting for a moment exactly what fatal mistake it was that lead Mother to take his nephew in the first place.

Dodd lowered his head. "Still, I'm so glad you could make it," he said, gently grabbing Dolan's shoulder.

"Mother sent me to bring you back," he said. The last words fell flat, realizing he was still talking to a Senior.

"Just as She was supposed to," Dodd said. "I told Her that if I should turn up missing – and conveniently enough, I did – She should send you to find me, to take you from Earth. She knows how disassociated you are from the world. You were the logical choice."

"Why me?"

"I wanted you here because you're an important part of my plan to separate us all from Her. And your being on Earth has only tightened Her grip on our abysmal situation here."

"Then you're a part of this movement, or rebellion? Whatever it is."

"I'm leading it, and we must REMOVE Her."

Dolan found it almost impossible to believe the animosity in Dodd's voice, but it was there nonetheless. "Why didn't you bring me back sooner? With all I was doing over there ..." The officer's face appeared again, bloodless, frozen in Dolan's head.

"I couldn't interfere, Dolan. In Her eyes, I'm no different than you. I'm one man, and one man cannot change this entire world."

Dodd offered him a seat at a table in the corner. Dolan eased himself into a rickety chair and rubbed his palms along the surface of the table. It felt different, like the table in his apartment. Mother hadn't created any of these things – *they* had, with their own hands. The genuine wood was imperfect, and that made all the difference in the world.

"First," Dodd continued, "let me tell you as much as I dare about the truth, a state of consciousness we call the *awareness*."

"Selmar told me earlier he knows the truth about Mother – Her birth, the primes, our hidden past, hidden thoughts."

"Being *aware* isn't simply a matter of me telling you. It comes from a chemical, the silver. Selmar's been injected, all of us who know the truth have had an injection. Those of us who wanted to stand up against Mother needed a way to release the memories She'd suppressed within us. The primes came to our aid."

"Give it to me, inject me." With the truth he could find the strength to turn his back on Mother for good, and return to Susan. But without knowing, he'd always be attached to Her by his thoughts, and his body.

"I can't give you the silver, Dolan. There's more I need you to do and part of it involves confronting Theman again. If I make you *aware*, he'll notice the change in you."

"Can't you at least tell me why Mother sent me to Earth in the first place? Why did She use me?"

"That reason is something you can't know yet. All in good time."

"We'll never break free from Her," Dolan said in a frustrated tone. This whole plan of Dodd's was only more secrets, more lies.

"Indeed. That is what Mother wants you to think. Your reaction is virtually instinctive, but what I retrieve from the mind of Mr Rayburne will change you forever."

"He came to me through Mother, out of a podium."

"Those that are *aware* can travel through Her unnoticed, but Selmar's no different from you or me. He has lived his entire life striving to please Mother, but what's hidden away in his mind can cut our link with Her. A few days ago, She detected the thought in him and took it from his KI, but it's not truly gone. Our thoughts are always with us. She just wants us to believe that we retain only what She allows. She can't actually *take* our thoughts from our minds, so She obscures them, hides them from us. The same way She's blocked out our past, and Her own."

"Even if I was *aware* I wouldn't remember the past before Mother. She's all I've ever known." Even while on Earth – Her choking grip reached that far.

"We were living here a long time before Mother came to be, very similar to how Earth exists now. At one time she was simply a figment of one person's imagination. Back then we all created the things needed to survive. We sold them and traded with each other for profit. Competition drove our world. A small number of us were getting rich very fast. So few were surviving in the deep pool of greed that had spread. At that time, there was no Unation.

"Decades passed, every year more prosperous than the previous one, and there were no signs of our economy slowing down. We'd all lost our sense of direction, money and technology had dissolved our ability to cope with each other on a personal level. We had become power hungry, self-centered. Every person's sole objective was to do whatever it took to rise to the top. If that meant infiltrating a competitor to steal secrets, then so be it – doing so made the winners rich. If it meant selling one's soul for the good of the business, then so be it – doing that made the winners indifferent."

"And Mother sprang from their greed. Eliminating it."

"No," Dodd said, shaking his head. "You're recalling part of the lies Mother told you. She did nothing so heroic as rescue the world from its own hunger for wealth."

From the other room Dolan heard a throaty, mechanical whine – a machine coming to life, trying to imitate Mother, but the sound was not Hers. It had a randomness that reminded him of Earth.

"The rampant theft of information and ideas," Dodd continued, "spread to every corner of this starving planet. The corporations became unbelievably powerful. Those who weren't prospering had to steal to survive. And I don't just mean the poor or underprivileged, even the most honest of successful business people were forced into illicit acts. At that point, the ability to earn a decent living, to merely survive with dignity, was all but eliminated by our greed. The world needed a new direction, something to manage our lives, something that would restore our integrity, our trust, our self-worth, while still allowing every one of us to strive for all the material wealth we've ever wanted."

"That's where Mother came in," Dolan concluded, finally understanding Her interest in the people of Earth. A chance to study a history She never knew by examining a group that still had their individuality. But that didn't legitimize kidnapping them. Dolan had never questioned his own actions before. He did what Mother told him to do, regardless of right or wrong. It was a matter of serving Her as best he could – that was inbred. Or was it *implanted?* "If Mother was so interested in individuality," Dolan asked, "why not just study the primes?"

"In comparison to Earth's population, there are very few primes," Dodd pointed out. "And someone in the prime camps would have eventually noticed. Those taken would have been missed."

Dolan shifted uncomfortably in his chair. "That's crazy. I returned everyone to Earth in a matter of days with no memories of what happened."

"Those were substitutes, fakes, created out of fissor. The real people are still here. At first, She was only curious how they could survive with such self-centeredness. She retained one or two for experimental purposes, but then Her agenda changed. She found that they too had minds filled with ideas and information She could use. Our thoughts were good, but theirs were better. With their ideas She massed more knowledge and gained even more power over us. Mother's nature is exploitation and nothing more. She doesn't care about consequences – so long as Her own survival isn't threatened."

"She's been stealing thoughts from their minds to provide for us?"

"Not just them."

"*Me?*" Dolan said, nearly choking. His actions, his behavior on Earth had meant nothing to Her; all the time it was his mind She'd been after.

"Earth is so different," Dodd said. "It intrigues Her, because here She controls everything, She *is* knowledge. On Earth, the greatest knowledge is kept hidden from most of the population, but occasionally a certain combination of random elements leads to important but often dangerous discoveries. You're familiar with their most destructive method of making war?"

Dolan nodded. "The atomic bomb."

"A mistake. Certain key pieces of information were brought together because there are too many people on Earth trying to monitor and control their understanding of technology. Mother has worked hard to eliminate that random human element in us, because fear and misunderstanding lead to misuse. She was finally in control here and could safely, and solely, exploit all of Earth's possibilities. Can you imagine the outcomes, Dolan? Earth's bomb was an accident requiring years to conceive and create. But in a single moment, Mother can explore every possible combination of thought and idea that a human can only dream about in a lifetime."

"You seem very intimate with the place."

"Because I was there," Dodd said, face washed with a grim expression. "Long before you were born, I was traveling to Earth, many of us were. It was quite a tourist attraction in its time, though it certainly wasn't as advanced as it is now. None of our nanochip and fissor technology. They had only crude vacuum tubes running elaborate, clunky machines. Centuries behind us ... until." Dodd lowered his head, a hint of shame showing through red blotches on his face.

"It was you," Dolan said. "You brought Her here."

"In an indirect way, yes." Dodd continued to stare down. "I was one of the few people who didn't like where our world was heading at the time of the corporations. So I went to Earth to work undisturbed, no chances for a competitor to steal my ideas. I assumed the identity of John Bardeen and worked on my plans that would become the brain of Mother Necessity. But in my many travels, I also unknowingly gave an Earth colleague of mine, Walter Brattain, a schematic, one that led to a great change in their world. He deciphered a section of it and combined that with a crude theory of his own. With his new idea he managed to create their first transistor, and from there ... " Dodd paused and looked up.

"What'd you do?" Dolan asked, haunted by the consequences coming to mind.

"I began a technological revolution on Earth that should never have happened. And what sprung from that disaster, the world those people have created, is the same technology Mother's been feeding on for the past forty *i*-years."

If Dolan had known any better he would have thought Dodd was about to weep. Though he prayed Dodd would remain strong, despite his mistakes, for the sake of explaining Dolan's role in Mother's great lie, for the sake of the memory in Selmar's head, for the sake of everyone that stood to lose if Mother won.

But first things first, and Selmar was at the top of a very long list. "What's in Selmar's head?" Dolan asked.

The old man breathed carefully, releasing a slow breath. He began chewing on his thumb nail as if he'd been spending the entire time working up to the truth, the *real* truth, and was only now ready to let it out. Suddenly Dolan wasn't sure that he wanted to know. What was in Selmar's head was his own business, even if it had everything to do with Dolan. Nevertheless, he still looked to Dodd and waited for an answer.

"The design for a REMOVAL device," Dodd said abruptly. "One we can use on Mother."

He didn't want to respond, rather just to sit back and take in Dodd's story. Minutes passed. Dodd remained sullen, staring into his lap. Dolan eventually looked down, too. He had a handful of questions, and rolling those over in his head brought to mind even more. But he'd had enough for now. The silence appeared to be easing Dodd as well as himself, creating a peacefulness that two people of such different social statuses could never have shared before. Their status levels hadn't been just a label, but a key that unlocked respect and intimidation as soon as the number was spoken. But there was no need to mention levels anymore.

He waited, as Dodd was waiting, for their plans to move forward. When the signal from Dodd's chron finally came, he looked up and passed a complacent smile. The end was coming and Dolan had never felt more out of his element, more alone, than right at that moment. All he wanted to do was go home, back to Earth, back to Susan, and forget that Mother ever existed. Nevertheless, he was ready, and he smiled back. To his surprise, it came quite easily.

Thirteen

The wiry, haphazard machine looked like it was digesting Selmar as he wiggled around inside, trying to get comfortable. Dolan knew Mother had had no part in creating it. The metal bars were thinner at points, bent awkwardly at others. Dodd helped Sheila make a number adjustments to the machine that encased Selmar, who looked like he was about to be REMOVED rather than redeemed. After a few more careful measurements, the vidcon screen lit the green light and Dodd, nodding with satisfaction, leaned through the criss-crossing metal bars. "Selmar," he said into his ear. Selmar didn't stir, but a soft wave of light moved across the screen as his voice echoed off the walls.

"I can hear you," Selmar said. "Is Sheila still with me?"

Dolan could sense Selmar's voice moving all around the room, resonating as Mother's would have.

"I'm here," Sheila said, turning from her work.

"Selmar, I want you to concentrate on the sound of my voice," Dodd said. "If you ever sense it fading away, I want you to tell me, but through the vidcon. Ignore every impulse you have to communicate with your voice – don't use your mouth. Can you do that?"

There was an eerie silence for a few moments, almost as if Selmar had taken the room into his mind and was observing it from a point high above. The scrutiny was unnerving. Only Mother had ever made Dolan feel like that before.

"I will speak through my KI," Selmar's voice reassured.

"I want you to concentrate on something particular," Dodd said, still leaning through the fingers of the machine. "An item, something concrete."

"All I can think about is Jay. There's blood on the carpet." Selmar's anxiety made Dolan shiver.

"Push that away." Dodd turned to Sheila and signaled for her to change a setting on one of the smaller control panels. The screen that had gone red switched back to green. "Don't think about him, or anything you two ever discussed. You must not force yourself to remember, let us take care of that for you. Simply concentrate on an item, anything." Dodd waited a few moments, chewing his bottom lip in the meantime. "Have you something?"

"Rose," Selmar's body said in a hollow voice. His lips were quivering.

"Think the words," Dodd said. "As you've been doing."

"A bouquet of roses," Selmar's voice filled the room again. "For Sheila."

Sheila reached out and squeezed his ankle, never taking her eyes from the vidcon. The waves of light floated up and down on the screen, Selmar's voice fluctuating in steady peaks and troughs.

"Excellent," Dodd said encouragingly. "Keep the image clear, as strong as my voice is to you right now. We're going to start slowly, moving into your mind one step at a time. Stay comfortable, even after you sense you're not alone."

"I don't want anyone inside me," Selmar pleaded. "Not like Mother used to be, not anymore."

"It will be Sheila," Dodd reassured. "She'll be the one coming in to release the memory."

"It won't be safe for her!" Selmar's body twitched. "Not safe for the baby!" Sheila leapt from her seat to a distant panel and adjusted Selmar's cerebral control until the screen went from red to green again. Selmar's body eased.

"Rest, concentrate." Dodd's tone was firm, but soothing. "Remember the roses." The waves on the screen resembling Selmar's breathing smoothed over, became less frequent; he was calm again. "Let's begin," Dodd said, then wiggled from the fingers of the machine. He nodded to Sheila who attached a cord to her own KI and worked a panel to her left. "Remember the roses," Dodd said. "Nothing but roses."

Sheila turned to Dodd. "I'm ready," she said confidently. She moved around in the chair until she looked comfortable, then braced her arms and closed her eyes. For a moment Dolan thought he saw a faint shadow of Selmar and Sheila rise up out of their bodies and converge in mid-air. A third reflection formed in the middle – a small, embryonic glow that hovered, then melded with the parent light and vanished.

Conception without Mother. *Was that Dodd's ultimate plan?* Dolan wondered. They would not be leaving Mother behind, but rather their children. But Dodd would have to prove they could succeed, because Dolan refused to lose another child. He couldn't live with that again.

Sheila's body jerked suddenly, then her muscles relaxed. There were now two wavering lines on the display. She had left her body behind. She was inside her husband.

"The flowers," Selmar said. "They're so beautiful."

An hour passed in utter silence. If either of them had moved a single muscle, Dolan couldn't tell. They looked like statues. Their breathing was imperceptible, even Dodd who was very much awake. He remained seated to the far right of the machine, staring at the waves on the display. Finally, Sheila signaled through the vidcon that she'd found the hidden memory. Dodd activated the vidcon projector and the transparent image of a short, hyper man appeared in the middle of the room. He was panting incessantly.

"Well, Jay, how are you?" Selmar's voice came from the vidcon.
"Hey, buddy, why're you out of breath?" Vickers' image looked toward the vidcon which was projecting the scene as Selmar had seen it.
"Don't talk so loud," Jay said, his voice squeaking. "Your office

isn't safe."

"Safe from what?"

"Those who shouldn't be listening right now. Selmar, I'm worried." Jay's image began to pace. "I think I'm in big trouble."

"A conspiracy?" Selmar chuckled.

"Don't make fun. You should know better when there's something really wrong. Whatever you do, you can't talk to anyone about this."

"About what?"

"I have something to give you, just in case I don't ... make it."

"You sound like this whenever you've spent too much time in a simulator. Did Ramie catch you again?"

Vickers whipped his hands back and forth. "No, no, nothing like that. Please, Selmar, this is serious. I may have given myself away earlier."

"To whom?"

The image twisted his head around scanning the virtual nothingness. "Mother," he whispered.

"What the hell are you talking about?"

"It's kind of a long story. Will you meet me after closing time?"

"Jay, Sheila is expecting me at home. Some important dinner thing tonight."

"Then meet me outside at midday," he said. He dug into his pocket and retrieved an access ribbon. "In the meantime hold onto this for me. Whatever you do don't lose it."

"I can't take your ribbon."

Jay shook his head. "Don't let anyone find it."

Out of the lighted mist in front of the vidcon a hand moved into the imaging area – Selmar's hand. He took the ribbon.

"It's almost time." Jay checked his watch. "I'll meet you right outside after the first tone." Jay's image moved out of the scanning area with short, rapid strides.

The vidcon crackled, cascades of white flowed across the lighted portion of the room. Blurry images of people moved like silver streams. Time was passing quickly.

The projection slowed once again and Jay appeared. He spoke to the vidcon. *"It's about time. They've been watching me. I just know it."*

"Who's been watching?" Selmar said. *"Jay, what's going on?"*

"Come over here." Jay turned and walked – or what resembled walking. His legs moving back and forth furiously, but the image stayed put.

"Jay, is everything okay? You're worrying me. Does Ramie know what you're up to?"

"Yes, she's in it with me. A lot of others are too. Look my friend, I've been there for you countless times in the past, and I need you now more than ever. I need you to help me."

"In? What are you in?"

He looked around, then bent closer. *"A movement that's going to separate us from Mother –"*

"You've got to be kidding me?"

"The truth about the Unation is not what you think. Can't you see it in my eyes?"

"I'm sure I have a good idea what the truth is. This conspiracy thing has gone a little overboard, don't you think?"

"This goes beyond conspiracy," Jay insisted. *"We don't need to depend on Her anymore, though. I found a way –"* He fell silent as a faint, mysterious image passed by. He waited until it was gone. *"I found a way to separate us from Her forever."*

"That's not breaking news. It's called REMOVAL. *You remember spending two status levels in the bays?"*

"Of course I remember, but you're not listening to me. During my time in the REMOVAL *bays I made a fascinating discovery. Mother hadn't even considered it –"*

Selmar's voice cut him off. *"There nothing new about how we make our Grand Contribution,"* he said, annoyed. *"What's your point?"*

"Selmar, you're missing my point. We can leave Her anytime we want."

"Jay, I can't believe I'm hearing this from you. After everything you've done, all those talks we had about striving to better ourselves. Now you start with this. Are you crazy?"

"*The primes' movement never vanished. It's still alive, and it's growing. You can't even begin to imagine how many people have the taste for change. Too many families have been divided. There's a whole truth to witness, one no one knows about, and so many have joined in because they're aware of it now.*"

"*Yeah, but leaving Mother? How have you been able to keep your insane ideas from Her?*"

"*I can't believe you're being so unreceptive. What about your father?*"

"*It's because of my father that I think your plan is absurd. The first revolt couldn't overpower Mother, so what makes you think you can? Jay, I can't let you do this. Mother is more vast, more perceptive now than she was forty i-years ago. She'll crush you, and Ramie. Think about your plans. You have too much to lose. You have children!*"

"*It's too late for me now. I know too much, and I lost control of my thoughts today. She got into my head. The idea of leaving Her makes my heart race.*"

There was a pause, and a long sigh from the vidcon. "*Tell me what you know,*" Selmar said.

"*We've survived this long by thought-blocking. Those who know how can control the core by masking thoughts we don't want Mother to see.*" He paused to look over his shoulder. His eyes were aimed straight at Dolan and that made Dolan shrink back, as if Jay knew he was there ... as if Jay were addressing him directly. Then he continued: "*I know it sounds strange, and impossible, and it's a little more complicated than that, but you need to believe me. It works, every time ... unless we happen to lose our concentration. Like I did. And that's why I need to talk to you.*"

Neither said anything for a moment. "*So what happened?*" Selmar asked finally.

"*This technique of thought-blocking, it's not a new idea, but it's very hard to become good at it. Mistakes can prove fatal. Sometimes extreme anxiety can make it impossible.*"

"*So the core read your thoughts, and now Mother knows what you know. Jay, why the hell are you dragging me into this? Do you*

*know what's going to happen when I connect? She's going to think
I'm in on this."*

*"Selmar, I'm scared. I remember every last detail of our plans.
She didn't erase any of the thoughts from my KI. She's up to something."*

*"Jay, It'd be a waste of Her time. She's going to remove you before
the sun goes down."*

*"You're the only one I can turn to. After all the i-years of offer-
ing, I'm finally taking you up on your help."*

"And how am I supposed to cover for you?"

"I don't need protection. I need reassurance."

"Reassurance of what?"

"That you won't lose that ribbon."

"Aren't you forgetting one thing, Jay?"

His image pondered for a moment. "I don't think so."

*"As soon as I connect this afternoon, Mother's going to know
everything you just told me."*

*"You need to learn to thought-block. I've already set up the meet-
ing."*

*"Jay, I can't believe you're roping me in like this," Selmar said
angrily. "I didn't ask to be part of your revolution."*

"I need you to go see this person before you connect."

"Why did you assume I was going to —"

*Selmar's voice was cut off by a muffled bellow. The image of an
ominous figure in a scout uniform slid up behind Jay and wrapped
a translucent hand across his mouth. The images blurred as they
whirled around the room, then the vidcon went dark.*

When Selmar managed to open his eyes Dolan was amazed to see
the change in them. Selmar had been released, wiped clean of
Mother's influence. He couldn't recall what color Selmar's eyes
were before, but they weren't as bright a blue as they were right
then. Selmar fought to turn his head to him. "I never did thank
you for bringing me here safely."

"I was happening by anyway," Dolan said through a half-grin.

Selmar attempted one of his own, but could only twitch his eyelids. The pain must have been awful. "That projection we saw," Dolan said. "The end, I mean."

"Neither of us saw it coming." He was trying hard not to work his jaw, and his words were falling flat.

"It's unbelievable She didn't REMOVE you," Dolan whispered, not wanting Sheila to hear their conversation.

"She would have soon enough, if She'd known where Jay's ribbon was." Selmar opened his hand and held up the ribbon. "I hid it from Her, before She blocked my memory."

"Then how did you remember where it was?"

"Very uncomfortable where I put it, pretty hard to ignore." Selmar winced as he shifted. "She let us both go. REMOVED Jay and his wife right in their home. Sent them, and their daughter, for the Grand Contribution long before their time. But She didn't care. She just wanted the ribbon." He paused to take a deep breath. "Sheila and I would've been next."

"Rest," Dolan said, reaching through the machine's metal fingers for the first time. "I'm sorry about your friends."

"Their REMOVALS weren't in vain," Selmar said, moving his mouth more freely now. "Now that we know the design plans are on the ribbon –" He turned his head away from Dolan. "– We can go on."

"You've done everything," Dolan reassured.

"Almost. I'm *aware* now of one more thing I have to do."

A soft hand come down on Dolan's shoulder and before he could turn Sheila moved in beside him. They both looked down at Selmar, who had closed his eyes. The ribbon lay half dangling between his thumb and forefinger. Sheila gently took it from him.

"Thank you, Mr Dolan," she said, holding wide with her kind, knowing eyes. They were as blue as Selmar's. "Thank you for bringing me my husband."

"My pleasure, Mrs Rayburne."

She walked away, open palm resting low on her stomach. A transparent barrier had enveloped both Sheila and Selmar, and nothing would ever penetrate it. Dolan imagined he could see the broken strings dragging along behind her as she walked away, frayed threads tied around her hands and feet and waist, a marionette that Mother would no longer manipulate.

Dodd passed Dolan a private grin as Selmar finished strapping him belly down to the examination table. Sheila started the anesthesia drip while Dodd instructed Selmar what to do with the REMOVAL device once it was complete. Selmar nodded nervously and secured the strap over Dodd's clean shaven head. His KI stuck straight out of his neck like a tumor waiting to be taken out so the rest of him could go on living. Dodd's last words to Selmar were mumbles as the drug took him over.

Sheila opened a case on the table in the corner, removed a glass jar and handed it to Dolan. The pink fluid wiggled inside as Dolan spun the jar, examining it. He held it up to the light.

"Genuine fissor," Sheila said.

Mother. In his hands. Aloft. A part of Her that he could control completely. Or destroy on a whim. "How did you get it?" he asked.

"Monty thinks it better you don't know. But soon enough."

Selmar wheeled over a makeshift podium, a tall awkward thing, riddled with jagged scrap metal edges. Yet another machine built by hand, without Mother's knowledge. Dolan constructed in his mind a world filled with machines like it, and so many others. Not to be used against Mother, but instead of Her. Everyone would live by their own means. In their own little private version of Earth.

Dolan reluctantly handed the fissor back to Sheila and watched as she poured the pink fluid into a spout on top of the podium. The machine sighed as the last of the fissor flowed in. Sheila turned to Selmar and passed him a look that said, *after all this I hope it works,* and then inserted the ribbon. It coughed and churned, spat the ribbon onto the floor by Selmar's feet and went silent.

Neither said a word, a tense silence, but Dolan knew there was too much at stake to discount that they may need to try a second time. Dolan had seen imperfection. On Earth it meant being unique. Here, the only definition was failure. Mother got everything right all the time, but the cost of losing Her meant embracing failure. Dolan wasn't sure if the Rayburnes were ready to accept that. In time, all in good time.

Dolan scooped the ribbon off the floor and reinserted it. The podium didn't spit it out, but did start to ooze fissor from a dozen different places. Selmar and Sheila quickly kneeled by the machine trying to scoop up the fluid. It came out too quickly, faster than their hands could collect it and force it back into the funnel. The sight was pathetic at best. Both of them, the most innocent of bystanders drawn into this coup, whose only resource for fighting the enemy is the enemy itself. *Does that mean Mother can never die?* Dolan wondered. The future history of the Unation would never tell this story, the real one, regardless of whether they succeeded, since history is always written by the winner. Mother would always find a way to go on weaving Her lies even after She was gone.

As Selmar and Sheila tried to save the last trickles of fissor along the side of the podium, the small pile that had collected in the bay began to reshape itself. It became elongated and reflective. Small spider-like legs grew from its sides, ten in all, and curled inward as the fissor hardened. The podium went dead, and Selmar and Sheila remained on their knees staring at the device, their hands dripping fissor onto the floor.

The beginning of the end, the real beginning. That was what Dolan saw in Selmar's expression. As if everything to that point had only been a test of character in preparation for the moment when they all would realize that Mother was not infallible. Like children suddenly realizing the faults of parents, the expressive signature of their humanity. In that light, Mother was human too. She was no better off than Dolan, than Selmar or Sheila. Not anyone.

Selmar wiped his hands on the seat of his pants and removed the tool with the curiosity and respect of handling a scorpion. He showed it to Sheila then held it up to Dolan. He didn't dare touch it, just nodded and turned to Dodd. "Are you up to this, Selmar?"

"I have to be. If I choose not to, then it'll be the first and last decision I ever make for myself." He turned to Sheila, wrapped his hand around the back of her neck, pulled her in and kissed her. "I don't want my life lived for me anymore," he said to her.

Dolan and Selmar stood on either side of Dodd, Sheila at his head. The scorpion tool was already in place, resting on its thin legs over Dodd's KI.

"How's it work?" Dolan asked.

"It's very similar in design to a KI. Apparently it slides inside the tendrils of the KI, attaches itself and then retracts, coming out as one piece. It's only good one time."

"Did your friend ever test this thing?"

"He never got around to making one," Selmar said. "This is the first."

"He and Ramie would be so proud to see it," Sheila said. "They deserve to be here."

"Probably better they're not," Dolan said. "This just might be the most horrible thing we've ever done." Besides the young cop, but Dolan reminded himself that killing him was unintentional. "If Dodd dies, our lives will always be the same. She'll make sure of that."

"He's not going to die," Selmar said.

Dolan ran his hand over the back of his neck. "Then turn the damn thing on and let's get it over with."

The scorpion tool hummed softly as Selmar gripped the handle. The tendrils curled further in, gathered around the port of Dodd's KI and seemed to leap off his skin just before burying itself inside him. Dolan winced, expecting to hear tearing flesh as the device seated itself into Dodd's neck, but there was only the muffled, artificial ticking of warming metal. Sheila dabbed at the small trickles of blood with a wad of gauze, though there was surprisingly little. Selmar held on, a white-knuckled finger wrapped around the trigger.

The humming and crackling stopped and seemed to reverse, the unnatural sound of retreat. The thing was on its way out, with the KI attached. Blood ran thicker, darker. Sheila swabbed faster. Selmar gripped tighter. Dolan could only picture the hole in the neck of the cop. The young man was lying there in front of him, strapped to the table, Selmar pressing down on the gaping bullet wound, Sheila dabbing at it with gauze. There was nothing he could do. It was too late to help him. Too late for Dolan. The damage was done. Freedom from Mother was the slightest of consolations.

The tool and the KI as one piece of twisted metal slid out of Dodd's neck with a wet, smacking sound. Sheila leaned over and applied pressure to the wound with a cloth until the bleeding slowed. Selmar placed an ear to Dodd's back, listened, then smiled and nodded to Sheila. With a suture gun, Sheila stapled the wound shut. Three evenly placed clicks, and the procedure was done. Dodd was alive, and free. Dolan felt that Mother's dues had finally been paid – a small part of Her was now dead too.

"Everything all right, sir?" Dolan asked. He had agreed to stay with Dodd while Selmar and Sheila got some sleep. Dolan tried to look under Dodd's bandage without actually touching it. Dodd turned, startled, his face riddled with fatigue. He didn't even come close to resembling the vibrant man who had scurried around the room less than three hours before. Whatever energy he had mustered earlier was gone.

"Dolan, you need to report back to Theman now," Dodd said, his voice tired, quivering. "Tell him I'm dead. Do you understand that? I'm dead. It's imperative you tell him that."

The old man's knees buckled and Dolan grabbed him by the arm. He urged Dodd to cross the room and sit at the table. The man's steps were uneven and Dolan had to use all his strength to keep him upright. Dodd sunk into the chair with a hard sigh and a thud. After catching his breath, he reached across the table and slid to Dolan a cloth bundle. Inside were a KI and a spider tool.

"Today," Dodd said softly, "dreams become reality for all of us." He pressed his fingers against the patch on his neck, then looked at his fingertips. "Now listen to me. You need to give the KI to Theman as proof ..." He paused for a satisfying breath. "... That I have died. Mother is well aware how brutal primes can be, so she'll accept your story that I was attacked and killed. Do not turn over this KI, whatever you do. It's a replica. Selmar tried to separate the asunder from it, but destroyed both in the process."

Dolan looked down at the asunder, then at the KI. Side by side, neither looked menacing, as if one had cancelled out the other. "What then?"

"Waste no time getting to section 421 in the processing building's left wing. The eightieth floor. That's where you'll receive the three of us – as you did Selmar at the plixport."

"Sir, if you return after –"

"The only way we'll succeed is to mass-produce the asunder. But there's no way we can create and distribute them by hand before Mother manipulates the entire Unation again."

"So how will we do it?"

"We won't have to. She will," Dodd said with renewed strength, "without even realizing the consequences until it's too late." Dodd held out a small vial filled with silver liquid, a clear plastic cap securing a small needle on one end. "Use this only *after* you've told Theman what you need to." Dodd slumped back in the chair, fighting for breath. He sat up again after a moment, Dolan reached out to help him up, but Dodd motioned to be left alone. Dolan could tell by the lingering expression on Dodd's face that he was waiting, unsure what was to come from this. But he seemed prepared, almost eager. Even after having survived a REMOVAL, Dodd was a resilient man. Dolan had half a mind to embrace him. But instead, he just put a hand on his shoulder. "I'll be fine," Dodd said. "Go now, Dolan. Your place lies in a different part from ours. Follow the path I've set for you. Your success will ensure ours, and our success will ensure your freedom."

Fourteen

Dolan knew Theman wasn't going to believe a word of his story. The *awareness* wasn't an issue – the silver was still in his shirt pocket. He was more worried about the fear and loathing that was sure to show up in every move and glance. Spending time in the prime camp had provided him a false sense of serenity, just as Earth had. But being back in the Eastern Central sector, back in Mother's world, had flung him into a reality that he wished never existed in the first place. The thought of conforming again, mingling and following the crowd of people, forcing himself to look as drawn as they did – even for a short time – turned his stomach into knots. As he made his way to the processing building, zero hour approaching, he felt he was the only one not wearing Mother's designer blindfold, an obscurer of the truth, one that let in just enough sanity to keep them all from walking into walls.

He looked in his shirt pocket at the vial of silver for a fifth time, deathly curious. He reached in and touched the glass. No, there was no way he could use the thing now. He had to wait until he told Theman his story. His mission was too important. Dodd and the Rayburnes were counting on him to be there in section 421 when they arrived. And their success ensured his freedom. He couldn't get Dodd's words out of his head.

But his mind kept returning to the silver.

Before entering Theman's office he removed the asunder from the gauze and returned the spider-like tool to his back pocket. He held onto Dodd's KI. The blood on it had dried to a rotten, flaky brown. He pictured the one just like it buried in his own neck. The thing in his hand looked too bulky, too awkward to fit inside him. As he rewrapped it in the gauze he tried to swallow, but coughed instead, choking on his own saliva, wondering who really controlled the workings in his own throat – he or it.

Theman's office was empty except for a single chair in the center of the room. Though it wasn't the typical stern, metal frame he'd have expected to see. The chair was plush; it looked very comfortable. Could this have been Dodd's doing? Was he still that powerful even after REMOVAL, the falsest of deaths? As he sank into the foam cushions he felt the tension – what would have been a sure sign of his concocted story – flush out of him. His problem was solved: Theman was sure to believe every word.

The overhead light winked out and the vidcon buzzed to life. Dolan glanced up to see the faint image of Theman appear in front of him. As usual, he was seated in his invisible chair. Even the shadow that Theman's image cast was ominous. Dolan slid his feet a little to the left, out of Theman's shadow, and breathed away his anxiety. Theman leaned forward, and for the first time ever Dolan saw his face. He looked more human than Dolan had expected, but his features were poisoned, his lips in an unnatural curl. There was a cold, detached haze coating his eyes. If Dolan had known any better he would have called it hatred. And it looked all too familiar. It was the same hatred he saw in his own bathroom mirror, while Jeremy Baines was still inside his head.

"Report." The word sounded like a malign roar.

Dolan imagined the rib cage of the metal insect in his neck squeezing his windpipe. Words would not come. He cleared his throat, swallowed hard, and then his voice sprang up unexpectedly. "Sir, all I can report is bad news. Shortly after Mr Dodd arrived at the Wick camp he fell captive to ... a group of rebel primes, many who don't take kindly to incorp visitors. I'm lucky *I* made it out alive." That last bit was true enough. He paused for a response which didn't come, so he continued with Dodd's story. *Remember,* he said to himself, *no embellishment.* "Mr Dodd's whereabouts when he ... during the time that he disappeared and I arrived is still unclear ... um ... but it appears that this group used him, alive of course, to spread their ... propaganda about Mother to the ... the other prime camps."

Theman showed his frustration with the jumbled story. His brow was creased and he'd started to make throaty grunting nois-es. "What do you mean they *used him?*" His skepticism was thick.

"Well, apparently they forced him to spread lies, but ... most of the camps still remain indifferent to Mother's policies ... so there's no cause for alarm."

"That is not what I asked you. Don't become a liar like the rest of them. I want to know how they forced him to spread their prop-aganda. *How* did they do it?"

Dolan hadn't anticipated needing to explain that any further, and neither had Dodd. He repositioned himself in the chair, feel-ing the pincers of the asunder digging into the small of his back. Opening his mouth to speak he realized his voice had vanished again. Theman's image crackled; the anger, the hatred had robbed its color. He was gray, like death. It was only a matter of time before the fear returned to Dolan's eyes. Then it would be too late. He had to let it out, he had to tell Theman something. "My report has the details," he said with slight hesitation. "This group of primes connected Mr Dodd ... to a crude communica-tions system." He paused to feign a cough. "That's how they trans-mitted the false information."

Theman's image winked out and reappeared in the same instant. "Mother concurs. We both find it very disturbing that primes have KI-compatible technology."

"Well ... I wouldn't go so far as to say that. Mother's in no dan-ger."

"Is that your *professional* recommendation, Mr Dolan? All of a sudden you're an expert on the primes?"

"I wouldn't feel comfortable giving my opinion on that, no."

"You'll tell Mother everything you saw there. Nothing more. No conjecture. It's the only way we can eliminate them."

"Eliminate who?" he asked, using all his breath in two words.

"One thing at a time, Dolan." Theman paused to lean forward

in his invisible chair until Dolan could have reached out and touched his colorless image. "Dodd's dead?" Theman asked.

"Yes." He hoped his eyes were as deadpan as his voice. Lying to Theman was easier than he'd expected. He wanted to keep going, to continue creating a whole new reality for himself.

"Don't guess. You saw his body?"

He unwrapped the KI from the gauze and held it out. The vidcon on the wall next to him, the one transmitting Theman's image, scanned the object in Dolan's hand. "He gave me this," Dolan said, quickly biting down on the tip of his tongue.

"Dodd handed it to you *alive?*"

"I meant *he*, the prime that killed Dodd. The one that took this out. He gave it to me as a sort of threat for us to stay away." *Excellent recovery. Keep going, you're doing fine.* "You see, when I first arrived I was a little skeptical because the border scouts wouldn't admit that Dodd was inside. That got me worried at first because I thought they were planning to hold him for ransom. But after I got in, I found out that both he and the woman ... what was her name again?" He tapped his chin, pondering what he already knew. "Sheila Rayburne. Both Mr Dodd and Mrs Rayburne had actually been killed several days before. Yes, the woman's dead, too. Though, strange I wasn't given her KI."

Theman leaned back, disappearing into his own shadow, his face falling dark again. Dolan felt panicked that he could no longer see his eyes, the anger.

"You were never told about Dodd's companion."

Shit. Keep talking. Don't stop now whatever you do. "S ... someone down there must have mentioned it." His mind raced for more, but no matter how hard he tried, the story had ended. There was nothing left to tell. Dodd's version and what he'd just concocted were now balled up into one convoluted thought. The confusing mess he'd made didn't even sit well in his KI – it was squeezing his throat. The asunder dug its pincers deeper into his back. He thought he saw something move in Theman's shadow.

"I want what's in your head," Theman said. "Right now, you lying little shit."

This was a Theman he had never seen before. The man's bitterness, his anger, made Dolan sink deeper into the chair, the asunder digging further into his back. He tried to move his legs, but they refused, paralyzed by the chair. It pulled him down deeper until he couldn't breathe. If Theman got into his head, if Mother saw what he knew, Dodd would fail. The *awareness* would be destroyed, Mother would rewrite their history again. How many times had She done it already? How often had someone come so close to discovering Her truth only to have their lives rewritten? How many different lives had he already lived?

"Don't make me have to cut your neck open myself," Theman said. "Stop fighting. It's only going to make the truth harder to accept."

He *would* fight. Whatever it took to keep Mother from knowing. He managed to slide his arm off the arm rest. The chair pulled him in tighter. He fought it, trying to reach behind him for the asunder burying itself into him.

"I'm taking what's in your head, Dolan," Theman repeated. He leaned forward, his eyes were two bloody bullet holes. "Then I'm going to kill you along with the rest of those little prime bastards."

Cool air rushed his neck as the head rest disappeared. He fought to look behind him. Out of the corner of his eye he saw a small mechanical arm moving toward his neck. His own arm was frozen behind his back, pincers of the asunder cutting his palm. Tiny rivers of blood ran down the tips of his fingers.

"Eyes forward," Theman whispered, and Dolan's head was forced around until he faced Theman again. "Mother has wanted nothing more than to survive. And now She'll kill for it." Dolan tried to fight the invisible hands of pressure against each side of his face, but there was nothing he could do, nowhere to turn. The mechanical arm attached itself to his KI and began sifting through the particles of truth hidden inside him. He closed his eyes and moved inside himself, trying to confuse Her with the insane labyrinth of his two separate lives. He had resolved that the solution was a paradox of some kind. Finding him was an impossibility.

But Mother wasn't fooled so easily.

After Mother was finished probing Dolan's mind and learning of Dodd's plan, Theman spared his life for the moment and ordered him to section 421 to meet the old man. She hadn't blocked out any of his memories of his journey to the Wick camp, claiming it was a gesture of kindness and sympathy. But he knew better; if She'd wiped his mind he'd be useless to Her, because he needed to be there to meet Dodd and the Rayburnes. She also wanted Dolan to remember exactly why he was turning on his friends. It was for the good of the Unation, for Her safety – and whatever other reasons She had forced him to believe. All he could focus on was Her new-found hatred for anyone that stood against Her.

He fidgeted with his access ribbon, waiting at the public podium in section 421 accompanied by eight armed, eager scouts. Their plans for a new world were about to end very shortly, and Dolan was dreading seeing the surprised, disappointed looks on his friends' faces. He inserted his ribbon and the podium began to hum, then it scanned him. Dolan stared at the machine, wanting to tell it to send them back. At least by staying at the prime camp they could live a happy life. He glanced into his shirt pocket, suddenly realizing he still had the silver. Mother had stripped him of the asunder, but with the silver, he could still know what might have been. What could have been if he hadn't ...

Pink globs of fissor began collecting around his feet. He stepped out of the way as the podium finished spewing the last of the initial delivery. The nodules merged and began to form a familiar shape. Dodd had come first, naked. Sheila was next, her body taking shape to the left of Dodd. Selmar appeared out of the last of the fissor. Dodd had already opened his eyes and was sitting up as Selmar's body hair separated and curled. Dolan moved in, more so to avoid being trampled by the advancing scouts. Dodd stood, shaking off the dizziness that was causing him to overlook the scouts, their unmistakable rifles raised to his eyes. "Clothes," he mumbled, looking around by Dolan's feet. "Where's the bag you were supposed to bring?"

Dolan didn't move, not even daring to step forward and help the Rayburnes who were just coming to their senses. "No bag, sir," he said in a pale voice. "I'm sorry."

Dodd blinked and turned to the line of scouts blocking the corridor. Dolan noticed the patch on the back of the man's neck was gone. The scar he expected to see wasn't there. The fissor had obviously healed him.

"This guy's a prime," one of the scouts said, taking two more aggressive steps forward, turning his rifle on Dodd. "Let's do away with this one right now."

"Yeah," another said. "Fuck waiting around. Get rid of him now."

"He's no prime," whispered the one nearest to Dolan. "Don't you know who he is?" Their conversation continued in low muffles.

"Patrick, how could you?" Dodd pleaded, taking no notice of his nudity. He held out his hands to Dolan and stepped forward. Sheila and Selmar had managed to sit up. Dodd moved around them. "After all I showed you."

"*Freeze! Don't move!*" the scouts shouted, still moving in.

"Don't," Dolan stepping between Dodd and the guns, his arms raised. "Don't you recognize this man?" The scouts didn't flinch.

"Tell me why," Dodd said, continuing to move, pulling at Dolan's shoulder.

One scout fired a single shot that rang through the corridor. Dodd fell onto Selmar's outstretched legs. Sheila screamed through her fingers. With a swift push, Selmar rolled Dodd off him, turning him onto his back. The beat of his heart pushed tiny pulses of blood from the hole in his chest. Selmar held his hand over the wound, but the blood continued to flow from between his fingers. Without a KI, a pain cap couldn't even take away Dodd's agony. It killed Dolan that he couldn't do a thing but watch the man suffer. The one man who had worked his whole life to make, and then break, an entire world.

"Answer me," Dodd managed to say. He coughed, choking on his own blood. "Why did you ... let Her in?"

"I was overconfident, sir. Selfish." Dolan said. "I forgot my place in this world."

Dodd opened his mouth and inhaled deeply. Blood rattled deep inside his throat. With a hard tug, he pulled Dolan close and whispered in his ear. "I should have ... made you aware of that ... I'm sorry." Then he let out the last of his breath.

Fifteen

The scouts took Selmar and Sheila away, ignoring Dolan's demands to wait for Mother to send them some clothes. He fumbled with his ribbon in front of the podium, fighting off the grip of one of the scouts. Even a blanket, if he could only get them a blanket. The scout leaned into his ear. "It's too late for them." The young man looked very sincere, but Dolan still itched to make his nose bleed.

Then they led Dolan away in the opposite direction, two of them toting Dodd's body by the arms and legs. When they reached the REMOVAL bays, one of the scouts pressed his rifle into Dolan's chin and threatened to shoot him if he didn't help Dodd complete his Grand Contribution. The demand might have been an act of pity for the old man, but Dolan didn't think so. The scout was just doing his duty, or Mother's duty. So he and two scouts fed Dodd's limp body into a REMOVAL chamber and closed the door. The look in the scouts' eyes told him he was next, but instead they escorted him to a holding cell a few doors down.

Dolan waited inside. He leaned against the wall as long as he could, then sat on the floor, refusing to climb up on the REMOVAL bed, no matter how comfortable it looked. At first he expected the doctors to come rushing in right behind him, strap him to the bed and get it over with, but hours went by with no word of his fate. Was Mother actually planning another assignment for him? He'd be damned if he was going to perform another day for Her. If She just wanted to drop him off on Earth and forget all about it, that suited him fine. Then he wouldn't need to know the whole truth. He would care less about being *aware* of anything.

He removed the silver from his shirt pocket. *Contains one dose of substitute knowledge,* he envisioned a label on the side of the tube. But not this vial, there were no markings at all. If Mother's decision was to REMOVE him, he wanted to make himself *aware* before She liquefied him and used his body for recreational toys, or engine parts, or a ham sandwich.

After undoing the protective cap he studied the injector needle, touching its tip with his finger, being careful not to stick himself. Not yet, anyway. He wanted to wait for word from Mother. Maybe then he'd be able to work up the nerve to actually shove the needle into his neck as Dodd had showed him. Even though the old man said there was no pain, the thought still made his stomach jump. He replaced the cap. All in good time.

The cell door swung open as he dropped the vial of silver into his pocket. A doctor entered, white smock sharply pressed, eyes concentrating on the floor as he scratched his bald crown. His remaining ring of hair was pure white.

"Patrick Dolan status level thirteen?" the doctor inquired, still digging his scalp mindlessly. He spoke so fast the sound of his voice was one long word. "My name is Dr Ronald Hagan SL17. Mother has sent me to help with your Grand Contribution." He made the process sound so formal and inviting. Far cry.

"She does have a way of ruining people's days." Dolan leaned against the wall and folded his arms, feeling the vial through his shirt. He was itching to use it, but not yet.

"Oh boy, you should be glad She made such a quick decision," Hagan said, arranging the bed that was going to carry Dolan down into the bay itself. "Many people have to languish for days, not knowing how it'll end. I can't even imagine. I mean, what would one think about? What would one do with all that time?"

"Think about what went wrong." He took the vial and tucked it neatly in his hand. "Obedience is a tricky business. If you're aware of the consequences."

"The consequences of defiance?" Hagan asked, stopping what

he was doing.

"No. Of knowing better." Dolan stood as Hagan motioned to the bed. "Being aware of an alternative."

"Oh, please don't start with that now." He waved his hands around like he was shooing a fly. "It's far too late to be paving your way to clemency."

"I don't mean for me, Doc," Dolan said, and stuck Hagan in the neck with the silver. The vial emptied quickly and Hagan yanked it out, dropping it, shards of glass scattering across the floor. Hagan remained stiff, tense from the surprise of the stick, even as Dolan cautiously circled him. Dolan watched Hagan's discerning eyes surface from underneath the hard, preoccupied glaze. As the silver continued to course through him, Hagan's muscles relaxed, his posture becoming more natural. Right before Dolan's eyes, he watched the man leave his world of deceit and enter the one of knowledge, of the *real* truth that Dolan had wanted so badly for himself.

"It all makes perfect sense," Hagan said, grabbing Dolan's arms as if trying to convince him of his revelation.

"What does?" Dolan pleaded. "Tell me what you know now. Tell me what you see." He wanted nothing more than to be inside Hagan's head.

"We shouldn't wait another minute." Hagan turned back to his station, sliding the bed back into the chute and closing the door. He turned back to Dolan, grabbing his arms again. "There's too much at stake. We must continue with the plan. Mr Dodd wanted it that way. Don't you realize?"

"I don't understand what you mean."

"The Rayburnes need to make their Grand Contribution," Hagan said. "It's meant to happen that way. It's the only way we'll find the truth." He hurried to the far wall where the bed had disappeared into the chute and opened the observation window. For the first time Dolan looked down into the vast warehouse where all life in the Unation ended. The REMOVAL bays were nothing but a macabre assembly line – rows and columns of beds shifting up and down, side to side, like tiny, insignificant pieces to a greater but unsolvable puzzle. Other doctors in white coats moved around the floor, tending to the people in the beds like fabrications. Mother's consumable goods. As the puzzle changed, the beds created various shapes, some that seemed paradoxical to their quick, linear movements. The room shifted again and another series of beds moved into position under tall funnels suspended from the ceiling. The people under the funnels, having had their KI extracted, lay helplessly as Mother turned their bodies into fissor and absorbed them. To Her, it was nothing more than an essential process to keep Her alive.

Dolan turned to see Hagan removing his clothes. Standing naked in front of the window, Hagan sighed in relief and pointed to a room on the opposite side of the bay. "They're in there, the Rayburnes, waiting for someone to complete what Montgomery Dodd started." He turned to Dolan, eyes wide. "I want it to be me." Before Dolan could pull him away, Hagan stuck his hand inside the podium and he instantly collapsed into a wiggling pile of fissor. The podium slowly took him in, as if it were drinking him through a straw.

Dolan turned back to the glass, leaned against it with his palms open, wanting desperately to be let out, to be spared the insane sight he was witnessing on the floor below him – an assembly line of people being absorbed and assimilated. So many by obligation, even more by force – but never any by pure choice, except right then. The Rayburnes were willingly giving themselves to Her, for reasons that he'd only know with the silver.

There was nothing to do but wait.

And in no time, Dolan saw two beds emerge from a chute across the bay and proceed along the line to the first station. He could see their faces quite clearly, Selmar and Sheila. They were different from all the others. The two looked relieved.

Sixteen

The naked man, eyes giving away his *awareness*, came to them wanting so desperately to be the one to give them to Mother. Selmar was grateful to the man as he checked on Sheila, making sure she was comfortable. He ran his finger through her hair, pushing it out of her eyes. The nervousness in them had returned. Selmar could see the familiar wrinkles set in on her temple and forehead. She gave Selmar a reassuring smile, then a single nod to the man. He slid the bed into the wall and latched the door. He came to Selmar and did the same, and as the door snapped shut Selmar knew that all he had left to do was wait for Mother.

Rewards, promotions, status – none of that had purpose anymore. Personal sacrifice now meant something completely different to him. The lessons his father had tried to teach him finally made sense. Giving yourself over entirely to what you believe, relinquishing yourself to the truth, is a person's greatest feat. Regardless of what the rest of the world observes as truth. He would gladly give his body to Mother, but not quietly. He had one last thought to give Her, and it would be his greatest contribution to the Unation and the greatest absolution of his father's memory.

His bed lowered into a narrow chute. Above him, the floor panel slid into place, sealing him inside. He could see Sheila through the glass to his right. Her eyes were closed, her hands resting on her lower abdomen. He prayed he would go first, to be there in the fissor when she and the baby were taken in. But Sheila's bed began to move into the pit first, and for a moment he had lost sight of her. She'd have to wait for him alone, but she was a determined woman, and she had already resolved to spend eternity with him. Mother wouldn't stand a chance against that kind of dedication.

But how strong could Mother really be? How powerful could one actually become by obscuring one's ideas, one's own consciousness, inside the minds of others? To REMOVE Her from this world all he had to do was destroy the minds in which She lived, and the bodies that kept Her alive. Her end seemed so close, so conceivable.

His bed began to crawl forward, taking its place in line. He heard the movement of instruments under his head. The sound of a small hatch opening and the grinding and sharpening of metal. A hot needle pricked him just below his KI. There was the sound of a drill getting louder and louder. He remained calm the entire time.

Seventeen

In spite of his desire to look away, Dolan remained glued to the window watching the REMOVAL of his friends. The beds moved along, the room changing shape as the conveyor chugged forward. Sheila was first, the doctors escorting her bed around the bay until she reached the final stage. The monstrous funnel looming overhead transformed her into fissor and took her in.

Dolan had committed himself to opposing Mother, but he was now caged, like all those people below him, without anyone left who could help him. Even Dr Hagan didn't seem to be coming back. However, unlike Sheila and Selmar, Dolan wasn't giving in without putting up a fight. He didn't belong inside Her, even if he was already buried too deep to pry himself loose. He was the last splinter trapped under Mother's skin.

He rapped his fists against the glass, screaming to be let out, and his throat shook itself into a broken silence as he watched Selmar move under the funnel. He looked as if he was welcoming it, reaching out with his arms despite the doctors trying to repress him. They all looked confused. Had they wanted him to scream instead? No need, Dolan was doing that for him. Even after it was over, when Selmar's body was unrecognizable, Dolan continued shouting until he felt something in his throat tear. The quivering pink pile rose into the funnel. At that moment, with his throat broken open and his fists swollen, he wished for one of two things: to be on Earth or in Mother. Either would have suited him. His last hope, the primes' last hope, was being taken up inside Her.

When the funnel stopped sucking, Dolan thought he heard a groaning sigh from the podium, Mother gloating over the defeat of those who'd threatened Her. First, Dodd with his knowledge of the past. Then Selmar and his ability to alter the future. The capacity for change only comes from those who had the will *and* the means. Mother was well aware that She had only needed to take away one, the other would crumble all on its own.

Dolan rested his back against the window and slid to the floor. He'd had enough, he wanted to be down there in the bay, in line with the others. "Send a doctor, Mother," he said in a torn voice.

The podium groaned again – a sharp, metallic cough, as if it were rejecting something foul or tainted. With his head in his hands, he turned to look at it, its door still hanging open from Dr Hagan's trip to the bay. His disdain for Her machine was so strong he thought he might be able to tear it right out of the wall if he tried. Where was his doctor? Did She only listen when there were words worth hearing? He didn't want to be insignificant any longer. He didn't want to be alone.

With little hesitation, he reached his hand for the opening of the podium, letting the muscles in the rest of his body fall limp as he prepared to be changed to fissor. He touched the inside, fingers hanging loosely, but nothing happened. The room continued to be the room. Traveling through the podium was still a mystery because the silver wasn't in him. Dodd had said only those who were *aware* could travel through Mother. So he had no choice. He'd have to wait until She came for him.

The podium had a third round of coughing fits. Dolan felt a sharp sting and pulled his hand out. Then the podium activated and small trickles of fissor started to leak into the bay. At first, he thought Dr Hagan was returning to finish what he'd begun. But there wasn't enough fissor to make a man. It was something different. As the fissor began to solidify, Dolan recognized the object's spider-like shape. It looked like a projection at first. He passed his hand in front of the podium, but the asunder didn't vanish. It was the real thing. Then from a small clump of the pink stuff a vial took form next to the asunder. The podium groaned one last time and Dolan swore he heard Selmar's voice, telling him to take the items, that they were his gifts to the people of the Unation.

Dolan removed the asunder and vial of silver. As soon as he did, more fissor leaked out and replacements appeared. He scurried across the floor to the foot of the bed, crouched down and examined the asunder, then the vial. Real enough, and sent for him. He glanced around the room, then out the window overlooking the bay. No one was watching him. No vidcons, no peering eyes. The place was safe. He uncovered the needle and held it to the side of his neck. He could feel the pressure of its end pressing against his skin and it made him itch all the way to his shoulder. He backed it off and the vial twisted in his fingers from the building sweat. *To imagine how small Mother will become*, he thought, then he stuck himself. The needle hit something hard; he heard metal against metal.

The silver was dense and cold. He could feel its thickness in his body. When it had finally soaked through his veins and made its way into his head, he watched the light and matter around him collapse into a fragment of reality so small that it could have passed right through without touching the tiniest piece of him. What followed was an explosion, an epiphany of simplicity. He sensed Mother as an equation that explained the most basic of his desires, and most complex of Her purposes. The visions he had of life and its meaning were so clear, explanations so obvious. He watched everything around him transform into its simplest element, Her element. His world became pink.

Then he began sensing the truth he was seeking.

His friends on the bay floor were meant to die. Selmar had known from the time of his *awareness* that he had to sacrifice himself, placing his knowledge into Mother and using it to manipulate Her, destroy Her, from the inside. There was no other way to persuade Mother to create the asunder and the silver – items lethal to Herself. And there was nothing Sheila wanted more than to carry her baby into the fissor and join with her husband. Selmar considered it an honor that he could free the Unation, knowing his father would have been so proud.

The truth of Earth was in him, too, and it was more involved than Dodd had explained. He sensed that the rudimentary brain machine Dodd had created for Mother was sitting idle, unused for *i*-years, deep underneath the processing building. The people Dolan had taken from Earth were in him, and they too were close by – very close by. But he couldn't sense their individual minds. Somehow, they had become one voice over everything else in the *awareness*. Through his mind he followed the one voice, as he would have followed Mother during his contributions. Dolan moved around inside the thought tank, through Her store of contributed ideas She used to sustain the Unation. But suddenly, he realized he wasn't alone. It was them – Mother was inside *them*, every person he'd taken from Earth. She'd transferred Herself into the human collective after Her mechanical brain had become too confining and unsupportive. The one voice told Dolan they wanted to go home.

But one by one they were dying. Or being killed.

"Selmar, *NO!*" He stood and tore at his clothes. The floor of the bay had fallen into disarray. The doctors were running around aimlessly, lifting people off the floor as their beds shook and tumbled. Some of them tore off their white robes and undergarments and ran around the bay screaming about freedom. He saw one woman stab herself in the neck with a vial of the silver. Hagan was among them, spurring them on.

Dolan turned from the welcomed madness and stuck his hand inside the podium, concentrating on a particular door many floors below him. Focusing, thinking hard. This time the room did change, melting away as if it, not he, had been transformed into fissor. Almost immediately the pink walls and floor thickened and reassembled, and he was lying next to a podium in a hallway just outside the door he had imagined.

The staircase beyond the door descended further underground than he'd ever been before. There were no lights, and with each next step he wondered if his foot would land on something solid or if he'd simply fall into the cold darkness. He shivered as the cooling air encased his naked body.

After some time, dim light appeared below and the stairs finally ended. In his head he could hear the fading screams of the people, the one voice dying off as Selmar continued to destroy Mother. But as Dolan moved away from the stairs he realized the screams were no longer in his head – they were coming from all around him. He had found all those who he'd taken, and She was trapped inside them. With a few more cautious steps he moved into the room which had no dimension. Even in its furthest reaches all he could see were bodies, hanging supine, suspended above the floor by fine wire. Their mouths were stretched wide, screaming in agony as She tried to protect Herself, the battle with Selmar raging inside them.

Dolan ran along one row of bodies, looking into their faces for some sign of their own lives, their individuality. "Selmar, stop! You're killing them!" He continued down the row, vague recognition of so many faces, real memories from his past. Then he saw two bodies fall, their tethers snapping back into the darkness, their voices falling silent. The fallen bodies aged and withered in a matter of seconds. Another small piece of Mother that Selmar had managed to eliminate, but he was killing them in the process.

Then the one voice spoke to Dolan over the screams of the people. The words were choked, unintelligible, but he recognized the tone – Selmar was fighting to speak. More garbled mess, then: "Dolan, I've found someone you know."

He stopped and spoke to the nearest screaming body. "Who?"

"Don't stop moving. Mother will find a way to get to you." Dolan continued down moving among the rows, passing another staircase on the way. The bodies continued to scream and fall, die and disintegrate. His own naked body shivered from the piercing cries. "Stop and turn left," Selmar said. Dolan did so and stopped by a group of females. "One of them has something of yours inside her. It's alive. I'm aware of it."

He saw Susan hanging in front of him, mouth wide open, hair pulled tight off her sheet-white face. The shrill of her voice was inhuman. He pulled at the tethers, sliding the thin cord off her ankles and wrists, detaching her hips and shoulders. He eased her to the floor and her screaming faded. Even as pale as she appeared, as little of her true self that had shown through, he thought she had never looked more beautiful.

"Run ... ru ... " and Selmar vanished from the one voice. There was only the wailing cries of the hanging bodies. Then one by one the bodies around him detached, landing softly on their feet. Their eyes grew wide, more white than color. They continued to drop from their wires – ten, twenty, marching in on him with slow, clumsy movements. With one arm he hoisted Susan onto his shoulder, with the other he warded off Mother's army of drones. She was purposely cutting off pieces of Herself to stop him – but they were no longer human. He kept repeating that over and over in his mind. It was all he could do to justify killing them. With a firm twist of his hand he crushed the throat of a man who had managed to grab Susan's legs.

They continued to move in, groping, permeating cold sweaty death through their skin as he searched for a way out. He dodged clumsily in and out, gripping Susan as a few tried to pull her from his shoulder. He felt the air being squeezed out of him, their hands taking his will, their empty eyes proving that even Mother was dead inside them.

He reached out and grabbed the hair of a small boy trying to bite him. He lifted the boy's head up. It was Jeremy Baines. Reaching over him was the other one, Justin Marcotte. Two more small pieces of Mother, but they were different from all the others. Their eyes were stained red with hatred, the same glare Dolan had seen in Theman. Mother was not learning about human emotions, She was acquiring them. She'd learned how to hate by acquiring it from Jeremy Baines, jealousy from Justin Marcotte. Missy Brenahan must have been Mother's new-found malice. The three things She needed to eliminate the primes without remorse.

Dolan began to see a truth the silver hadn't given him. Mother's desire was never to study the people of Earth, but to become them by constructing Herself a personality. She was using them to experience all the facets of sorrow and joy, love and hate, greed and altruism. She wanted nothing more than to be human.

He pushed the boys to the floor and forced his way through to a set of stairs that ascended into the blackness. Suspended bodies continued to die off, Selmar's battle still raging. Dolan lumbered up a few steps, Susan's weight making each one a challenge. Once he was out of reach he stopped to watch his attackers tumble on top of each other as they tried to navigate the first stair. The two boys had managed to fight their way over the fallen bodies. They glared at Dolan, hissing and spitting as if their single emotion was all they knew. Their eyes had become instinctive, murderous. The crowd writhed under the boys and they fell backward into the pit of bodies.

Naked and shivering, Dolan made his way up, his grip on Susan tighter than ever. Out of the darkness he could still hear the waning screams and the sounds of the bodies hitting the floor.

The crossover room was just down the hall, but Dolan paused, knowing that walking around the corner stark naked would surely catch the scout's attention. Regardless, he carefully lifted Susan and made his way down. "Henry Douglas, a pleasure to see you," he said, trying hard to walk casually.

Douglas stood quickly and reached for his rifle laying on the patrol desk. "Sir, what are you doing?" He raised the rifle like a klutz. "This is a restricted area."

"Douglas, you can't say you don't remember me. It's only been, what, a few days?"

"Sir, I'll have to ask you to stop." The rifle was in the air now.

He kept walking, stopping at the desk. Just beyond that was the crossover room. He could hear the faint whirl of the way mechanism initializing. Tuft was in there, and he had to catch him before he went back. Otherwise, there'd be no way mechanism to follow him.

Dolan shot his hand up and grabbed the rifle. It slipped easily from Douglas's hands. The young scout tried to reach for it, but in one twisting motion Dolan turned the rifle in his free hand and clocked Douglas in the ear with the butt. The man fell hard into the wall and slumped into the chair head first.

Dolan opened the door. He turned the rifle around, putting Tuft's forehead in its sights. Tuft's eyes grew wide. A KI cord dangled like a limp tongue from the base of his neck. Beside the table was Susan's doppelganger, the one who was to take her place on Earth. He set his Susan down against the wall.

"Dolan, you pervert. What the hell are you doing?" Tuft asked. He sounded genuinely frightened.

"Take that cord off," Dolan said flatly.

Tuft lifted a trembling hand and slid the cord off his KI. "Do you know the trouble I went through to get that bitch over here?" Tuft asked. "She's a little fighter." He grinned, becoming snide. "A hearty lover, too, I imagine. Eh ... daddy?"

Dolan felt sweat break out on his palms, his eyes burned inside his head. He flinched the rifle. Tuft didn't move, but glanced down at Susan's double. As Dolan looked at the body, he saw a flash of movement in the corner of his eye. Tuft reached out and grabbed hold of the barrel. The rifle slipped out of Dolan's sweaty grip. They struggled with the weapon, Dolan trying to slip his finger through the trigger guard, Tuft continuing to twist, making it impossible for Dolan to fire it.

He could feel Tuft's hot breath in his face above the grunting. Tuft's strength easily matched his own. Getting the weapon back was impossible, so Dolan turned his body, drove his shoulder into Tuft's folded arms, the rifle still between them, and pushed. They fell back toward the wall, crashing into the podium. Dolan pushed down on the rifle, driving the butt hard into Tuft's lower stomach, throwing him off balance and sending him stumbling to the side. The rifle went with him, sliding out of Dolan's sweaty grip. Tuft regained his balance and turned the rifle on Dolan. He smiled and took two controlled steps toward him. Dolan stared straight up the sights.

"Well pervert, looks like this situation has taken a little turn," Tuft said, almost in a laugh.

He pulled the trigger.

Click.

Complete silence. Dolan peeled his eyes open.

Click. Click.

Without another thought Dolan rushed him. The *tick-tick* of the rifle hitting the floor was muffled slightly by the thud of Dolan's body on Tuft's. Tuft rolled away toward the wall. Dolan scurried to his knees and scurried after him. He caught his foot on the leg of the chair and dragged it with him. His legs were tangled under the chair as Tuft turned, pulling Dolan closer to him and connecting with his jaw.

A bright flash of light erupted inside Dolan's head. He flashed his hands in front of his face, protecting himself, until the white pips of light subsided. There was Tuft, still sitting in front of him, arm now raised above his head, and in his hand was a glittering blade. He hammered it down into Dolan's shoulder. A fire spread through his upper body, scorching every nerve ending. He lay his head softly on the floor. Every breath seemed like a mouthful of burning air.

The outline of the room faded, then softly returned. He forced himself to hold on to consciousness, refusing to let Tuft re-enter his world. And he would not have Susan either. For her sake, he'd kill the man if he needed to.

Tuft didn't move, merely sat in front of Dolan, leaning against the wall trying to catch his breath. Dolan sought desperately for any muscle that would move. His back and left arm were frozen, his right arm trapped under Tuft's leg.

My legs ... are free.

He forced them to move, heard metal scraping metal. Were they broken? Or was that the rifle ... ?

The screeching was the chair still entangled between his legs. Moving was difficult. He wiggled his feet, feeling his legs tremble. The knife bit his arm, reminding him of his wound. He found it difficult to overcome the pain. Flesh tore as he twisted his body, knife still inside. He forced his head slightly off the ground, turning his eyes upward. Tuft remained slumped against the wall, laboring for breath, eyes closed. He had no idea what he was about to meet with.

Dolan moved the chair closer, bit down hard on his tongue to mask the pain in his shoulder. He reached out with his right hand, stretching his fingers. He both felt and heard the ligaments in his right shoulder snap as he turned his arm over. He grabbed the leg of the chair, worked his sweaty fingers around it, planted a grip upon the smooth, round metal. Then with all his strength he pushed up with his arm. Beyond the chair, he could see Susan slumped against the door, and her doppelganger lying on the floor. They both looked utterly helpless; they both looked dead.

The chair moved upward. As it rose, he took care to balance it, praying it wouldn't fall onto his back or land on the knife. He moved it up, higher, over his head. With a last burst of strength he pushed it over. The top edge of the metal back came crashing down onto Tuft's face, catching him between the cheekbone and his nose. A rain of blood sprayed Dolan's face. The chair fall to the floor.

Tuft tried to open his eyes, but couldn't. He reached for his nose, the blood flowing in a steady stream through his fingers and into Dolan's hair. Dolan shoved one leg underneath him and pushed himself up, cradling his left arm. The hilt of the knife was out of reach. His body wouldn't let him twist far enough to let him remove it, so he left it there.

As Tuft tried unsuccessfully to stand, Dolan glanced to his right. On the wall next to the podium was a core node. He drew out the KI cord and attached it. Then he slid his fingers through Tuft's thick brown hair. Tuft grabbed his wrist; the blood on Tuft's hand was already cold. The knife tore into him, cutting away more muscle. He dragged Tuft to the node, grabbed the cord and jammed it onto Tuft's KI.

Tuft stumbled to his feet, disoriented by whatever battle was still raging inside Mother, now inside him, too. "You can't stop me from following you," Tuft said in a thousand different inflections. "She'll find a way."

"I'll be waiting," Dolan said, backing away.

Tuft raised his arms and screamed as he rushed at Dolan full force. The KI cord snapped like a whip. Dolan heard a wet, tearing sound. Tuft stopped short and fell flat on his back, one last spray of blood shooting from his nose in a fine red mist. The KI cord landed on the floor near the wall, Tuft's KI still attached. It fluttered around like a disemboweled fish.

The knife dug deeper as Dolan stood. Holding his arm steady against his chest and keeping his head forward helped to alleviate the pain. He removed the asunder and vial of silver from the podium bay and slid the chair to the table. He considered sticking Tuft with the vial, but decided that he didn't deserve to know, even if he was as good as dead. He waited by the podium for the replacements. Nothing more appeared; the podium went silent.

After fitting Susan – the real Susan – with crossover goggles, he attached the KI cord to himself, activated the way mechanism and sat down. He labored for a satisfying breath and waited. As the green globes rose and the crossover room melted away, he wondered how Susan would feel about going away for a really long time. Maybe Fiji. He was sure she'd love it.

Eighteen

Dolan slid his arms from the sleeves of his sweaty, dust covered t-shirt, leaving it around his neck. He propped himself against the push broom and watched as the tar spreader pressed a layer of steaming asphalt onto the road. Behind him, a rusted-out backhoe in desperate need of a tune-up loaded bucket after bucket of earth into a waiting dump truck. As soon as it was full he would hop in and drive it away. Until then, he decided to take a break and watch the traffic roll on by. Beyond the line of cars, a group of skidders barreled over the make-shift dunes of sand and rubble, lugging the day's cut of trees off the land that was to be the new route 101B, a more direct run north straight into Garrison, a quicker way home for him and Susan.

Dolan laughed to himself, watching his co-workers as they continued to swap stories of their newer, richer lives that were so close each of them could taste it. He had spent every day for the past eight months listening to those same dreams repeated again and again. They all longed for what they couldn't afford. Dolan realized that only their elaborate dreams could drive them forward, make them get up in the morning. But another day would pass and the men were no better off. They were all still right there, doing the same job they'd been doing for years, wishing they had more. Dolan had been keeping to himself mostly, happy to have a place to call his home, and a woman to call his wife. There was nothing else in the world worth wanting.

"Dolan!" he heard over the roar of the machinery. He looked

across the street. Freddy Talbot, the site foreman, was pointing over his shoulder. Behind Talbot he could see Susan's red Mercury pulled off to the side of the road. Dolan wiped the sweat and dirt from his face with the shirt around his neck. Cars rolled slowly by, tires humming and thumping on the cracked asphalt. A tractor trailer rumbled past, the driver winking at Dolan as he adjusted the truck's sun visor and downshifted the transmission. The engine gave a throaty belch and crawled away. When the traffic came to a standstill Dolan edged out to cross the road. A small blue Chevy was stopped in front of him. He glanced at the man behind the wheel, then turned to look again – a real hard look. The man turned and smiled at Dolan.

"Selmar?" Dolan asked. The uncanny resemblance brought back a mountain of memories, ones he'd given up the day he left the Unation. He had accepted Mother's demise as part of his truth, but Selmar's death had seemed inevitable as well. And if Selmar was here, then–

"Excuse me?" the man said over the roar of the machinery.

Dolan leaned in the passenger side window. The eyes – there was nothing in his eyes that Dolan recognized. "Sorry, I mistook you for someone else." He scooted around the car, moving to the shoulder. He watched as the Chevy drove away. Susan grabbed him by the arm as he began to walk past her.

"Where do you think you're going, mister?"

"Sorry," he said, still looking down the road. "Got distracted." He placed his hand on her stomach. "How's our little one?"

"Baby's fine, and so is mom." She smiled. "Are *you* okay? You look a bit peaked. Have you been drinking enough water like I told you?"

"Drink," he muttered, looking back at the blue car. "Right."

Susan turned his head to her and rubbed her hand against his beard. "Out in this heat, I can't imagine why you're persistent about keeping this thing."

He looked away from her eyes. "A necessary evil."

"You don't look like you."

He said nothing. He didn't want her to ever know, never wanted their child to discover how far Mother had pushed him, what he had done just to survive. To be with her. He ran a finger through the grooved scar on his arm. He still thought he could feel a trace of pain.

"I was unpacking some boxes," she brought her other hand from behind her. "Came across these." The contorted, fused metal of the asunder and his KI. "You still want to put them where no one'll ever find them? Thought this would be the perfect place. We'll drive over them every day with no one the wiser."

He didn't want to touch it. In nine months he had almost forgotten how just glancing at it took his breath away, as if the KI could still squeeze the life out of his body. But Susan was so comfortable handling it. That made him uneasy.

"There's not a hole deep enough," he said. "I'd feel better holding onto it. I don't like the idea, but there's nothing I can do."

"It has to go, Patrick." She handed them to him. "You might start sleeping a little better."

"It's beyond that."

"You've kept it long enough."

"It'll never be long enough. I figured I'd eventually consider it junk. Easy to throw away."

"If you can't then let me." She pointed to the waiting dump truck, now full of dirt. It churned choking diesel smoke into the air.

He held her wrist and brought her to him, embracing her. He spoke into her ear. "For twelve years, I saw so many awful things, did so many. I don't ever want to forget that it wasn't my fault. And for that, I can never let Her go."

"There's nothing to be afraid of. None of that matters anymore."

"The day I learned that one man had the power to alter this entire world–" He turned and looked off toward the new high rises in the distance. "– I realized that everything matters. Every little thing."

She sighed heavily. "I love you, Patrick," she said. "For facing that fear."

"So little is from courage," he said, kissing her on the forehead, then placing his hands on her belly. He felt the baby move.

They both turned their backs on the road. Garrison was not far beyond the line of trees. Home.

Behind them, the spreader groaned as it laid more asphalt. Susan looked up at him, shielding her eyes from the sun. "What a terrible stink. How can you stand it?"

"You get used to it," Dolan said, glancing toward the sky and breathed deeply. "After a while."

Tim Kenyon

Tim Kenyon is a writer, editor, and publisher, making his living in the United States on the seacoast of New Hampshire. He is currently at work on his second novel as well as a teleplay for a new science fiction television series. In his spare time, Tim also runs Clockhouse Press (www.clockhousepress.com), a publishing company for his alma mater, Goddard College.

Other science fiction from Big Engine

The Leaky Establishment

1 903468 00 0

David Langford
£8.99

Langford's 1984 comedy classic, not at all based on the author's work at a nuclear establishment nowhere near Newbury, with a brand new introduction by Terry Pratchett. Black comedy overtakes the unfortunate defence-scientist hero Roy Tappen when a "harmless" theft of office furniture lands him with his very own doomsday nuclear stockpile at home. Chain reactions of insanely comic escapades follow, with disaster piled on disaster, leading the increasingly desperate Tappen to the borders of science fiction as he seeks a way out of the mess.

The Leaky Establishment was first published in 1984 to great reviews, and has lost none of its charm since. Terry Pratchett has written a new introduction to take it into a new century.

Other science fiction from Big Engine

BIG ENGINE

Bad Timing & Other Stories
Molly Brown

1 903468 06 X
£9.99

> *"One of the most popular contributors to Interzone, Molly Brown's short stories are extremely crisp, clever and a joy to read... a collection is long overdue."*
>
> – SFX

That long overdue collection is here!

An Earthman's stranded spaceship is besieged by thousands of cuddly aliens whose idea of war is to commit ritual suicide; a teenage princess is kidnapped by an army of undead skeletons; a Chinese demon rides through the streets of Soho; and Toni Fisher tells Joanna Krenski, "I'm working on a calculation that will show density of shoulder pad to be in directly inverse proportion to level of intelligence. I'm drunk by the way."

From the satire of the award-winning *Bad Timing* to the horror of *Feeding Julie*, via the mind twisting paradoxes of *Women On The Brink Of A Cataclysm* and the out-and-out comedy of *Agents of Darkness*, these stories from the first 10 years of Molly Brown's writing career show her range and her versatility, and never fail to enthrall. Several of the stories have been specially updated for this collection.

Other science fiction from Big Engine

The Ant-Men of Tibet & Other Stories 1 903468 02 7
David Pringle (ed.)
£9.99

Interzone is still Britain's best selling science fiction and fantasy
short fiction magazine, and the only monthly one. *The Ant-Men of
Tibet & Other Stories* is a brand new collection of ten of its most sig-
nificant stories in recent years: flamboyant space opera, chilly
thrillers, contemplation and comic fantasy. All are by authors who
had their first or near-first sales to the magazine and every new
story opens up a completely new world with new visions and ideas.
This collection is a celebration of the diversity that is British science fiction.

The stories:
- Stephen Baxter: The Ant-Men of Tibet
- Alastair Reynolds: Byrd Land Six
- Chris Beckett: The Warrior Half-and-Half
- Keith Brooke: The People of the Sea
- Eugene Byrne: Alfred's Imaginary Pestilence
- Nicola Caines: Civilization
- Jayme Lynn Blaschke: The Dust
- Molly Brown: The Vengeance of Grandmother Wu
- Peter T. Garratt: The Collectivization of Transylvania
- Eric Brown: Vulpheous

Other science fiction
from Big Engine

Maps: The Uncollected John Sladek 1 903468 08 6
David Langford (ed.) £9.99

"Across five decades John Sladek's work has burned like a dark fire at the heart of modern science fiction. One of the most technically gifted writers of his generation, the products of his ferocious intelligence are at once inventive, funny, melancholy and sharply satirical. His stories are skewed mirrors, revealing with remarkable clarity the technological, social and moral fractures of our day and the next."

- Stephen Baxter

"Thanks for a chance to see the intro. My eyes are still moist with laughter. Lord, John was a funny guy! And such titles. What contents pages he could boast! I'm pleased to be present at such a distinguished wake. I hope I have the good luck someday to have so conscientious and quick-witted a memorialist. Were there a heaven and were John in it he'd be raining down suitable blessings, I doubt not."
- Thomas Disch

Big Engine is proud to publish a final collection of the late John Sladek's fiction, assembled by David Langford and a team of helpers with the full co-operation of Sladek's estate.

Sladek's satire still bites, his stories still compel with their unique mix of wit and melancholy, his obsessive inventiveness still amuses and impresses. Langford has gathered *all* the solo stories — the science fiction, the detective puzzles, the mainstream (or what passed for it with Sladek), the unclassifiably off-beat "non-fact" pieces — that Sladek is known to have published but did not appear in his previous collections. Also included are poems, playlets, pseudonymous fiction, all the short collaborations with Thomas M. Disch (including three never previously published), and some witty autobiographical essays — testimony to a hugely talented man who stood a little aside from science fiction but for two decades helped shape it, because his achievement was impossible to ignore.

Other science fiction from Big Engine

BIG ENGINE

Coming Soon

The Journal of Nicholas the American   1 903468 11 6
Leigh Kennedy   £9.99

"A powerfully written, introspective novel ... Unquestionably one of the most mature of the year, and one of the best to deal with ESP."
- SF Chronicle

Originally published in 1986, *The Journal of Nicholas the American* tells the story of college student Nicholas Dal – a tele-empath who experiences the emotions of other people. In company, he can only feel what those around him feel, and too-powerful emotion can induce seizures, so he must live in semi-drunken solitude simply to stay sane.

In the past the family talent, or curse, has led to insanity, persecution and murder, and the Dals even fled Russia to escape its deadly legacy. But now a psychiatrist is on Nicholas's tale and his feelings for a fellow student in his history class, and her dying mother Susanne, threaten to break through his isolation. Will he risk his love, his sanity and his life to be with Susanne on her journey past the edge of existence?

Other science fiction from Big Engine

Festival of Fools

Charles Stross

1 903468 13 2

£ 9.99

In a universe where the unseen but never unfelt force known as the Eschaton maintains the laws of relativity and cause-and-effect with an iron fist, the Festival comes to Rochard's World and changes it forever. The Festival seeks only to entertain and be entertained: it promises whatever you want and has the power to deliver it, even to the poorest beggar on the planet. Rochard's World belongs to the New Republic, a state governed rigidly by hierarchy and tradition and ideology. The New Republic despatches a war fleet to deal with the threat, never imagining what will happen when ideologies and technologies from either side of a Vingean singularity collide.

Other science fiction
from Big Engine

Weird Women, Wired Women   1 903468 14 0
Kit Reed   £ 9.99

"She is the SF writer par excellence of the war between the gener-
ations... Kit Reed frees us as we read her."
                    John Clute, Science Fiction Weekly

"The dread and fascination of sex is only one of the themes Reed
holds up to her unyielding magnifying glass... superb work."
                    The Washington Post Book World

"These stories embrace, with fearful lucidity, contemporary
trends, like the passion for the perfect house... the fiercer side of fem-
inist combativeness and the obsession with fashion. There is no
doubt about the prescience of Reed's earlier stories, or about the
despairing sense of the consumer media that infuses the later ones."
                    Publishers Weekly

Kit Reed is a veteran US author and we are delighted to be able to
publish her in the UK. She says, "I've been accused of being a
writer of literary fiction, a comic novelist, a feminist science fiction
writer and of writing psychological thrillers that give readers night-
mares. This may be because I am easily bored, which means I
never do the same thing twice." To the *New York Times Book Review*,
the stories in this collection are "less fantastic than visionary,

uncovering humour and horror where others have seen only clothes, make-up and recipes snipped from the newspaper."

The Big Engine edition of *Weird Women, Wired Women* includes two stories not published in the US edition, "The Attack of the Giant Baby" and "Empty Nest".

Other science fiction from Big Engine

The Holy Machine   1 903468 12 4
Chris Beckett   £ 9.99

> *"Perhaps I should start this story with a description of my dramatic escape across the border in the company of a beautiful woman. Or I could begin with myself picking up pieces of human flesh in a small room in a Greek taverna, retching and gagging as I wrapped them in a shirt and stuffed it into my suitcase. That was a turning point. There's no doubt about that. Or perhaps I should open with the spectacle of the Machine itself, the robot Messiah, preaching to the faithful in Tirana?"*

Illyria is a scientific utopia, an enclave of logic and reason founded off the Greek coast in the mid-twenty first century as a refuge from the Reaction, a wave of religious fundamentalism sweeping the planet. Yet to George Simling, first generation son of a former geneticist who was left emotionally and psychically crippled by the persecution she encountered in her native Chicago, science-dominated Illyria is becoming as closed-minded and stifling as the religion-dominated world outside ...

The Holy Machine is Chris Beckett's first novel. As well as being a story about love, adventure and a young man learning to mature and face the world, it deals with a question that is all too easily forgotten or glibly answered in science fiction: what happens to the soul, to beauty, to morality, in the absence of God?

Other science fiction
from Big Engine

The Starfarer Saga
By Vonda N. McIntyre

Starfarers I *Transition* I *Metaphase* I *Nautilus*

The Starfarer Saga is a quartet of novels describing Earth's first contact with galactic civilisation. *Starfarer* is a giant university starship, two counter-rotating cylinders made of moonrock and propelled by a solar sail. On board are a fascinating mix of characters: an alien contact specialist who of course has never actually contacted any aliens; an exiled Russian cosmonaut who dares not return to his homeland; a sculptor who likes to bury fake fossils of impossible beings in geological strata (including the rock of *Starfarer*'s hull); an accountant; an assortment of scientists, journalists and grandmothers; and above them all the enigmatic and seldom seen Blades, chancellor of the starship, whose control over everyone's lives might be more absolute than any dare believe. Each with their own agendas, many embittered or badly hurt by earlier traumas, these are the people who must work together to bring *Starfarer* safely home and to convince galactic civilisation that humanity is worthy of inclusion.

Other science fiction
from Big Engine

**BIG
ENGINE**

Starfarers

1 903468 15 9
£12.99

Still undergoing preparation for its first voyage, starship *Starfarer* faces delay after delay and possible cancellation. Yet its eclectic inhabitants are forced together into an early transition to Tau Ceti with a nuclear missile embedded in the hull by a combination of politics, treachery and greed.

Transition

1 903468 16 7
£12.99

Arrived in orbit around Tau Ceti, *Starfarer* begins to receive strange transmissions from its second planet. Meanwhile, on board, trouble with Arachne — the bioelectronic entity that controls the ship — seems to have been the result of sabotage. And to their surprise, the people on board find they have something the locals badly want.

Other science fiction
from Big Engine

Metaphase

1 903468 17 5
£12.99

The first contact team prepare to meet the reclusive alien squid-moth, a creature shunned by all civilised worlds. But the Starfarers must make a terrible decision — return home for possible trial before they are stranded in space, or trust an offer from the enigmatic squidmoth Nemo before it dies.

Nautilus

1 903468 18 3
£12.99

Bequeathed the starship *Nautilus* by the dying Nemo, the Starfarers finally make contact with the elusive representatives of galactic civilisation, from which Earth has long been barred. But they must convince the representatives that humanity should be allowed to join rather than simply quarantined, and there is still the matter of the saboteur on board *Starfarer* ...

A series discount is available for orders for the entire Starfarers *series. Contact the publishers for details.*